MW01124262

Copyrighted Material

www.wispvine.com

978-1-939997-97-5

1st Edition

Dragon Dojo Brotherhood

Reign of Dragons

Fate of Dragons

Blood of Dragons

Age of Dragons

Fall of Dragons

Death of Dragons

Queen of Dragons

A Legend Among Dragons

Blackbriar Academy

The Trials of Blackbriar Academy

The Shadows of Blackbriar Academy

The Hex of Blackbriar Academy

The Blood Oath of Blackbriar Academy

The Battle of Blackbriar Academy

The Nighthelm Guardian Series

City of the Sleeping Gods

City of Fractured Souls

City of the Enchanted Queen

Demon Queen Saga

Princes of the Underworld

Wars of the Underworld

Sentinel Saga

By Dahlia Leigh and Olivia Ash

The Shadow Shifter

STAY CONNECTED

Join the exclusive group where all the cool kids hang out... Olivia's secret club for cool ladies! Consider this your formal invitation to a world of hot guys, fun people, and your fellow book lovers. Olivia hangs out in this group all the time. She made the group specifically for readers like you to come together and share their lives and interests, especially regarding the hot guys from her novels.

Check it out! Everyone in there is amazing, and you'll fit right in.

https://www.facebook.com/groups/LilaJeanOliviaAsh/

Sign up for email alerts of new releases AND an

exclusive bonus novella from the Nighthelm Guardian series, *City of the Rebel Runes*, the prequel to *City of Sleeping Gods* only available to subscribers.

https://wispvine.com/newsletter/olivia-ash-email-signup/

Enjoying the series? Awesome! Help others discover the Dragon Dojo Brotherhood by leaving a review at Amazon.

QUEEN OF DRAGONS

Book Seven of the Dragon Dojo Brotherhood

OLIVIA ASH

As the world burns, I must walk through the fire —and emerge a queen.

I never wanted to rule. I never wanted to have men follow me. Die for me.

But now, they do it anyway.

The power in me—it's growing.

If I'm not careful, it will consume me. It will consume *everything.*

And the gods want it back.

They come to me in a vision. Through the smoke and the screams of dying men, they give me a choice.

Bow before them, or die.

My choice is easy—I defend what's mine.

It's easier said than done, of course. I have to build an army unlike anything the Bosses have ever seen. It's the only way to survive this world that wants to kill me and the men I love.

Thank the gods I have my evil butler with me to help me navigate the chaos…

CONTENTS

IMPORTANT CHARACTERS & TERMS

CHARACTERS

Rory Quinn: a former Spectre and the current dragon vessel. Rory was raised as a brutal assassin by her mentor Zurie, but escaped that life. When Zurie tried to force Rory to return, Rory was forced to kill her former mentor. Rory's newfound magic is constantly evolving and changing, and now that she has shifted, her magic continues to defy all known limits. Her diamond dragon is the only one of its kind, and the only other diamond dragons known to exist were the fabled dragon gods themselves. But Rory was born a human, so she can't be a *goddess*... can she?

Andrew Darrington (Drew): a fire dragon shifter. Drew is one of the heirs to the Darrington dragon family. With no real regard for rules or the law in general, Drew tends to know things he shouldn't and isn't fond of sharing that intel with just anyone. Though he originally intended to kidnap Rory and use her power for his own means, her tenacity and strength enchanted him. They have a pact: if he doesn't try to control her, she won't try to control him. Drew sees her as an equal in a world where he's stronger, smarter, and faster than nearly everyone else.

Tucker Chase: a weapons expert and former Knight. Tucker's a loveable goofball who treats every day like it's his last—because it very well might be. He was forced to kill his father, the General of the now-defunct Knights anti-dragon terrorist organization, when the man brought a war to Rory's door. Tucker was originally assigned to hunt Rory down and turn her in to his father, but as he spent more time with her, she became the true family he'd never had. To protect her, Tucker fed his father false intel about her abilities—and gave up his old life to stay at her side.

Levi Sloane: an ice dragon shifter and former Vaer soldier who went feral when his commander killed his very ill little sister. When he was feral, Rory saved him from a snare trap on the edge of the Vaer lands, and he has been by her side ever since. Feral dragons slowly lose touch with their human selves, but Rory helped bring him back from the brink. Though all dragons can communicate telepathically when they touch, Levi and Rory can also communicate this way in human form. To save Rory's life, he and his dragon healed their relationship, and Levi can once again shift and retain full control. He's the only dragon to ever come back from being feral.

Jace Goodwin: a thunderbird dragon shifter and former Master of the Fairfax Dragon Dojo. Jace grew up in high society and has the vast network to prove it. A warrior, he used to operate as the General of the Fairfax army—and his only soft spot is for Rory. He gave up his position at the dojo to take her as his mate, and now his full attention is devoted to her. As Rory's mate, he is deeply connected to her and her magic, and he's the only person who can soothe her wild power. If she dies, his dragon will go feral, so he has quite a bit at stake if one of Rory's many enemies comes after her.

Irena Quinn: Rory's sister and former heir to the Spectre organization. She betrayed Zurie when she discovered her former mentor wanted to sell Rory as an assassin-for-hire, which would mean they would never see each other again. A brutal fighter, Irena's only purpose in life is to keep her sister safe and destroy the Spectres organization that almost killed them both. A powerful bio-weapon created by the Vaer gave Irena strange super-strength and bright green eyes that are eerily similar to Kinsley Vaer. Irena might develop magic or even a dragon of her own, though no one knows for sure what Kinsley's experiments have done to her.

Zurie Bronwen (deceased): former leader of the Spectres and former mentor to Rory and Irena. Zurie was a brutal assassin and held the title of the Ghost. Cold-hearted, calculating, and clever, Zurie considered both Rory and Irena as failed experiments—and she was determined to kill them both. The war she started between the Fairfax family, the Vaer family, and the Knights will have lasting consequences, and it's unclear if Zurie realized just how terrible the outcome would be.

Diesel Richards: a former Knight turned Spectre.

With Zurie dead, Rory out of the picture, and Irena excommunicated for her betrayal, Diesel is now the Ghost. His incentive is to kill both Irena and Rory to ensure no one threatens his rule. He's helped Rory once and tried to kill her on other occasions, so Rory isn't sure what Diesel really wants or what game he's playing with her life.

Harper Fairfax: a thunderbird, the Boss of the Fairfax dragon family, and Jace's cousin. Harper is friendly and bubbly, full of life and joy, but Rory knows a fighter when she sees one. The young woman is smart and cunning. As Rory's first friend, Harper has a special place in Rory's life. She will do anything to protect her friend—including going to war to protect her.

Russell Kane: a thunderbird and new Master of the Fairfax Dojo now that Jace has stepped down. He endured brutal trials to earn his place as the new dojo master. He grew up with Jace and Harper in the dojo and has a deep love for both the castle itself and the people within it. He will do anything to protect the Fairfax dragons—and Harper, for whom he seems to have a soft spot.

Eric Dunn (deceased): a fire dragon and part of the Fairfax family, Eric was the one man Irena was beginning to let herself love. After a betrayal by someone she adored, Irena had shut down. Eric's death broke her, and she left Rory's side shortly after.

Brett Clarke: a former Knight and once the General's second-in-command. With the General still out of commission after his last run-in with Rory, Brett led the Knights' charge against the Fairfax Dojo. When the Knights lost, Brett was captured, and he realized everything he knew about dragons was wrong. He helped Rory defeat the Knights, but they're still not sure if he's trustworthy.

William Chase (deceased): mostly referred to as the General. William is a former military man who was discharged from the army in disgrace for his terrorist connections to the Knights. He now runs them in a brutal regime that kills defectors, and he now has his sights set on his son Tucker.

Guy Durand (deceased): an ice dragon and former second-in-command to Jace Goodwin at the dragon dojo. Guy always wanted power. When he lost the challenge to Jace for control of the dojo, he joined the Vaer and gave over top-secret intel about Rory and the dojo itself. He was killed by Jace after he tried to kidnap Rory and return her to Kinsley.

Ian Rixer (deceased): a fire dragon, Kinsley Vaer's half-brother, and a master manipulator. Ian was smarmy, elitist, and arrogant. He was often referred to as honey-coated evil for his ability to speak so calmly and kindly, even while torturing his prey. He treated everything like a game, and playing that game with Rory cost him his life. He tried to control her and Jace's magic with specially designed iron cuffs to block their power, but Rory's magic can't be contained. She destroyed the cuffs—and him.

Mason Greene (deceased): a fire dragon and sadistic Vaer lord tasked with dismantling the Spectre organization. Irena gave him access to their sensitive Spectre intel in exchange for giving her and Rory a fresh start, but he betrayed them both. His attempt to kill Rory backfired massively and ultimately cost him his life.

Kinsley Vaer: an ice dragon shifter and the Boss of the Vaer family. Her power and cruelty make most grown men tremble in fear. She's utterly ruthless, cruel, vindictive, and vengeful… the sort to kill the messenger just because she's angry. She's increasingly frustrated that Rory has slipped through her fingers so often, and she's done giving her minions chances to redeem themselves. Now, it's personal—and Kinsley is coming after everything Rory loves.

Jett Darrington: a fire dragon, the Boss of the Darrington family, and Drew's father. He wants Rory for reasons not even Drew fully knows, but everyone's certain it can't be good. He disowned his son when Drew wouldn't hand Rory over, but he promised Drew everything he could ever dream of—including ruling the Darrington family—if he betrays her.

Milo Darrington: a fire dragon, Drew's brother, and current heir to the Darrington family line purely because he's older than Drew. Not much of a fighter, but an excellent politician and master manipulator. He's been growing increasingly resentful of his younger brother's skill and charm. When he tried to kidnap Rory and blackmail Drew into doing his bidding, she shifted into her dragon to beat him into submission. He knows her secret, but he's too terrified of her to tell a soul. Probably.

Isaac Palarne: a fire dragon and the Boss of the Palarne family. A skilled warrior and empowering speaker, Isaac can rally almost anyone to his cause. He's a deeply noble man, but there's something unnerving about his eagerness to get Rory to come to the Palarne capital.

Elizabeth Andusk: a golden fire dragon and Boss of the Andusk family. Vain and materialistic, Elizabeth can command attention without even a word. She exudes power mainly through her beauty and has a knack for getting people to share secrets they wouldn't have shared otherwise. She's determined to obtain Rory and considers the girl to be nothing more than another object to control and display.

Victor Bane: a fire dragon and Boss of the Bane family. He's a brutal fighter, excellent negotiator, and never gets caught in his many illicit dealings. With his hot temper, he picks fights whenever he can. He has very little direction and purpose, as he is merely looking for the next thing—or person—he can steal.

Natasha Bane: a fire dragon and Victor's sister, Natasha has almost as much influence and control over the Bane family as her brother does. She's smart, clever, and cunning. A sultry temptress, she enjoys bending men to her whims. Though both demanding and entitled, she knows when to keep her mouth shut to get her way.

Aki Nabal: an ice dragon and Boss of the Nabal family. He's excellent with money and can always see three moves ahead in any dealings—both financial and political. Clever and observant, he can pinpoint a fighter's weaknesses fairly quickly, though he's not an exceptional fighter himself. He believes money is power—and that you can never have enough of either.

Jade Nabal: an ice dragon and Aki's daughter, Jade is young and not much one for words. As a silent observer who prefers to watch rather than engage, little is known about Jade. She and Rory have met once, only briefly, and Rory knows there's far more to Jade than meets the eye.

Other Terms

The Dragon Gods: the origin of all dragon power. The three Dragon Gods are mostly just lore, nowadays. No one even remembers their names. But with the dragon vessel showing up in the world, everyone is beginning to wonder if perhaps they're a bit more than legend...

Dragon Vessel: According to myth, the dragon vessel is the one living creature powerful and worthy enough to possess the magic of the dragon gods. Rory Quinn was kicked into an ancient ceremony pit—the one Mason Greene didn't know was used to judge the worthiness of those who entered. With that ritual, Rory unknowingly brought the immense power of legend back to the world.

Castle Ashgrave: the legendary home of the dragon gods, said to be nothing more than ruin and myth. Drew believes he's found the location, but he's not yet sure.

Mate-bond: the connection only thunderbirds can share that connects two souls. The mate-bond is not finalized until the pair make love for the first time.

Even before it's finalized, however, the mate-bond is powerful. The duo can vaguely feel each other's whereabouts and, if one should die, the other would go feral.

Magical cuffs: complex handcuffs that cover the entirety of a shifter's hands when they're in human form. These cuffs are designed to keep thunderbird magic at bay. The Vaer have designed special cuffs just for Rory, with the ability to block her magic. These cuffs come with a remote that allows the captor to electrocute their captive to help subdue them, as thunderbirds are notoriously powerful.

Spectres: a cruel and heartless organization that raises brutal assassins and hates dragonkind. The Spectres specialize in killing dragons and are known as some of the fiercest murderers on the planet, in part thanks to their highly advanced tech that no one else has yet to duplicate. They're a spider web network that spans the globe, all run by the Ghost. Often, Spectres are raised from birth within the organization and are never given the choice to join. Once a Spectre, always a Spectre—quitting comes with a death sentence.

Override Device: Spectre tech. Very frail and easy to break, it fits into USB ports and can grant access to sensitive files. Though imperfect and obscenely expensive to create, it *usually* works.

Voids: Spectre tech. Fired from a gun with special attachments, a void can force a camera to loop the last 10 seconds and allow for unseen access to secured locations.

The Knights: an international anti-dragon terrorist organization bent on eradicating dragons from the world. Run by General William Chase, they'll do anything and kill anyone it takes to further their mission. There are some rebel Knights organizations that think the current General is too soft, despite his brutal rampage against dragons and his willingness to kill his own family should the need arise.

Fire Dragons: the most common type of dragon shifter. Fire dragons breathe fire and smoke in their dragon forms. They're found in a wide array of colors.

Ice Dragons: uncommon dragons that can freeze others on contact and breathe icy blasts. Usually, ice dragons are white, pale blue, or royal blue. The only known black ice dragons belong to the Vaer family.

Thunderbirds: dragon shifters that glow in their dragon forms and possess the magic of electricity and lightning in both their dragon and human forms. They're the most feared dragons in the world, and also the rarest.

The Seven Dragon Families: the seven dragon organizations that are run like the mob. Each family values different things, from wealth to power to adrenaline. Usually, a dragon is born into a dragon family and never leaves, but there are some who betray their family of origin for the promise of a better life.

Andusk Family: sun dragons who prefer warm climates, almost all of which are golden or orange fire dragons. They're notoriously vain, focused on beauty and being adored. Fairly materialistic, the Andusk dragons hoard wealth and gems and exploit those in less favorable positions.

Bane Family: ambitious fire dragons who deal mainly in illegal activities. They view laws as guidelines that hold others back, while they aren't stupid enough to follow others' rules. They like to see what they can get away with and push the limits.

Darrington Family: the oldest and most powerful family. Darringtons are mostly fire dragons, and angering them is considered a death sentence. They're well situated financially, with a vast network of natural resources, governments, and businesses across the globe. They're notorious for thinking they're above the rules and can get away with anything… because they usually do.

Fairfax Family: a magical family known as the only one to have thunderbird dragons. They have innate magic and talent, but sometimes lack the drive it takes to use those abilities to obtain greater power. They prefer to think of life as a game, and the only winners are those who have fun. To the Fairfax dragons, adrenaline is more important than money, but protecting each other is most important of all.

Nabal Family: wealthy fire and ice dragons. Money and information are most important to the Nabal, and they have an eerie ability to get access to even the most secured intel. Calculating and cunning, the Nabal weigh every risk before taking any action.

Palarne Family: noble fire and ice dragons known for their honor and war skill. Ruled by their ancient dragon code of ethics, the Palarne family operate as a cohesive military unit. Their skills in war are unparalleled by any other family.

Vaer Family: a secretive family of fire and ice dragons, they're known to be behind many conspiracies and dirty dealings in the world. Some see them as brutal savages, but most fear them because they have no ethics or morals, even among themselves.

CHAPTER ONE

Cold December night air whispers across my skin as I flatten myself against the closest tree, my body tense and ready for battle.

Through the dense smattering of snow-covered evergreens, I spot the corner of the Vaer research facility we will be attacking tonight.

We have to succeed.

No second chances.

This is life or death.

I'm risking everything by being here, and though my years as a Spectre let me stalk silently toward the compound, this mission isn't going to be easy.

If one thing goes wrong, people might die tonight. People I care about.

I *can't* let that happen.

Tonight's mission is straightforward—get in and divert the Vaer's attention long enough for Drew to hack their network. The program he's planting will allow us to spy on all of the Vaer's dealings from here on out.

But honestly, I have a second reason for being here tonight.

A vendetta.

So, yes, we're going to hack their network. But we're also going to free the shifters being held against their will. These people are being used by Kinsley. We think she's testing them for some type of new bio-weapon. A weapon that I refuse to let see the light of day.

I glance down at Ashgrave, in his mechanical dragon body, as he stands near my feet. I can't help but smirk. I can't deny it—I love having my murderous castle close by. His metallic head swivels as he takes in our surroundings, still curious about the outside world.

From my vantage point of about fifty yards from the front doors of the Vaer compound, I watch three armed guards pace back and forth, weapons strapped at their waists as they scan the forest. The thunder of boots hitting the pavement lets me know there are more guards in the back.

Time to blow their night to hell.

Drew's voice booms through the comm in my ear. "I have eyes on the front."

"Same," I respond in a calm and steady voice. "If this works, we're going to have a huge advantage."

"Yeah, it's risky," he admits. "It'll work, Rory."

"I know."

It's only a partial lie, really.

This *will* work.

It has to.

"Let's do this," Drew says with a tense sigh. "Standby."

"Stay alert," I warn everyone.

The crunch of footsteps in the snow catches my attention, and I stiffen impulsively even though I recognize the gait.

Tucker.

"Hey babe," I whisper without looking over my shoulder.

"I thought I was being quiet," he mutters, a twinge of disappointment in his tone.

I shrug, my attention still trained on the guards. They haven't seen us yet, thank the gods.

I feel his gaze on my body, and I take a quick glance back at him to find his eyes observing my curves.

I smirk.

"Are you going to watch the enemy, or my ass?" I ask as I quirk an eyebrow.

"I can multitask." Tucker says as he puts a hand on his chest and sticks out his bottom lip, pouting as I call him out.

The ex-Knight gestures toward the sniper rifle slung over his shoulder, indicating he's ready to use it at a moment's notice.

As I turn back around to observe the facility and time our little invasion just right, he moves behind me, pressing his muscled body against my back and ass. I suck in a deep breath, my dragon immediately stirring in response. Heat burns through me as desire pools between my thighs.

"You know I'm ready whenever you are," he breathes into my ear.

"Jerk," I whisper teasingly. "How the hell am I supposed to focus on getting us in there when you're pressing against me like this?"

I playfully brush him off and he gives me a peck on the cheek. Tucker jogs over to his tree of choice and hoists himself up, readying his sniper rifle and falling into silent mode.

Now, he's focused. I guess he just needed to mess with me first.

I glance upward. The skies overhead are empty.

Good.

I know that Jace and Levi will be here at my signal.

With a steady breath, I try to shake off the brewing tension in my shoulders. This is going to be an unusual fight.

Mainly because we aren't here to win.

According to our little plan, I have to leave the facility standing and some of the Vaer guards alive, even though the Vaer are torturing people inside it. Our hack won't work, otherwise. But we *do* get to throw a wrench into their operations which thrive on dragon experimentation, bio-weapon development, and drug trafficking.

Kinsley makes her money by destroying the lives of those around her. I think it's high time I give her a bit of her own medicine.

The Vaer Boss will think I'm here to rescue her prisoners and piss her off. But I will also walk away with the hack firmly planted in the heart of her telecommunications system.

I can hardly wait.

The snow falls lightly around me as I watch the armed guards pace back and forth. Their strides aren't changing, and if they have any hint that we're here, they aren't acting on it.

Something tells me they aren't good actors—we're in the clear.

"Drew, how many are around back?" I whisper into my comm.

"Eight. And no doubt there are more inside."

"We can handle it." I reach for the gun at my waist and prepare for battle. "Are our decoys ready?"

"Ready," Jace's voice chimes in. "Levi and I will charge in and take them out, clearing the way for Drew."

"Good," I say. "Get ready, on my mark."

I nod to Tucker and then Ashgrave.

"I WILL SMITE AS MANY AS I CAN, MY QUEEN," Ashgrave promises, barely keeping his booming voice to a whisper.

What a good evil butler.

My gun weighs heavily in my palm, a comfortable reminder that I'm going in armed and ready to kill. It feels a little unnecessary, since I can summon a dagger with my magic. It would be easy to use my power to take out the guards. Problem is, my power fluctuations have been wild lately, and they're only getting more uncontrollable.

Not great.

Besides, I don't want to overwhelm any of the prisoners the Vaer have locked in there. Who knows what hell they've experienced, and how terrified they're going to be as it is? Fear makes people do crazy things, and I want to make sure I get them out uninjured.

A magic dragon-lady running in with a glowing white sword might scare the shit out of the people I'm here to help.

So… I'll play nice.

For now.

"Let's do this," I say into the comm, my voice tense and dark.

Within seconds, my blue ice dragon flies silently through the air near the back of the facility. My black thunderbird flies at his side, and the two unleash a flurry of ice and blue lightning against the eight shifters.

It's not even a fair fight.

I give Ashgrave a firm nod, and a dark plume of smoke escapes his nostrils as he flies toward the front entrance and unleashes fire from his throat at the three guards. Flames crash against two of them, consuming them in moments.

They don't even have time to scream.

The third guard dives out of the way and tries to

run for cover, but a muffled gunshot cuts through the night. The third guard's head jerks back, his body going limp as he tumbles toward the ground.

Tucker's an excellent shot.

These guards weren't prepared for us. The men only seemed to be paying attention to their surroundings. They were too comfortable and felt too safe here. Their location is almost completely off the grid. The Vaer probably thought no one in their right mind would launch an assault on this facility. Well, they were wrong.

"Tucker, let's go," I say into my comm.

My weapons expert descends from the thick tree branch he perched himself on and slings his rifle back over his shoulder. He draws two pistols and runs alongside me. As we approach the entrance, Ashgrave circles us, as if daring anyone to come near his queen.

The roars of dragons fill the air, but I don't have time to watch Levi and Jace wage their war against the shifters now taking to the sky. They can handle this.

I trust them.

With a quick glance toward the camera that's watching the front door, I do my best to suppress the desire to hide.

After all, I'm the bait. We all are—Drew's the one doing the heavy lifting on this mission, not me. I have to give him time to do his thing, and for that to happen, I need to draw as much fire as possible.

Oh *joy.*

"Make them work for it," I remind Tucker.

He growls in frustration as I type in the code Drew managed to steal for us—though, to my irritation, he still won't tell me how he got it—and I can't help but nod.

I hate the idea of leaving a place like this still standing—even if it's on purpose.

The digital pad on the wall glows green and the door opens to a small reception area—which I was definitely not expecting in a place like this.

It's a military-style compound, for gods' sake. Not a damn dentist office.

The clatter of footsteps echoes down a nearby hallway as four men come around the corner and race toward us with their guns drawn.

The guards rush into the well-lit reception area and open fire, but we take cover behind the partition with a built-in desk. I cover Tucker with a few shots as he leans out just enough to take out one of the guards.

Ashgrave barrels in through the open door, fire

building again in his throat, unleashing it on the other two.

One left.

I bolt toward the last guard standing. He's barely eighteen, and his uniform is a little loose on his thin frame. His eyes dart from Ashgrave to Tucker, then to me, and I can tell he's not ready for this.

He's not ready for war.

I can't really blame him—this may be a military-style facility, but it's an outpost in the middle of Alaska with few Vaer soldiers to staff it. That's what made it the perfect target for us. They won't withstand the trouble my men and I are bringing.

The kid lifts his gun at the last second, but he's too slow. I duck out of the way and swing my fist hard into his groin. He groans, doubling over onto the floor, and I deliver a kick to his head and knock him out.

"Ouch," Tucker says, wincing as the kid goes limp.

"Hey, at least I didn't kill him." I shrug. "By my standards, I'm being *nice.*"

"Fair point," my weapons expert says as he cocks his handgun. "After all, they did try to kill us."

"Hold this room," I tell Ashgrave and Tucker.

According to the blueprints Drew swiped for us,

all the hallways funnel through the front lobby. Tucker and Ashgrave will be in the perfect position to kill anyone who tries to come after me—or get Drew.

"Phase two, go," Tucker says into his comm with a short nod.

Time to find Drew.

I run down the main corridor and turn the corner. Gunfire echoes down the hall, and it takes me a minute to place where it's coming from—the front, where Tucker and Ashgrave are.

I hate letting my men separate. I hate letting them put their lives on the line for me. I hate letting them risk everything—because they're *everything* to me.

But if we want this to work, we *have* to.

"Vaer reinforcements are on the way," Drew says, his deep voice booming through the comm. "Let's make this quick."

"Did it work?" I ask my fire dragon over the comm as I race down the hallway toward our rendezvous point.

"It did," he confirms. "Cameras are down, too."

Short and sweet. Just the way I like it.

I breathe a sigh of relief. With the spying program planted, that's one less stressor on my plate.

Now, to rescue the Vaer's prisoners and get out of here alive.

Bonus—Kinsley can't watch what we're doing or where we're going in her compound. With the cameras down, we won't even need voids to stay hidden.

I glance at the number on the wide, metal double doors in front of me.

"I'm in Area Twelve. Where are you?" I ask Drew.

The thunder of footsteps echoes down the hall, and sure enough, my gorgeous fire dragon rounds the corner seconds later. I can't help but grin as our eyes meet.

"Let's do a good deed," he says, cocking his gun before kicking open the double doors we're standing in front of.

The doors open into a large room with about two dozen beds lined against the far wall. Half are empty, and the rest are filled with people—shifters to be exact. The prisoners are young men and women who don't appear to be older than Tucker. Most of them are cuffed to their beds, while the rest lie so still that I'm tempted to check if they're still breathing.

No wonder the Vaer didn't bother restraining

them. They couldn't escape on their own if they tried.

I knew I'd find something rotten in this compound. What I didn't expect to see was seven shifters, severely beaten and chained to their beds with a terrified look in their eyes.

There's some kind of nurse's station set up on the far side of the room. Small glass vials, syringes, and charts sit on the counter in front of the beeping medical equipment.

I don't know exactly what's going on here. But judging by the bruises and open cuts on these people, I figure none of it is good.

The doors slam closed, and every face turns toward me. A few shifters watch me through half-closed eyes, barely able to hold their heads up as they study us, while others hold their breath. They freeze. Eyes wide, they simply watch me like I'm some kind of grim reaper, here to finally take them to their graves.

Not today.

"We're here to help," I say, while my face stays calm and I hide how pissed I am.

Pissed at how Kinsley can be so cruel. Pissed that shifters would do this to each other and that this kind of injustice exists.

It makes me want to burn this place to the ground—plan be damned.

Deep within, my dragon coils with fury. She's seething at how these shifters are being treated.

I get it, I tell her. *We will make sure these bastards pay for everything they've done. Just not now.*

My beautiful diamond dragon snarls at me, but accepts my promise to destroy the Vaer when the time is right.

One of the shifters, a man with a shaved and bloodied head and dark bruises beneath his eyes, sits up and stares at me with the look of a man who believes his death is near.

"Kill me," he wheezes. "Please."

Oh *gods.*

I can't do that.

"I won't do that," I say gently as I lift his thin arm over my shoulder. "But I *can* help you get out of here in one piece."

Drew breaks the cuffs off of the trapped shifters. Seven of them are strong enough to walk, and one by one, they pair up—the strong with the weak, carrying each other toward the door.

A redheaded woman walks up and places her arm around the bleeding bald man. "I'll get him to safety," she says as she assists him in following the other freed prisoners.

Toward the exit.

Toward *freedom*.

"Shit," Drew mutters.

Oh, good.

A complication.

"What is it?" I ask tensely as the last of the freed prisoners shuffles into the hallway. A patter of gunfire comes from down the hall, and I stiffen, wondering what fresh hell *that* could be.

Drew wraps his strong fingers around my shoulders and guides me toward the hallway. "We have to get to the security room."

"What happened?" I ask as Drew drops his hands.

I should know better, though. Drew never tells me *anything*.

"Tucker, escort the shifters out," I say into my comm as Drew gestures for me to hurry the hell up.

"BUT YOU NEVER GET MY VOICE RIGHT," Ashgrave says through the line before Tucker can respond.

"Got it," my weapons expert says.

"And stop pissing off my castle!" I add as I race after Drew down the hallway.

"Eh," Tucker replies, and I can practically *hear*

him shrugging. "No promises."

"Tell me what's wrong," I demand, glaring at my fire dragon as he and I bolt down the corridor.

"I didn't exactly have the luxury of time when I set everything up," he answers, scowling. "It looks like some asshole is trying to block the upload."

"Damn it," I mutter.

We silently race out of Area Twelve toward the security room.

This time, the hallway opens to a wide area with large crates lining the walls of the room. A few desks are scattered throughout, some of them overturned, and I guess it's been a while since any secretaries filled *this* space. Broken chairs litter the floor, and a large dark door stands ajar at the opposite end.

The security room.

The air is stale and eerily silent, but I know better than to think we're getting off that easy.

"Hey, Tucker, did those shifters get out okay?" I ask into my comm as Drew charges ahead.

The line is silent. With a pang of dread, I wonder if something happened to him.

Seconds tick by, and a deep, brewing tension builds in my chest.

"Tucker, what the hell?" I snap.

Still no response, and flashes of worst-case

scenarios start playing in my brain. I grip my gun tighter, more for comfort than anything else. "So help me gods, if something happens to him—I'm slitting throats."

"Whoa, whoa… easy there, Rory. I'm okay. Sorry, my comm got knocked off by your stupid steam-punk-robot-bird."

"Damn it, Tucker," I mutter as my heartbeat slows.

I release the breath I was holding just as muffled screams filter through the line.

"What's going on?" I ask.

No one had better hurt a single hair—or scale—on my men.

"Oh, just Jace and Levi kicking Vaer ass while I help these captives out to the chopper. Really, babe, you're missing all the fun."

"Someone's gotta do the legwork," I say with a smirk as I enter the security room and join my fire dragon.

Drew's already huddled over a computer, typing furiously as he curses under his breath. While the man who tried to stop the upload lies dead in the corner with a broken neck.

"I'm restarting my software. This should only take a few seconds," my fire dragon says.

With my back to Drew, I keep watch, my gaze scanning from left to right across the large—and definitely unused—room. I'm used to battle and gunfire, not silence.

Silence sets me on edge.

Through the line, I hear more gunfire and an explosion. Tucker's voice chimes in. "Just blew up a crate full of drugs. Mind if I take out a few more?"

"Be my guest." I chuckle.

Let the Vaer think we're here to free their captives and destroy their illegal goods while we sneak into their network.

"Ror-rry," a man's voice echoes down the hall in a sing-song kind of way, like we're playing hide and seek.

I tense as the soft thud of his shoes on the floor echoes lightly toward me with each slow step.

I've never heard his voice before. I have no idea who this is—but it's pretty obvious he knows me.

"Oh Ror-rry, dear," he sings, his voice louder this time.

I look over my shoulder to find Drew tense, his fingers hovering over the keyboard as he glares out into the large room. Our eyes meet, and I simply shake my head.

He needs to focus.

I'll deal with this new asshole myself.

"Rory, don't," Drew snaps.

I glare at him, daring him to stop me.

Without a word, I turn my back on my fire dragon and cock my gun as I head out into the large room.

Searching the cavernous space, I notice bare light bulbs that hang down every ten feet or so from the ceiling. No wonder it's dark in here. The Vaer are saving money on electricity.

"Ror-rry," the new voice sings again from around the corner.

Let this poor fool *try* to hurt me.

After all, Tucker said it himself—he's been having all the fun so far—time for me to have some fun of my own.

I raise my gun and slip into the hallway, eyes narrowing as I follow the soft trail of the stranger's footsteps. I strain my ear, listening for any guards that might be following behind him. Sure enough, he's not alone. There are four—no, five soldiers with him.

"Come out and play, Rory," the man says—so close, this time.

The hallway ends in a T, where the three corridors meet, and a man's shadow stretches from the hallway to my right. I raise my gun, my shoulders tight and tense as I let out a slow and silent breath.

I fire.

The bullet lands in the wall across from me, and the soldiers gasp with surprise and panic. The stranger, however, merely chuckles.

"You missed me," he mocks.

"I never miss," I correct him as one of the suspended light bulbs falls and hits him in the head.

His shadow pauses, and both of us wait for the other to make the next move.

"Come out," I demand. "Leave your guards."

"Very well," he says.

With a few steps, he appears from around the corner and lifts his chin. Dark hair. Dark eyes. Not a wrinkle on his baby face. He's a kid, nineteen at most, with a sneer plastered across his lips—like he has me right where he wants me.

Despite my training, despite my experience, my blood runs cold. There's something about this guy that just isn't right.

The hatred on his face has me searching my memory for this young Vaer. But there is nothing there. I know I've never met this man before. He's probably just another of Kinsley's lackeys, eager to prove himself to their psychotic Boss.

"What do you want?" I demand.

"You," he says simply, with confidence beyond his years.

My heart aches with how the Vaer manipulate their youngest members.

"Join the club," I snap, lifting my gun toward his forehead.

To his credit, he doesn't flinch.

"Put the gun down, Rory," he says calmly, glaring at me like he can't even see the weapon. "Just give in."

"You're new," I say with a chuckle. "That's not how this works."

"Oh?" he tilts his head inquisitively. "How does this work?"

"You make some longwinded speech about how I'm going to lose. We fight. I kick your ass. You die." I roll my eyes.

"Or," he says with a gentle shrug, "we skip to the part where I chain you in a room until my Boss can have a word with you."

The clamor of footsteps down the hall catches my attention. My ear twitches briefly, zeroing in on where the sound is coming from.

It's coming from—shit, it's coming from *everywhere.*

They're trying to surround me. This little asshole is trying to set a trap.

"Call them off," I demand, narrowing my eyes as I aim my gun at his forehead.

"You can kill me, Rory," he says with another gentle shrug. "But you're still not getting out of here. You have no idea what you're up against. Not really." A loose lock of black hair falls in his face, and he smirks.

Something in his voice makes my blood run cold. I need to get out of here, and I need to get out now.

Rule 12 of the Spectres—always know when and how to escape.

I have to choose my next move carefully. My dragon stirs within me, coiling and ready for war.

I'll only have one chance to make this work. And I'll do it by using the magic of the dragon gods that runs in my veins.

The coward darts behind the corner for cover as the chak-chak of over twenty rifles being cocked at once has me staring at the surrounding guards.

A little handgun won't help me now.

Shit.

In a fluid motion, I holster the gun and reach inward for my magic. Ribbons of white light dance across my skin, familiar and safe.

My magic.

My power.

But as it ripples through me, the magic burns suddenly hot—too hot. Far hotter than it ever has. In a flash, it's cold as ice, and I can practically feel my blood freezing.

What the hell?

This can't be good.

I grit my teeth as I try to control the power surge. This is a really bad time for my power to fluctuate like this. Not now—not with over twenty soldiers barreling down on me from every direction.

I need *control.*

But the surge hits—and in that moment, the world goes white.

I lose track of everything. Time. Direction. Which way is up. My stomach churns as I fly through the air, suspended in nothingness as my magic explodes out of me. I'm a leaf in a storm, at the whim of the fury burning within me.

The world fades in and out. For a second, I see that stupid kid's face as he sneers down at me. I blink, and the world goes dark.

Gods above, I want to slap that smile off his face.

Even if it takes every ounce of magic I have.

CHAPTER TWO

I awake with boards stabbing me in the back while I lie on the floor in the middle of a large unfurnished room. Drew stands over me with his fists out in front of him.

Damn. I must have flown through the wall and landed here. My fire dragon growls at the guards and Kinsley's new lap dog who are circling us. Some of the guards are wiping blood from their lips and noses. Drew must have landed a few punches while I was out. Good.

I roll to my hands and knees and force myself to stand on unsteady feet. The ringing in my ears is deafening. My head is spinning and it's hard to focus my eyes.

Shit.

I have to get a hold of my magic before these power surges do something worse than just knocking me out.

"Are you sure you want to be a foot soldier in this war, kid?" Drew asks the young Vaer, as he bumps me lightly with his shoulder.

Drew's lips turn upward in a grin that could charm a snake, as he faces the young commander and the other guards.

An echoing bang comes from the front of the compound, and everyone in the small room turns his head to the hallway. Even though my head is pounding and spots are still floating in front of my eyes, my lips draw up at the thought of Tucker trying to draw attention away from me and Drew.

"Kinsley wants you alive. That is the *only* reason you're still breathing." With that, the young man in charge turns his back to us and struts to the rear of the building, his form lost in the darkness as I continue to fight to stay on my feet.

That must be where more of their victims are.

The Vaer guards make a loose circle as they surround us.

Spreading my feet apart, my dragon hums to life. My head's still foggy and I shake it to clear the haziness.

Drew's eyes meet mine as he raises a questioning brow. I give him a slight nod and answer his unasked question.

"I'm fine," I say.

My dragon is *pissed,* yet she attempts to calm me as we try to figure out what the hell just happened to our power.

She's eager to fight. I chuckle at her impatience, as my eyes scan across the heads of the soldiers in the dimly lit room, and my hazy brain tries to count how many Vaer we're up against.

Twenty-something, maybe thirty armed guards.

With the ringing in my ears and the fuzziness starting to clear from my aching brain, I'm ready to fight. Let's rock and roll.

The rustle of fabric tells me the soldiers are just as hungry to get this over with as I am. The clicks of guns being cocked has me and Drew dropping to the floor with a heavy thud just as the thundering of gun fire deafens me. The Vaer are out for blood, that's for sure.

Mine.

Time to save more prisoners and get the hell out of here.

Drew jumps up like he's got springs in the soles of his boots and roundhouse kicks the advancing three guards. His long muscled leg takes all of them down. I smile, as I admire my fire dragon.

I jump to my feet and notice my ear stings as something warm lands on my left shoulder. Shit. One of the bullets must have grazed the tip of my ear.

I hiss through gritted teeth, while my left hand reaches up to wipe away the blood dripping down my ear lobe.

Drew's handsome face is marred by the tight scowl he's giving the surrounding Vaer. His eyes take on a subtle red glow, and his body is giving off heat. He is out for blood. My Darrington is fighting the urge to shift.

Drew throws himself through the wall on the far side of the room, drawing startled yelps of surprise from the Vaer.

"Hey assholes," Drew shouts from a dark corner in the large room with the scattered desks.

Damn, that was quick.

The guards rush him but only hit him with the butts of their guns. I guess the Vaer aren't interested in killing a Darrington heir. If the Darringtons enter Kinsley's war on the Fairfax side, it could be the end. And not the *end* Kinsley wants.

After a few grunts and fists thudding as they hit

flesh, bodies drop to the floor. Drew has just taken out eighteen Vaer guards. Alone.

His strength never stops amazing me.

I face two of the remaining five guards and punch them both in the face with my magic-infused fists. Their bodies tumble to the ground unconscious.

"Do you want to play?" Drew asks the three guards surrounding him.

"Easy," I tell him. "We don't want to fuel the fire any more than we already have."

The plan was very clear. But none of us expected to find the atrocities we've found here. And I am not the running away type.

"On second thought, fuel it a little bit. We need to send the Vaer a message. Kinsley needs to know she is *not* in charge. But get out before you put yourself in danger," I tell Drew.

"Danger?" He asks in irritation.

Drew tenses and raises a questioning brow. I smile. I can't help it. He's so damn sexy when he's mad.

"You're right." I roll my eyes and chuckle. "I don't know what I was thinking."

I wink at him, and his shoulders relax.

He's going to use that against me later. If I'm *lucky.*

My eyes rove over his large form. The way his muscles tense and bulge in all the right places. It's a turn on. We may be outnumbered, but we sure in the hell aren't out-muscled.

Even if we were, worst case scenario I can always shift. Hell, an extra set of razor sharp teeth and bone crushing claws will help. But with the way my magic is acting, I don't want anyone to know about my fluctuations. The less they know, the better.

My dragon pouts. She really wants to rip out some throats.

Patience, I tell her.

"We're running out of time. I'll hold these guys off, get to the rear of the facility. Be sure to search every door," Drew demands.

He is so bossy. I love it.

I laugh and give Drew a small salute, as I run toward the back of the building.

As I make my way down the hallway, a door opens behind me, silently. A bullet ruffles my hair as it passes my head.

I do a one-eighty and come face-to-face with the cold stare of a Vaer guard. I lunge forward, yanking the gun from his hands. I lift up the butt and use it to hit him in the face, before tossing the rifle off to the side. His body drops with a satisfying thud. I turn around to start my search for more prisoners and notice that I just drew the attention of a few of his friends.

"Are you just gonna stand there and let a girl hit your friend like that? Who's next?" I taunt them, hoping to get their blood boiling.

Angry guards are less focused, more fueled by emotions than logic. More likely to miss if they shoot. Two guards raise their weapons. Now I'm staring at the business end of cool steel barrels.

Fan-freaking-tastic.

I step back, searching for a way to end this. The guard to my left gives me a sinister chuckle. Cocky bastard thinks I can't escape. Good. Arrogant guards are bad shots.

The clicking of a gun cocking has me throwing myself onto the ground. As I turn over onto my back, I drag my leg in a circular motion, hitting the ankles of the surrounding guards. It happens so fast that they can't do anything except shoot randomly as they lose their balance and fall to the ground.

I somersault to the nearest moaning guard, yank the gun out of his hands, and hit him in the head with the butt of it. As I jump up, I grab the gun off the floor and toss it further down the dark hallway.

Even though I have weapons of my own, I may need it to fight Kinsley's young friend. There's something poetic about fighting people with their own weapons. I smile as I walk toward the dark hallway.

"Stop!" A young guard yells while charging after me.

His gun hangs in his hand by his side.

Silly boy. You shouldn't have a gun if you're not willing to use it.

He runs up to me and I pull my fist back to punch him in the nose. My knuckles land in the center of the boy's face with a sickening crunch. Blood pours from the guard's nose and he drops his gun as he bends over to catch his breath.

I know he won't be able to see for a while. His eyes will tear up and swell closed. The guard's head will ache and his face will feel like it's on fire.

I've had my nose broken a few times. Irena broke it once accidentally, and Zurie broke it twice to teach me to fight through all types of injuries. Fighting with a broken nose is hard. *Very* hard.

I hop over one of the men I've knocked out and head to the back of the facility.

Keeping low, I stick to the shadows until I approach the "T" in the hallway.

The gun. It's lying right here. I bend over and pick it up.

The cold steel in my hand is a comfort as I silently stalk deeper into the compound.

I keep my senses tuned in to any changes around me. On alert for any sudden noises. My borrowed gun is cocked and ready to shoot. But it's quiet here. Almost too *quiet.*

There's light shining from the end of the hallway on my left.

I quietly move down the corridor and head toward the light.

As I leave the darkness of the hallway, I notice the hanging light bulbs are gone from this area of the compound. The light is coming from old-fashioned fire torches that are bolted to the wall every five feet or so.

Strange.

What the *hell?*

Where are we? In the 15th century?

Then again, if there is no electricity, they can use this part of the compound off the grid without being detected. This hell reminds me of Zurie's dungeons. Like Zurie, Kinsley is a genius strategist and a master manipulator. Gods, this has to be another of the Vaer Boss's evil strategies. Especially if my instincts are right and there are prisoners held in this corridor. And my instincts are *always* right.

I move slowly down the medieval hallway as I search for signs of the prisoners. Wooden doors with some kind of metal reinforcement line the passageway. The doors remind me of the ones you would find in ancient dungeons.

What in the *hell* are the Vaer doing?

One thing is for sure. The entrance of the building is just for show. This corridor is where the action is.

As I walk further down the hallway, my stomach clenches at the coppery stench filling the air. I know I'm on the right path.

Anxiety washes over me as I realize this is a true place of horrors.

Damn it. I don't like this at all.

Gunfire comes from the room I left Drew in.

"Drew, how are things going out there?" I whisper low into the comm.

"Good. You?" He asks.

"Drew, there's something weird about this place. It's like a dungeon, metal reinforced wooden doors. Torches on the wall."

I take a moment to study my surroundings as the steady, sure-footed steps of my fire dragon come closer.

"It's *weird*," we say at the same time.

"Rory, Let's get out of here. We've done what we came to do."

"We need to release the dragons the Vaer are experimenting on. I'm not leaving until I'm finished," I remind Drew.

Still whispering. Still paying attention to any sudden noises. Still constantly searching for Vaer.

Reaching one of the doors, I peek in through a tiny window at the top. I can't see a damn thing. The window is thick, probably bulletproof. The glass is so dirty it's hard to make out anything.

"Damn it, Rory," Drew growls as he heads to the other side of the wide hallway. The passageway is so wide it can easily fit twenty shifted dragons. He needs space.

Drew's the one who urged me to hurry over here in the first place. I know he's just concerned, but it really pisses me off when he gets all overprotective and controlling. I'll talk with him later. For now, I'm going to do what I came here to do.

I stand on my tiptoes as I struggle to see through the dirty window. The filth is concealing whatever is on the other side of the thick glass. I lick my thumb and use it to wipe away some of the grime from the window.

Finally, I see something or someone move. In the corner, there are at least five—maybe more silhouettes. A soft shuffle of feet comes from behind me. I immediately turn around, hoisting my gun, and pointing it where my attacker will be.

A small black dragon stares back at me and growls low in response.

For a moment, I'm dumb struck. Another victim? Or a feral? I can't tell.

It takes everything in me not to scoop the little guy up in my arms. I want to take him out of here and then burn this damn place to the ground.

A *child.* Seriously? What the fuck are the Vaer doing here? I force myself to calm down, before talking to the small dragon child.

"Hi," I whisper gently, "Are you okay?"

The little dragon nods his head, but his body is shaking.

I motion for him to come to me, but he doesn't move an inch. I don't blame him, I just had a gun aimed at his little head.

"I'm sorry," I say as gently as I can.

I'm still struggling with my rage at the fact the

Vaer could stoop so low. The fact that Kinsley has captured and probably tested on children has me struggling to control my dragon.

Now we both want every guard associated with this place dead. No questions. My blood is boiling.

I need to control my angry thoughts. I *have* to care for this child.

Lowering the gun, I bend down and try again to urge him to come to me.

"I promise I won't hurt you. I'm here to help," I whisper with a gentle smile.

I'm trying to keep my tone low and soothing, but to be honest, I'm not the nurturing type. The instincts are there, and I really want to protect him. If I could, I'd wash his mind of the horrors he's seen. But the best I can do is get him out of here.

We have to leave—now. But he won't move. He refuses to approach me. So, I slowly walk toward him.

When I get close enough to touch him, I reach my hand out and gently place it on his head. He trembles under my touch, and I notice that he has fresh wounds on his side. Whatever the Vaer are doing to these dragons, I'm going to put an end to it. Tonight.

I open a mind-to-mind connection with the

young dragon, and I'm flooded with the memory of the pain of blood being taken. Vials and vials of it. The image of a small boy dressed in rags and chained to a steal bed floods my mind. Kinsley's young commander's face is furious as he stares down at the light haired boy. The small dragon child is shaking in fear. His blue-green eyes are filled with terror.

I'm so sorry that you had to go through that, I tell the little dragon through our bond.

I pour my hurt and sorrow at the way he was treated through the bond as well. I don't want to believe any dragon could treat their children like possessions instead of little beings that need love and nurturing. But that's exactly what the Vaer are doing.

Do you know if there are others? I ask my new companion.

He nods.

Images of all types and sizes of dragons spring into my mind. My stomach lurches with disgust at what is being done to these people. I force the bile back down my throat at what is being done to these *children.*

"I'm going to protect you," I promise as I remove my hand from his head. I motion for him to stay close to me while we search for the others.

My anger is begging to burst free, to level this place and everyone associated with it. But I have to stay focused. We are supposed to run away today.

I close my eyes for a moment and suck in a deep breath. I have to calm down. These dragons need our help.

The loud rumble of a growling ice dragon comes over the comm.

"Get your heavy ass claw off of my head before you crush it, and I'll ask her Levi. Damn, brother. Calm down!" Tucker shouts.

"Levi wants to know if there is a child in there," Tucker says calmly.

Things must have settled down outside if the dragons have landed and are being updated on what's happening. Tucker must have been telling Levi and Jace what I was saying while I was talking to the young dragon.

Children being imprisoned here isn't going to sit well with any of my men. Especially my master of stealth. Being a Vaer, Levi knows they treat their children cruelly, brutally, and with a total lack of compassion.

"A dragon child. I don't know if there are more," I

answer. "Ask Jace to call Harper and see if she can help us care for the prisoners we're freeing today."

The little dragon tilts his black scaled head up at me and gives me a questioning stare with his blue-green eyes. I don't want to tell him there is help outside waiting. There could be recording devices or a Vaer guard within earshot. I have to keep him and my men safe.

"Can you take me to the others?" I ask my new little friend.

The dragon child shakes his head. His eyes are wide and terrified.

"I promise I'm going to get you all out, but you have to help me. Okay?"

"Oh, he's not going anywhere," the young commander's voice says as he and five guards step through a hole in the wall just a yard away from me and my little companion.

"You're going to let him and any other dragons you have here go," I demand as I stand tall and take a fighting stance.

"Those are big words for someone who's very outnumbered and dumb enough to walk right into my trap." The snobby man-child chuckles.

The hallway brightens, and fluorescent lights descend from the ceiling.

Hidden lights. Secret passageways. Why go to all the trouble?

"So, you do have power in this hallway?" I ask.

I'm surprised. And I don't like surprises. Surprises are a sign that I'm unprepared. I can't be unprepared. Not ever.

Why go to the trouble of appearing off-grid, when they aren't? Unless it has more to do with their dragon victims? Why bother keeping up the appearances of being in an underground dungeon? They must be trying to make their victims feel like they're somewhere they're not. The Vaer are confusing their prisoners.

Confused people are easier to control. Easier to manipulate, so you can get what you want from them.

The young Vaer doesn't answer my question about the lights. He's too busy blowing his own trumpet to notice what's going on around him.

I give Drew, who's silently stalking toward me, a subtle nod of my head. Raising my eyebrows slightly, I let him know to hang back and keep quiet.

"I have a little counter offer for you. I'll let him go, if you stay?" Kinsley's apprentice asks.

I don't know if the public image that Brett has helped me to develop has the Vaer believing I'll put my life on the line for a single small dragon without a plan. But this punk thinks he can get me to just lie down and be taken to Kinsley.

Not gonna happen.

I have to get this young dragon out of here safely. But more dragons are being held in this dungeon, and one just isn't going to cut it. I need to free them all.

"What? Do you think I'm just going to trade my life for his?" I ask.

"Oh, absolutely. Especially if a news channel picks up that you sacrificed yourself for a little dragon. Poor Rory, always the martyr," the overly confident Vaer mocks.

My dragon pushes against me. She wants out. *Now.*

I dive toward the Vaer commander and knock him to the ground. After pinning his arms under my knees, I sit on his chest and pummel the punk's face with my magic filled fists. His eyes roll back into his head, blood pools beneath him, and he stops moving.

The brutality of what I've just done hits me like a hard slap in the face. I jump to my feet and shake out my arms to get rid of the memory of killing someone with my bare hands.

When I look around for Drew, my eyes land on

the little dragon who is staring at me with beautiful blue-green eyes as large as saucers.

He shouldn't have seen that, but he has probably seen worse in this hell-hole.

How dare Kinsley's apprentice insinuate that I was only saving this little boy for my own self-image? I curse up a storm in my mind, but I don't say a word out loud.

The guards quickly jolt out of their shock and rush at me. A tall, skinny guard tries to grab the dragon child. I jump in front of him and aim the gun from my waistband at the guard's head.

"Touch him and you die," I say.

The clicks of guns being cocked have me sucking in a deep breath. I'm willing to die if it will save this little boy.

Drew's heavy footsteps thunder toward us. He's done being silent. Drew slams his fist into the face of the guard closest to him, then sweeps his long leg in a circle, knocking the remaining four guards off of their feet. My fire dragon stands over the downed guards with pure hatred in his eyes.

"Move and I'll end you," he growls.

I'm out of time. I need to find the other dragons and get them out of here. And we all need to get back to Ashgrave.

"Can you distract them while I look for the others?" I ask.

Drew gives me a firm nod, and I set off to find more captives.

I break down the door to the first room I had looked in, and I yell for the dragons to leave. But they can't. They're bound to the floor in the corner with chains that are attached to manacles around their ankles and fastened to a metal loop in the concrete floor. I call my magic axe into my hands and cut through the chains at their ankles. It takes a little while to free all ten of them from their chains.

"Get out, now," I tell them.

"This way," Drew adds as he directs them where to exit the building safely.

Their bodies barrel down the wide hallway, clumsily fumbling toward the entranceway while their large talons scrape against the concrete surface.

Whimpering comes from across the hallway. I can barely hear it above the sounds of fleeing dragons. Little dragons.

I break down the door, and there's a group of dragon children huddled together. Several pairs of yellow, green, and brown eyes stare at me in terror. Small pearlescent fangs curl over their dragon lips, as they watch my every move.

There are at least twenty of them locked in this cell. These little dragons are being kept like trash, just piled together in a quiet corner of the building with no signs of food or water. My heart pangs with dread at the way their little bodies tremble in fear. I lower my gun and suck in a steadying breath.

"Hi," I whisper. "I'm going to get you out of here."

I know they don't believe me. And I don't blame them. They've been abused, starved, and tested on.

The little dragon who's been my companion since entering this hallway steps up beside me. Like a silent, trusting sentinel. He stands next to me as a symbol of faith.

"Can you follow me?" I ask. "I'll keep you safe. There are a lot of people here to help you get out. We have to leave now."

One of the dragons, with white scales and stunning blue eyes, nods at me. He's the first to stand, and I can tell he's the leader. Once he moves, the rest of the dragons do too. They head toward me and my friend, we exit the cell, and I lead them down the hallway. I do my best to keep them close to the wall and together. The last thing I need is to lose one of them in the compound before we get outside.

Drew knocks the four soldiers he's guarding unconscious and joins the back of our line.

Witnesses. Kinsley needs to know that we were here and that we left without burning down the compound or killing all of her guards.

During our trek to safety, I have to shoot a few guards that wander too close to me and my precious cargo. As we move down the corridor, I kick open every door I pass. They're all empty. As we make it to the front hallway of the facility, I inform Tucker of my little party.

"Tucker, the dragon children are free. Can I get some help with them?" I ask.

Running footsteps head in our direction, and Tucker joins us.

As he slides to a stop in front of me, his eyes widen at the size of the group behind me. I can tell he's counting how many children we're freeing as his mouth takes on the shape of an "O."

"Time to get out of here, babe." Tucker kisses me on the forehead.

I want to ask if the hack went as smoothly as it seemed to, but I can't say anything until I know we are all safe.

As I walk up to Jace, I lay my hand on his leg. *Did Harper agree to heal the survivors and care for the children?*

She is more than happy to help, especially if it means

throwing a wrench into Kinsley's plans, my mate says with a toothy grin.

We regroup by the chopper. Jace, Levi, and Drew choose to fly to the Fairfax capital in dragon form to flank the chopper and the dragon survivors. I get back into Tucker's second favorite toy, and Ashgrave hops inside with me. My little metal dragon seems excited that he finally got to smite some enemies.

I take the time to observe the survivors inside the chopper. Some of the former captives stare at Ashgrave with gratitude, and I wonder what my evil little butler had to do to keep these people safe.

A high pitched growl has my gaze scanning the outside of the chopper. I spot an incredibly small ice-blue dragon touching Levi's outstretched wing with its own. My ice dragon gently picks up the dragon child in his front talons and cradles it to his chest as Jace roars into the air to tell the thirty dragons to take off.

The helicopter whirs to life, and within minutes, we're all airborne and on our way to see Harper.

I start to get comfortable as our group heads to the Fairfax capital.

My phone starts buzzing in my back pocket. I take it out and stare at the screen. Unknown number.

As I watch the dragons and dragon children fly with my men back toward safety, I plan the destruction of the Vaer.

My phone buzzes again, so I click the talk button and wait for the caller to say something.

"Rory?" my sister says, and my shoulders instantly relax.

"Irena," I sigh. Gratitude warms my heart, until her next sentence hits me in the chest and makes my heart skip a beat.

"I need to meet with you as soon as possible. Face-to-face. It can't wait."

The fact that she wants to meet in person means something has gone very, very wrong.

"All right, I'll be home tomorrow night."

"I'll meet you at Ashgrave in a couple of days. Don't die, little sister," Irena says before the line goes dead.

CHAPTER THREE

As we fly over the helipad at the Fairfax capital, I suck in a steadying breath as I spot Russell, Harper, and a few dojo soldiers standing by one of the Fairfax's choppers waiting for us.

Jace makes an earthshattering roar, telling the group of dragons to land, as Tucker brings the chopper down on its pad.

"Who needs help getting to the infirmary?" I ask the shifters in the chopper.

"I think we can manage to help each other ma'am," a young redheaded woman not much older than me says. "Thank you for saving us. We would have died if we had stayed in that hell-hole much longer. We're in your debt."

"You're all welcomed to stay here," I tell them.

"But realize we will need to check you for trackers. I won't put everyone who calls this place home at risk."

"Understood," A black haired man says as he wraps his arm around the woman who spoke.

I exit the chopper and watch as Jace, Levi, Drew, Russell, and Harper hand out dark colored sweat pants and jackets to the dragons who shifted to their human forms.

A little blond-haired boy with blue-green eyes waves at me as he rolls his pant legs up. A dark haired pre-teen boy bends over to roll up the sleeves of a young girl with chubby cheeks and freckles.

"You saved them, Rory." The Fairfax Boss touches my arm and gives it an affirmative squeeze.

"They're so young, Harper," I tell my friend. "Why would anyone do that to these children?"

"Because Kinsley Vaer only thinks of herself. I'll get these little ones settled and talk to you later," Harper says.

The Fairfax Boss helps the children finish getting dressed and lines them up in pairs before she walks them into the castle.

My men, Russell, and some dojo soldiers make their way to me as the last of the children disappear inside the capital.

"Can you please help the shifters in the chopper to the infirmary?" I ask Russell and the dojo soldiers. "Some are in very bad shape."

"We will take care of them," a dojo soldier with kind eyes says.

Jace carries the shaved and bloodied man who had asked for his death into the castle. Drew follows with a blonde woman lying unconscious in his arms. Tucker and Levi are each carrying young men who are as skinny as rails. Their skin is so thin that I can see their veins. What were the Vaer doing to these people? They are clinging to life because of Kinsley and her selfishness.

Russell lifts a woman with blue hair into his arms as though she weighs nothing. I run to the side of a tall girl with long brunette hair who is stumbling and unsteady on her feet.

First things first.

These people need to be healed. And not only from their physical injuries. No one knows what horrors they've lived through. But I do know that Kinsley won't get away with this.

As I stand on my balcony breathing the cool morning air, I watch the sun rise over the mountains and breathe a sigh of relief.

Harper has taken on the twenty-one dragon children and assigned them caretakers and teachers.

The teachers have already set up three school rooms in the children's wing of the Fairfax capital. And a few of the teenage children have been placed with the dojo soldiers to train so they can learn practical skills along with the basics.

The Vaer didn't care enough about these children to teach them to read or write. It's almost like they didn't want them. The Vaer didn't even place trackers in them. They only wanted their blood and dragon magic to use as Kinsley saw fit.

My dragon coils with fury at how the Vaer treat their children. And I feel the same way.

The Vaer *need* to be punished.

We had to bury three of the four severely injured dragons before we left the capital last night. We didn't get there in time to save them all. But the bald man who was ready to face death is walking the halls of Harper's infirmary with a walker. *Bonus*—he's the only one left in the infirmary.

A total of eighteen freed prisoners have had their trackers removed and have joined the Fairfax family.

By the looks in their eyes, they are ready to give Kinsley a taste of her own medicine.

If I didn't hate the Vaer Boss, I would worry for her safety. *Not.* After everything she's done to these people, the children, and to me and my men, one thing is certain.

Kinsley Vaer is going down.

"YOUR SISTER APPROACHES, MY QUEEN." Ashgrave's thundering voice draws me from my thoughts.

"Bring her to the main dining hall," I tell my castle.

"YES, MY QUEEN. WOULD YOU LIKE YOUR LORDS TO JOIN YOU?"

"No. I'll meet with Irena alone," I tell my castle.

The wall to my left swings open and I take the staircase down, two steps at a time. As the wall opens into the formal dining hall, I step through.

"Rory!" Irena says from the entrance of the massive dining room.

We run to each other and she throws her arms around me, squeezing me like her arms are bands of steel and she's trying to make sure I can't wiggle away.

"Glad to see you escaped Kinsley's compound of horrors," my sister says with a smirk.

"That's old news," I tell her. "I'll introduce you to some of the shifters we saved some time."

"Then the chatter is right, you broke out all of the Vaer prisoners from the testing facility," Irena says with a smile pulling at her lips as she punches me playfully in the arm. "Way to go, little sister."

"Why did we need to meet in person, Irena?" I ask.

Irena doesn't look at me. Instead, she looks around the room and plucks some grapes from the fruit bowl in the center of the table.

"Rory, my Spectre rebels are growing in number every day. It's honestly getting a little out of hand. I need a way to keep them organized. A way to give them direction, and an enemy to take out, before they get hurt."

"This is all stuff you could have said over the phone," I say with a small nod.

Something is off with Irena. Part of me wants to believe she had to see me because she just really missed me. But my sister knows better. We keep our meet-ups limited because it's too dangerous. Both Quinn sisters in one place is tempting to all the wrong kinds of people.

"Spill it, Irena. Why did we have to meet?" I ask, allowing my frustration to show.

My sister sets her bright green eyes on me with a stare that could peel paint. But I don't back down. I want answers.

Irena plops a few grapes in her mouth as we continue to silently stare at each other.

"You're going to want to sit down for this."

I pull out a chair and take a seat. Not because I'm worried about what she has to say, but to let her think she's won the staring contest.

Tossing a grape into my mouth, I sit back and put my feet up on the table, trying to give the impression that I'm relaxed and ready for anything. Irena paces the dining room floor and wrings her hands. Something has her on edge. I haven't seen her like this in years.

"Diesel has become the Ghost and is remaking the Spectres into his own twisted image. The rebels who join me are risking their lives. He even hacked my phone to find out who is working against him. I think he knows I've planted moles among his Spectres. This is why I couldn't go into details over the phone. I don't want him to know that I'm aware of his hack," Irena blurts out as she sits with a thump into one of the dining room chairs.

"Sounds to me like Diesel is being Diesel. He's grabbing for as much power as he can and he will take out anyone in his way," I say with a hard edge to my voice.

"What's worse is he's trying to take over where the Knights left off," Irena adds. "I have intel that Diesel has allies all over. People who want to destroy every dragon who walks the planet. You included, Rory," Irena confesses with panic in her eyes.

"We both knew this is what he would do if he ever became the Ghost, Irena. But, he's only one man. And you said it yourself, the rebels are growing in number every single day. We will take care of Diesel," I reassure my sister.

I'm not afraid of him. The destruction this power hungry man could cause, well, I need to make sure that doesn't happen.

"That's not the worst of it," Irena whispers.

Finally. She's going to tell me the rest of what's going on.

"Kinsley's developing a new bio-weapon," my sister blurts out. "And Diesel wants to get his greasy hands on it."

"Yeah. I figured that's what the dragons were for."

I think back to the compound, to the people chained and bloodied. To the three shifters who are now dead because of Kinsley. To the countless night-mares the dragon children have lived through because of the Vaer Boss's lack of compassion and need to dominate the world, no matter the cost.

"Tell me more about the dragons you freed, little sister," Irena demands with a frown.

"We found chained dragon shifters at the Vaer facility we raided. They were all bruised and bloodied, and the worst part is there were dragon children being held there. It was clear they were being abused and tested on for some reason. A new bio-weapon makes perfect sense," I say, shaking my head.

Irena shakes her head, and I know it's to try and remove the images of children being abused from her mind. We grew up without a choice of what we would become. Both of us have a soft spot in our hearts for children who are forced to be something they're not.

But our lives are different now. *Very different.* I picture each of my men in my mind, and my heart swells with the love I have for them. I would do anything for them. Absolutely anything.

That is why Kinsley has to die.

"Diesel is paranoid and trusts no one," Irena says. "But I do have a mole—someone he would never suspect as one of my rebels—who keeps tabs on him."

"He must be getting desperate," I add. "The new

Ghost is trying to track what you're doing and who you're talking to. That makes life a lot more interesting."

I scoot my chair back, stand up, and start pacing the length of the long dining room. Pacing helps me think.

"We can use this to our advantage, if we do it right," I say.

"You might be onto something there," Irena says as she stands in front of me.

"How much do you think he knows?" I ask my sister.

"Not much. I have software on my phone that alerts me to hacks and bugs."

"Good. If we feed Diesel false intel, we could use the hack against him," I say nodding.

"What kind of false intel?" Irena's bright green eyes watch my every move.

"We just say what we need him to hear on your hacked phone."

"Ah!" Irena smiles. "Then we can set him up."

"Exactly. He won't know what hit him."

Brilliant. It's like the universe itself has aligned to help us take down Diesel. I can hardly wait.

"How do we talk in the mean time?" she asks.

"And don't you think you have enough on your plate? You do have a dragon war brewing."

"Let me take care of the dragon war, and nothing needs to change. You call me as much as you normally would. Give me fake intel, tell me about Kinsley, things we usually talk about. Just don't say too much. When we need to see each other, we can say we need 'sister time'. That will be our clue to meet here within two days."

"So, how do we decide what lie he needs to hear when it's time to take him out?" Irena asks.

"I haven't decided that yet. We can meet up again to talk about it."

My sister nods in agreement.

"We need to figure out exactly what he knows. So we can finally stop him."

"Rory, you've got this," Irena says with a smirk as she puts her hands on my shoulders. "Between you, your magic, your men, and Ashgrave, you've got it handled. I promise."

"Yeah. Having a team and magic is helpful," I wink. "Maybe you should tap into your dragon magic?"

"I'd rather not think about the magic that runs in my blood right now. Thanks." Irena drops her hands.

Irena doesn't want to accept that part of herself.

The part that Kinsley changed with the bio-weapon. The part that is a dragon.

The more time my sister spends with me and my men, she can see that dragon magic isn't all bad. And that's a step in the right direction. The direction of having Irena accept the dragon that lives inside her.

I step closer to my sister and wrap my arms around her before she leaves.

"Just let me know if you learn anything new," I tell her.

"Yeah, I will. Just try not to die," Irena says, teasing me.

CHAPTER FOUR

My sister's words tumble through my brain all night, making me step back and look at the problem like my dead mentor would have. I have to take out Diesel and Kinsley. And to do that, I have to control my magic and bring Ashgrave back to his full power.

As the morning sun warms my room, I grab a pair of jeans and a sweatshirt from my closet and get dressed.

"Ashgrave?"

"YES, MY QUEEN?" my castle's voice booms.

"I'd like to go to the treasury."

"RIGHT AWAY, MY QUEEN."

A section of the wall swings open and I step inside. I follow the secret stairwell Ashgrave has made for me toward the treasury. For as long as I live here, I will never stop marveling at the magic that is my mysterious castle. My home. *Home.* The word still feels strange to me, even as I descend the stairs and come to an opening in the wall. I know we won't be completely safe here. Not until every orb is found and placed in their domains, and Ashgrave has all of his abilities online.

I step through the opening at the bottom of the staircase and stand in front of the giant double doors that lead into the treasury. The huge ornate doors open, and I walk through them. Bright sunshine streams in through the windows and reflects off the piles of gold, jewels, and silver.

The three suits of dragon armor grabs my attention, and I take slow, steady steps over to them. I get close enough to touch the one in the middle, but I don't. Instead, I stand next to the polished suit of armor and search its white and gold filigree surface. The beautifully decorated armor belonged to Morgana, and it served a purpose at one point. Yet, the deep gouges in the metal tell of a much darker time. A period when dragon wars were normal and Castle Ashgrave was a force to be reckoned with. With the threat of a new dragon war hanging heavy on my shoulders, I know it is coming again. A war I *have* to win.

It's essential to Ashgrave, to all of us, to find the remaining orbs. Having Ashgrave at full power is the only way to ensure our safety. I don't have to give much thought to which of his abilities I want—no, *need*—online. Ashgrave's army. The idea of a metallic, magically replenishing dragon military that's impenetrable sounds very comforting.

"Hey babe," a familiar voice fills the room, and I turn away from the armor to look at the dorky grin on Tucker's handsome face.

"Hey," I reply.

"How did your meeting with Irena go?"

"As well as can be expected, I suppose." I shrug my shoulders. "Have you talked to Drew? Was he able to get the software installed?"

My gorgeous weapons expert nods.

"Are you okay? You have a weird look on your face." He observes my facial expressions.

"Are you sure you're okay? You are being extremely annoying," I respond with a smirk, so he knows I'm kidding.

I don't want to be serious right now. I've wasted enough time being serious in coming up with a plan to stop Diesel and Kinsley.

Tucker steps up to me, wrapping a strong arm around my waist. He pulls me against his hard body. He's so distracting. My dragon stirs, rumbling with desire, the traitor.

"Trying to get me to talk?" I ask.

"You've figured me out," he confesses as he leans forward and presses his warm lips to mine, which immediatcly has warmth pooling between my legs.

"No. Not now," I laugh as I take a step away from Tucker. "I have to focus."

"I know that. I'm just trying to cheer you up." He gives me an adorable smirk—it works.

"You're impossible," I say with a huge smile.

"You love it."

"We need another orb. I need to get Ashgrave's army online. We're going to need it, sooner rather than later."

Whether the world is ready for it or not.

Really, I don't think our world can understand or trust everything that Ashgrave has to offer, but I've seen what the Vaer are capable of. As long as Kinsley Vaer is around, there will be a need for Ashgrave's power. All of it.

But, the question of whether or not I can command it—command him—that's a whole other matter.

"Possibly," Tucker says with a nod of his head.

"Possibly? What do you think I should do when we get our hands on another orb?" I ask.

Tucker is many things. He's a skilled fighter, an expert with every weapon under the sun, a pilot, and hotter than hell. But in this case, I need his opinion as my weapons expert.

"I think having an army of indestructible metal dragons is necessary," he says as his lips turn up into a charming smile. "The bee drones are a huge plus too. And don't get me started on the magically infused weapons that come with the placement of the orb in the army domain."

"You would be the one to think about the weapons," I chuckle.

I try to hide my worry over how the world will change when the orb brings even more of the dragon gods' magic to life, but he catches the slight furrow of my brow before I can hide it from him.

"You know it's what we need, but you're doubting yourself—your abilities. Aren't you?"

I can't answer. It's not that I doubt myself. My shoulders tense as I try to pinpoint exactly what's irritating me.

"If you're worried about leading us all into the pit

of hell, don't. We're already here," he says with a grin.

But I can't smile or move in response. I'm stuck in my thoughts.

"Listen babe, if you're worried about being a bad leader, stop. There are no bad leaders, only bad choices made from dishonorable intentions. And I, and everyone else here, don't think there's a dishonorable bone in your body," my weapons expert confesses.

Oh, Tucker. You're so sweet.

As I stare past him at the dragon armor, my mind drifts over the dishonorable things I've done in my past. My body tenses as I remember all of the dragons and people I've killed. The first few were murders I didn't want to commit. But the last of them I had taken out only because it was absolutely necessary.

"Rory, you're nothing like my father. He didn't have a single noble cell in his entire body. But you... you have the makings of a great leader. Hell, Ashgrave calls you queen."

"I'm no queen," I say, shaking my head.

"Bullshit!" Tucker shouts.

His normally playful tone is replaced with a

serious one. It's kinda hot. It means he's being real, and that's a side he doesn't show very often.

"You are a true queen. Whether you accept that or not," he says.

Tucker grabs my hand and places it on his chest. The heat and muscles beneath my fingertips warms my hand. The sincerity in his eyes warms my heart. He traces the edge of my chin with the fingertips of his other hand, and I close my eyes with a soft moan.

"Rory," he breathes heavily into my ear as he pulls me in close to him. "You're going to be one hell of a queen, and you know... I'm always ready to bring a few bazookas."

The seriousness is gone from his eyes, replaced with a sparkle of mischief. My weapons expert kisses my neck as he slips on some coins and we fall to the floor.

My arms hold him tight as I reach my hands up and run my fingers through his hair. Tucker's lips collide with mine. I want him, now. He pulls me on top of him. His erection presses against my stomach, and a gasp of pleasure escapes my lips.

"Tucker," I sigh.

My dragon is wide awake and horny as hell. I'm fighting the urge to strip off our clothes and make love to him here in the pile of gold coins.

There's a knock on the double doors, and we stop.

"Go away!" Tucker shouts, desire dripping from his gorgeous green eyes as his gaze runs over my body.

Expecting the person on the other side of the door to obey, his fingers leave a trail of heat up my stomach, as they make their way to my breasts.

"I need to talk to Rory," Brett demands through the closed door.

Shit.

My own little harbinger of bad news.

He's a mood killer for sure.

"Forget him," Tucker says in a voice that washes over me like sunshine, warming my entire body inside and out.

I wish Brett would just disappear. I try to ignore him, but the door handle jiggles. Quick as lightning, Tucker is on his feet and pulling me up to mine as Brett walks into the treasure-filled room.

"Damn you, Brett," Tucker growls.

My weapons expert barely tolerates the guy as it is. This isn't going to help. Brett just made life harder on himself, at least where Tucker is concerned.

"Why can't you just go away?" Tucker mumbles under his breath.

The ex-Knights stare each other down, and I'm reminded of the way peacocks strut around with their feathers on display. I cover my mouth to stifle a giggle, breaking the tension in the room.

"Uh, sorry to interrupt, but Drew needs to see you both in the war room," the public relations expert says.

A million obscenities fly through my mind as I think of how much fun me and Tucker could be having if Brett hadn't interrupted.

"Did he tell you why he needs to see us?" I ask as my shoulders slump.

"It has something to do with the bugs that were planted at the Palarne and Darrington capitals."

I sigh heavily as I straighten my clothes and grab Tucker's hand. We don't have a choice—intel is more important. For now, at least.

Tucker looks pissed as hell and I know why. I give him a sexy smile and a flirty wink. I'll make it up to him later.

Ashgrave leads us to the war room through his private tunnels. When we exit the tunnels, we stand outside the door of the war room and knock.

Levi opens the door and gives me a kiss on the

cheek. He ushers us inside, and I find Drew and Jace sitting at the large mahogany table, and even though their eyes are sad, they're sexy as hell. My men—I smile.

Levi takes his seat as Tucker and I make our way to the table. Tucker pulls out a chair for me and then takes the seat on my left. Brett walks to the far end of the table to sit as far away from Tucker as possible.

"Brett said that you have some new intel," I say, not being one to waste time.

"Yes, we've learned from our bug at the Palarne capital that Isaac is choosing to side with us—with you, Rory. He believes in you. Believes in your cause. The Palarne Boss hates what Kinsley's doing and that she has no regard for humans or dragonkind," Jace informs us.

I let out a sigh of relief as my muscles unclench. That's good news. Finally. I needed something good to happen after the skirmish at the Vaer facility three days ago. I shake my head to get rid of the images of the people who suffered because of the Vaer Boss.

"Another thing," Drew adds, "he thinks that Kinsley is absolutely insane. Judging by what we found at the Vaer compound, and the state and ages of the dragons we found there, I wouldn't doubt it."

"This is good news, but you're not telling me something." I shrug.

Drew grabs the recorder from the center of the table and fast forwards through some of it. Payton Palarne's voice comes over the speaker. He's eager, too eager if you ask me.

"I want to make the delivery," Payton says a little out of breath.

"What delivery?" I ask as I quirk an eyebrow at Drew. He pauses the recording.

"We don't know," Jace intervenes.

At the sound of his voice, my dragon is immediately on alert for our mate. My dragon is turned on, especially since she wasn't satisfied earlier. My mate's voice has warmth pooling in my core.

"Good or bad?" I ask as I sit up in my chair.

"We think good, considering that Isaac is on our side. But we will take measures to make sure. However, Isaac has asked Payton to wait to make the delivery until he gives the okay. Whatever it is, he's made it clear that it's a delicate matter. And Rory, there's one more thing."

"What's that?" I ask Jace.

"Something Isaac said. He's hoping that you'll share what you know about the dragon gods," Drew adds.

That's information I'm not willing to give, mainly because I don't know everything myself. The things I do know, I don't really like—I need to know more. I *need* the other two Astor Diaries.

"So, what else is happening with the Palarne?" I ask.

I'm thankful we were able to get the bugs in undetected. It's finally working to our benefit.

"Payton doesn't like that Isaac seems obsessed with knowing more about the dragon gods. That's it. The bug has been quiet lately," Drew says.

"We should keep the bug in place," I say. "At least until we find out what this delivery is all about. And until we fully trust the Palarne as allies."

Jace and Tucker nod.

"We need to keep it in place, as a precaution," Levi says, breaking his silence.

"I hope the Palarne are going to deliver something we can use in this war. Maybe even stop it before it kills hundreds, if not thousands, of people," I tell my men. "What about the bug at the Darrington capital?"

"We're getting to that," Jace says with a sexy smile.

"Maybe we should listen in," Brett pipes up.

Drew messes with the audio coming in from his family's capital.

"Is this a recording?" I ask Jace.

He nods. Moments later, Milo's voice fills the room.

"I don't know how it happened," Milo says, his voice shaking.

"How in the hell does someone break into your warehouse and you don't even know it happened?" Jett's voice thunders through the room. "I noticed you were off the grid the day of the break in."

The room is silent. We're all frozen, waiting to see what will happen next.

Will Milo tell his father that the Fairfax took him and threw him into an arena to punish him for killing Jace's brother? If Jett finds out what happened, he will definitely turn on the Fairfax and side with Kinsley. Unless Milo does the right thing. This is his chance to be honorable.

"I... I didn't want to anger or disappoint you. But, I went out with some friends and I had a little too much fun. The toilet was my best friend on the day the warehouse was robbed," Milo apologizes. "I guess I need to be more disciplined."

My men and I gasp in shock. Milo actually

covered for the Fairfax. I never expected that from him.

Never.

"Just make sure you take care of the warehouse situation. I don't want to see any more raids on our facilities. Got it?"

"Yes father," Milo murmurs.

It seems like the incident in the arena has changed Milo. Time will tell if he's changed for the better or not.

"I thought you wanted to be my successor," Jett growls.

Don't fall for it, Milo. No matter how much Jett may deny it, Drew has always been the Darrington Boss's choice to take up the title. But Drew has found a new purpose. He's found a new family. My fire dragon has me.

"Milo, if you want to be my successor so damn bad, track down the thieves and kill them. I don't care who it is. Dragons, Spectres—whoever it is—I want them dead." Jett's voice sends a chill up my spine, even over the recording. "I suspect it's the Spectres going for a weapons grab. It's too bad that the greatest weapon in history is sitting with my other son in a well-protected castle. I wish I could control the dragon vessel."

As the recording continues, a door creaks open and bangs as it closes. Someone just left the room.

"The others aren't ready for her yet," Jett whispers, almost as an afterthought.

It'll be a cold day in hell before I'll be some pawn in Jett's game. No matter who the players are.

CHAPTER FIVE

I stand with my feet in the snow on one of the mountains that surround my castle with my eyes closed. The wind whistles a deep and resonant tune through the trees.

Concentrate, I tell myself.

But I can't.

Jace is standing only a few feet away. My dragon is dancing at his closeness, and my thighs are clenching with need for my mate.

"Would you mind moving over there?" I point to the mountain across from us.

"Are you serious?" Jace asks with a grin that could melt the ice surrounding us.

My dragon coos her excitement. She doesn't care where we are, what time it is, or who's close by. If our mate is near, she wants to play. But, I don't have time today. I have to learn to control my magic so that it doesn't control me.

"Work now. Play later," he promises with a flirty wink.

My dragon pouts.

"Focus on the blue magic that makes the dagger," Jace says.

I focus my power, drawing on the ancient magic that lives inside me. It's not just some random force living inside my body, but it's a part of me—mine. As long as I remember that, I can stop the fluctuations.

My dragon is pacing, the energy flowing through both of us. She wants to use it as much as I want to understand it.

"Make a dagger, Rory," Jace commands.

The air around me is displaced by something being thrown at my head. Holding my right palm up, my blue magic sparks to life, and with it, my magic dagger. Spinning the dagger in my right hand, I swipe the knife Jace threw at me out of the air.

My thunderbird rewards me with a wink. I know he's challenging me to get better. Faster. To push the limits so that I learn everything I'm capable of.

"What if that hit me?" I ask with a hand on my hip.

"I would never let that happen," he promises. "I'm just trying to keep you on your toes."

"Thanks." I roll my eyes.

"Do you want to try again?"

Hell yes, I do. Our training sessions keep me sharp so I can focus on the real danger. They also give me the chance to watch my mate in action, and my dragon and I are always in the mood for that.

"I suppose," I yawn, pretending to be bored.

Jace takes a fighting stance and flashes me a wicked smile. His gaze doesn't leave my face as he draws his sword from the scabbard hanging at his side.

Looking down at the dagger in my hand, it feels extremely small compared to the four-foot long blade my mate holds.

"What the hell, Jace?"

"Focus, Rory. You can do this," my thunderbird urges.

His eyes drift to the dagger, and I know what he wants. Shit. I can't sword fight without a sword. Jace starts walking toward me, making figure eights in the air with the tip of his blade.

Holding out my palm, I close my eyes as the magic dagger hovers in the air slightly, and I focus. The crunch of footsteps in the frozen grass grows louder. I imagine that he's the enemy. In a real life situation, I only have a split second to act. The dagger starts to morph and change into an elegant glowing sword made of magic.

Jace's sword sings as it slices through the air, and I lift my sword to block his blade. The clang of metal is like music. It echoes into the valley surrounding Ashgrave. He pulls the blade back and then thrusts with it toward my waist. But I deflect it with a twist of my wrist. I swing in an arc, aiming for my mate's head. He spins away and brings his blade up to meet mine. As we parry, there is fire in his eyes, so I give him a wink. He rushes me, and I trip him. Jace's blade flies from his hand and lands tip-first in the frozen ground as he falls to his knees.

"WELL DONE, MY QUEEN," Ashgrave's voice thunders from his little mechanical dragon body.

Jace uses the distraction to somersault to his sword. He yanks it from the ground and lunges at me while still on his knees. I jump back, slip on the ice, and end up flat on my back with Jace straddling my waist. My mate gently places his sword across my shoulder.

If I was fighting an enemy, I'd be dead. But for me and Jace, this is foreplay.

"Now, you're my prisoner. I'm taking you captive

to show you why you can never make a mistake like that again," my sexy thunderbird jokes.

As he straddles my waist, he gives me a playful smirk and puts his sword in its scabbard. I use this moment when his guard is down to roll to the side, pushing him off of me. I use my momentum to roll on top of him and pin him by hooking my leg between his knees. I summon my magic dagger again and stab it into the dirt next to his head.

"Looks like you're my prisoner now," I tell my mate with a flirty smile.

He groans in desire. His erection grows against my thigh. I fold my body over Jace's and explore his mouth with mine. The heat of his chest burns through our clothes, and it takes every bit of my self-control not to rip his clothes off right here on the top of this mountain. My dragon is practically begging me to let her have fun. The *hussy*.

"Damn it, woman. We're never going to finish your training if you keep pulling stuff like this."

Jace lifts his head off the ground and plants a gentle kiss on my shoulder. The warmth of his lips sends shivers down my spine.

I jump off of him, laughing.

My mate rolls over and pulls himself up. Once

he's standing, he shakes his head and rubs the back of his neck.

"Back to work," Jace demands.

"Screw you," I retort.

"Oh, you will. When we're done training for the day." He gives me a wink. "I want you to try one more thing."

A heavy sigh escapes my lips.

"If you can create magic weapons at will, then there's no reason why you can't exchange one for another. I want you to remake your sword and then shift it to an axe," he says calmly.

"I'm not amused, Jace Goodwin."

"Just try it?"

I place my right palm up, facing the sky as I try to concentrate on making the long blade in the middle of my hand. I'm not at risk of an attack, so it takes a little longer to form the sword.

As I focus on changing the magic blade in my hand to an axe, my magic falters. It sputters like a fire going out. My vision goes grey and my head feels faint. I refocus, fighting the power surge. Moments later, my hand wraps around the sloped handle of a large battle axe.

"EXCELLENT WORK, MISTRESS. BOTH THE BATTLE AXE AND YOU ARE EXQUISITE."

I laugh out loud at Ashgrave's choice of words as I stare at the axe. I did it. I fought through a power surge. But I don't want to let Jace know, at least not yet.

"Great job, beautiful. You need to get control of those surges, though," my mate says with a scowl. "Part of me wonders if your power is growing too fast for you to handle."

"I don't know what the hell to do, Jace," I admit. "I refocused and fought through it. It's not like I can predict when they're going to happen."

"Drew told me what happened in the Vaer compound. It had to be a power surge—a fluctuation —that knocked you out.

I nod in agreement. If I don't get this under control, I won't ever win a fight with Kinsley, or Diesel. Using my magic in a battle will be too risky. Controlling the power inside me has to happen before I can even think about taking them on.

"Let's practice switching between the three weapons."

With my feet shoulder width apart, I place my right palm face up and concentrate. My dragon is calm and focused as we both pay attention to the making of our magical weapons. From axe to dagger —dagger to sword—sword to axe again.

A large shadow crosses over me, and I look up and spy my fire dragon circling over us. His brilliant red scales reflect the sun, making him appear to be on fire. I let go of my magic and the dagger disappears. Jace shakes his head and folds his arms across his chest.

"You're not off the hook, woman." My mate sighs in frustration.

"I know."

I imagine the ways Jace will punish me for not finishing my training, and heat creeps up my neck as I blush. Shit.

The mountain shakes as Drew lands nearby. His large, naked human form stalks toward me. My eyes take in his gorgeous body, and I know I'll never get tired of looking at him.

"Ashgrave?" I call out.

"YES, MY QUEEN," he says as his small metallic body saunters toward me.

"Some clothes for Drew, please?"

"AT ONCE, YOUR HIGHNESS," he responds.

Within seconds, metal hands emerge from the mountain and leave a sweatshirt and jeans lying on a dry patch of dirt.

"Is this really necessary?" Drew asks as he stares at me.

"Absolutely. I need to focus on my training and I'm having a hard enough time as it is."

Drew grumbles but pulls the clothes on.

"What are you doing here?" my mate asks.

"Rory, I've been going over the notes you made on the Astor Diary. Since there's no way I can read the magic book, it's all I have to go off of," Drew says as he buttons his jeans. "But I think I finally have a general map of the remaining orbs."

"YOU HAVE SERVED THE QUEEN WELL. YOU MUST KNOW THAT ONE OF THE ORBS HAS BEEN DESTROYED—OR PERHAPS WELL SHIELDED BY SOMEONE VERY POWERFUL."

"I'm only focusing on the orb that I can track down. I've already lost a few good men on our hunt for the remaining Astor Diaries. The ones we've found so far have all been cursed fakes. At least we know the orbs aren't cursed. I've been able to trace an orb to Reims, France. When do we want to leave?" Drew's gaze meets mine.

"Thank you. This is great news, but getting the orb and restoring Ashgrave's powers isn't enough to win the war. Have you received any updates on the Palarne?"

Drew opens his mouth to answer me when

Ashgrave's metal hands appear and deposit a dirt-covered Tucker on the mountain top with us.

"TUCKER HAS ARRIVED, YOUR MAJESTY."

"I see that. Thank you, Ashgrave."

"What the hell, Ashgrave," Tucker shouts as he brushes the dirt from his rumpled clothes.

"YOU SAID YOU WISHED TO SEE THE QUEEN, IMMEDIATELY. THIS IS THE FASTEST WAY I CAN ACCOMPLISH THAT WITHOUT CAUSING YOUR DEMISE."

Poor Tucker—he and my murderous castle will never be friends.

"It's fine, Ashgrave," Tucker says as he faces the three of us. "I don't want to break up the party, but I need to show you something in the surveillance room."

"Let's go," I say.

Training is over for the day. Without saying a word, Drew, Jace, and I shift into our dragon forms. I give Jace a quick nod and he gently grabs Tucker in his talons and carries him back to the castle.

I shift on the fly and somersault in through my balcony. I roll to my feet in my bedroom. As quickly as I can, I put on a pair of jeans and a long sleeved T-shirt. I rush through Ashgrave's secret tunnels to the surveillance room.

Jace and Drew are already in the room waiting when I walk in. Tucker enters, out of breath, a few moments later.

The surveillance room is brightly lit with large counter tops that have eight stations set up with double monitored desktop computers, headsets, and plush computer chairs. There are also two sets of floor-to-ceiling shelves with twenty gallon plastic totes that are labeled cameras, bugs, voids, override devices, and more. In the center of the room stands a round wooden table that Brett is sitting at while he types away on a laptop. Levi stands behind him, looking over his shoulder.

"What the hell is going on?" I demand.

Brett holds his hand up in the air to silence me, which pisses me off. I need to know what's going on. His phone rings, and the public relations expert puts a finger to his lips to tell us to be quiet.

"Who the hell has your number?" I ask the ex-Knight. "You know better."

"It's a burner," he says as he holds the phone up so he can study the number. "Besides, it's not like Ashgrave has a landline."

"The eloquent queen is on the premises. I dare you to talk to her, for I am Ashgrave the Vengeful,"

Tucker mocks Ashgrave's voice as he pretends to answer a fake landline.

"DO NOT MOCK ME, PUNY HUMAN," Ashgrave butts in. He's clearly agitated by Tucker's humor.

"Shhh, I need to answer this," Brett urges. "Drew's network tipped us off to the Andusk Boss trying to reach out to Rory, so I threw them a breadcrumb." Brett holds out the cellphone and puts it on speaker so we can all hear.

"I'm calling on behalf of Elizabeth Andusk. The Andusk Boss is requesting a meeting with Rory Quinn. Elizabeth has acquired video footage of her battle with Kinsley Vaer and finds the emergence of the diamond dragon... *fascinating*. Ms. Andusk is agreeing to open up negotiations," says the young man on the phone.

I shake my head vigorously.

"Trap," I mouth silently.

"On behalf of Ms. Quinn," Brett starts to say, but is interrupted.

The caller clears his throat, and I wonder who this guy thinks he is.

"Ms. Andusk is promising to bring an artifact of great value to the negotiation table as a sign of good will. Do you accept?" He asks in a crisp voice, and I wonder how much of a pawn he plays in Elizabeth's little game.

"What is this artifact?" Brett demands.

"Tut-tut. I've already said it's of great value," the young man says, shutting him down. "Something your Ms. Quinn will be very interested in possessing."

"Orb? Diary?" I ask silently, and Brett shrugs his shoulders.

There's no way of knowing what the Andusk have. The only way to find out is to meet with Elizabeth.

"Fine," I say to the dismay of everyone in the room. "I'll meet with your Boss, but we meet on my terms. Let's meet at Reggie's castle. Otherwise, no deal."

"Hold please," the caller says curtly, and the line goes silent.

A moment or two later, the caller returns and clears his throat. "Elizabeth agrees to meet you at the castle of Reginald Greaves in two days."

I nod my approval and Brett ends the call.

"Why the hell would you agree to meet with her, Rory?" Jace asks as his face screws up in a scowl.

"Watch it, Jace," I caution him.

My mate knows I don't like being told what to do.

"I am going," I state. "If Elizabeth is serious and she's willing to join us, then good. Kinsley already has the Bane on her side, and we don't know how many of the Bosses she has her claws in. I assume the Nabal will be the next to join the Vaer, considering Jade is here and Aki has every reason to come at me."

A pang of pity hits me in the stomach as I think about the look on Jade's face when her father disowned her. Once she's settled in at the castle, I'll have to check in on her.

If Aki Nabal joins the Vaer, we will be outnumbered. As long as there's any chance the Andusk will join us, we have to try.

Jace watches me with a concerned look on his face.

"If my meeting with Elizabeth doesn't work out, our next stop is Reims."

My men stare at me with tense jaws, like they're biting their tongues. We have to meet with the Andusk Boss. We don't have another choice.

CHAPTER SIX

Tucker sleeps with his back facing me. At some point after our naked workout session, he untangled himself from my legs. With the tip of my finger, I trace the strong muscles of my weapons expert's back. His slow, steady breathing is soothing.

I should be asleep. But after our little talk with Elizabeth's assistant, I can't stop thinking of my meeting with the Andusk Boss tomorrow.

The moonlight shines through my room, highlighting Tucker's naked body, and I consider waking him up for round three of naked aerobics. I shake the thought from my head as I slip on my silk robe and sneak out into the hallway. I pull the door shut carefully, making sure not to wake the sleeping man in my bed.

The plush carpeting in the long hallway is soft and cool under my feet. I lose track of where I am as I follow the bends and turns of the corridor. I'll never get tired of this castle. I know that I'm privileged to call this place home. The paintings, the décor inlaid with gold, the statuettes that line the halls. It's heaven here. My *heaven*, with my men.

"MY QUEEN, WOULD YOU CARE FOR SOMETHING TO DRINK?"

Ashgrave startles me, and my foot catches on a step. I trip—nearly falling down a flight of stairs. Thank the gods for lightning fast reflexes, because a fall down this stone staircase would hurt.

"No, thank you, Ashgrave," I answer as my heartbeat slows to its regular rhythm.

"PERHAPS A BLANKET? OR A GOOD SMITING OF AN ENEMY?"

I can't hold my chuckle in. The fact that he would offer a smiting in the middle of the night is funny.

"I'm okay, Ashgrave. Thank you."

I love my castle. No matter what I'm going through, his wicked but devoted nature always makes me laugh. When we recover the other two orbs, I'm sure he will be happy to go to war and kill our enemies.

I continue walking the length of my castle, still

unable to pinpoint why I feel so uneasy, until Jade crosses my mind again. I'm overcome with sadness for her, and I'm not sure why. Maybe it's her connection to my magic? I realize that I still haven't checked in on her to see how she's holding up. I was trying to give her space, time to grieve, and allow her to make her own decisions to stay here without influencing her one way or the other.

"Ashgrave?"

"YES, MY QUEEN. HOW MAY I SERVE YOU?"

"To the treasury, please."

"AT ONCE, YOUR MAJESTY."

The wall on my left opens and a stairwell appears. At the end of the stairs, the wall in front of me opens to the double doors of my treasury.

The moment I enter, an uncomfortable chill creeps down my spine. None of this treasure feels like it's mine, it's Morgana's. And I wonder how loyal Ashgrave will be to me if Morgana ever returns.

I walk over to a pile of gold bars and run my finger along the top. As I look around the piles of jewels, I wonder if Elizabeth would like any of them.

Probably not. The Andusk Boss already has riches. She doesn't want any more—not from me anyway. Elizabeth wants to control the dragon vessel. Or maybe she wants my power? It seems like that's what everyone wants. Or, she could just want to hand me over to the highest bidder. Unless one of my men are ·the highest bidder. I smirk and shake my head at how ridiculous I'm being.

Which brings me back to what Jett said a few days ago. Something about others?

"The others aren't ready for her yet," I mumble.

I wonder what the Darrington Boss meant by that? Who are these others?

"MISTRESS?" Ashgrave questions.

"Never mind, Ashgrave. I'm just talking to myself."

"VERY WELL," the castle's voice booms, causing the coins in the treasury to jingle. "MY QUEEN, YOU HAVE YET TO WEAR YOUR CROWN."

I don't know if he's trying to cheer me up or annoy me, but I'm not wearing that crown. Not now. Probably not ever.

"It's not really my style, but thank you."

As an afterthought, Morgana pops back into my mind. I hate that the thought of her has me questioning Ashgrave's loyalty.

"Ashgrave, when you were fully functioning, what did Morgana use you for?"

'A GREAT MANY THINGS, MY QUEEN.

CLEANING, PILFERING, STEALING FROM HER GUESTS, KILLING ANYONE SHE DID NOT LIKE, CAPTURING MEN TO BE HER PLAYTHINGS, TAKING—"

"I get it," I interrupt him. "So, how do you feel about that?" I ask.

Can he feel? I mean, he's sentient, but he is still a castle.

Ashgrave doesn't speak for a moment. "IT IS MY OBLIGATION—DARESAY MY HAPPINESS, TO SERVE MY QUEEN."

His response makes my stomach churn. I can't bring myself to ask him if he's truly mine to command, or if I'm just a placeholder for Morgana.

My eyes scan over the piles of jewels, stacks of gold and silver bars, and finally rest on the beautiful sets of dragon armor.

Walking around the piles and stacks of treasure, I make my way to stand in front of the elegant white and gold armor. As I study the grooves and etchings in its well-crafted metal, the gold begs me to reach out and touch it. I become overwhelmed by the feeling, so I lay my hand on the face plate. The metal becomes an electrical conductor as my fingers brush against it.

The air around me shimmers blue and white,

glimmering and rippling like water. An enormous sense of déjà vu rushes over me. I've been here before. A familiar voice speaks to me.

"Petulant child, did you think we would never come?" A male voice asks.

I'm immediately pissed off. *The gods...* I'm in the presence of the dragon gods.

"You will give us back what is ours, or we will take it," the second male voice says coldly.

He's trying to scare me, but I'm not afraid. I stand with my back straight and my chin lifted in defiance. I will never cower before them. *Never.*

"Pretender... fraud," a woman says, her voice still grating against my soul.

Let them come for me. There's nothing they can do. My dragon is having none of it, even while the angry voices threaten me, promising they will come for their magic. My dragon is awake and furious. She stretches her wings and legs, and I can feel her rage pour from her.

My diamond dragon wants to fight, and suddenly I'm being sucked through a black hole. Something is gripping me around the throat and pulling me through some kind of magical portal. I fall to the ground, surrounded by treasure.

I'm back home—at Ashgrave. Did I even leave?

My head is throbbing. I can barely see through the black spots floating in my eyes. I pull myself to my feet and look around. Everything appears the same, but my dragon's fury burns inside of me.

Enough sightseeing for one night.

Time to go back to bed.

CHAPTER SEVEN

As I awake to the sun shining through the windows of my enormous bedroom, my mind returns to my visit with the dragon gods. Did I really travel to see them, or was it all in my mind? They were so angry and demanding that they woke my dragon and made her furious. Being sucked through the black hole did nothing to diminish her anger, and it took me a few hours to drift off to sleep after coming back to bed.

I roll over onto my back and start thinking of the meeting with Elizabeth Andusk that will take place this afternoon. We need more allies, and her assistant said she has something that I'll want. That's the only reason I'm doing this.

The Andusk Boss will probably try to capture

me, which is why my men and murderous castle will
be with me. None of the neutral zones are truly
neutral anymore, but I feel generally safe at Reggie's.
I've already talked with him about my concerns and
I know he will be prepared if Elizabeth tries
something.

Reginald Greaves doesn't like the thought of her
— or anyone—disturbing the peace he's created at his
castle. If she does try to capture me on his turf, there
will be hell to pay. That's the reason why I've chosen
his castle as the meeting place.

Ashgrave seems pleased with the fact that he will
travel with us to our negotiation meeting, and I
know why. The bloodthirsty beast of a building will
skin Elizabeth alive if she so much as touches me.
Not that I'd let him hurt the Andusk Boss—I'd rather
he save his thirst for blood for Kinsley and the
coming battle. But we need more allies, the missing
Astor Diaries, and the other orbs before I can even
think about the brewing war.

I sigh in frustration. There are so many things I
need to do, and I'm running out of time. I'm not
worried about Elizabeth though, and I'm ready for
anything she may try to throw at me. I slide over to
my side of the bed and suck in a deep breath as I
prepare for the day.

"Hey babe," Tucker whispers as he rolls over in bed to look at me.

He's so adorable with his messy mop of dark brown hair hanging over his green eyes. I can't help but lean over and kiss his stubbly cheek. Tucker runs his hand over my thigh, drawing a needy groan from my lips. The groan has him grinning from ear to ear.

"Don't you dare start with me this morning, Tucker Chase. You know we have a busy day ahead of us."

"I've got some business you can take care of right under this sheet," he jokes, and I can't hold back my laughter.

I push the covers off of me and sit up before Tucker can grab me and change my mind about staying in bed with him all day, instead of meeting with the Andusk Boss.

My weapons expert rolls over and sits up. He slides on his pants and shirt while I put on my jeans and sweatshirt. After dressing, we walk down to breakfast together. The aroma of fresh brewed coffee is heavenly as we round the corner outside the dining hall.

As we walk through the doors, I'm greeted by Jace. My mate kisses my forehead and gives Tucker a quick nod. He puts a large cup of coffee in my hands, and I give him a grateful smile.

"My hero," I tease, and he gives me a smile that touches his stormy grey eyes.

My dragon notices how hot he is, dressed in a tight black shirt and dark jeans. And we both sigh at the sight.

Drew walks into the room carrying a tablet that he's tapping away on. He's probably double checking that everything is ready for us to head to Reims after our meeting with Elizabeth.

Levi follows my fire dragon into the room, and his smile has my dragon begging to be touched by him. I need to spend time with him soon. My body is craving his.

My master of stealth has hunger in his ice blue eyes as he takes in my curves. He grabs a few pieces of toast and some fruit from the buffet as we all sit down at the table.

"Are you going to eat your tablet, Drew?" Tucker asks, while Levi and Jace chuckle.

"No, but you can if you want to." Drew gets up to get some breakfast from the buffet at the side of the room.

My fire dragon taps the tablet on Tucker's head as he comes back to the table and sits down. My men all start laughing as my weapons expert looks around to see what hit him.

These men of mine tease each other like they're brothers. I love it. My men. *My family.*

Jade enters the room and pours herself a steaming cup of coffee before taking a seat across from me and next to Brett. I'm surprised she's finally joining us. She usually prefers to have breakfast alone in her room. I understand that she needs space to come to terms with her loss. I know it's not easy being yanked from the only family you've ever known, even though they've forced you to do things you didn't want to do.

"How did you sleep, Jade?" Jace asks.

But I can't hear her answer because Levi and Tucker are arm wrestling for the last banana, and their laughter booms around the room.

Jade smiles at my men's silliness, and I can tell she's getting more comfortable being around them. Being around all of us.

I watch as Brett slides slices of fresh fruit from his plate onto hers. Jade flashes Brett a huge smile that lights up her whole face. She still seems hesitant though, like she's holding back or that she's afraid to become a part of our family.

When I'm full and see that Jade is finished, I

silently invite her to take a walk with me by curling the index finger of my right hand and pointing to the door. She nods in response, and we leave the men to tease each other while we talk.

"Jade, how are you doing?" I ask as we walk down the hallway.

She looks at her feet, probably to distract herself from looking me in the eyes. "It's curious, watching you all laugh and share together. My family is not that way. Meals are for eating. We don't laugh or talk about our lives. There's no time for those things." Her voice comes out monotone and even though she tries to hide her emotions, I know she's hurting by the way her breathing hitches.

"I understand, Jade," I say softly. "Spectres aren't big on family ties and camaraderie either."

My heart pangs with hurt that anyone would grow up without the natural affections of family, but she is here. I hope in time that she will be able to feel love.

"The Nabal family—my father—has always said that emotion is weakness. To express anything other than strength and leadership is to lose respect. It is failure."

It makes my heart skip a beat to hear her say these things.

"The Spectres have the same beliefs, Jade. But I assure you that emotions are not a symptom of weakness. In fact, emotions make us stronger. *Love* makes us stronger."

She nods her head in agreement but doesn't say a word.

"How are you adjusting to living here?" I press.

I want her to be happy, and to feel comfortable and safe.

"I love it here. Ashgrave is beautiful, and everyone has been so kind. Much kinder than I deserve, but I don't want to be a burden," she says as she stares at her feet, "or a charity case."

I can almost hear her father in the last part of her statement, and I want to beat it into her head that I could never think of her that way.

"We have more than enough to go around here. And I would never think of you as a burden or a charity case. Never."

She's a scared child. A child who needs to be taught that it's okay to just be alive. She doesn't owe the world a damn thing. I know it'll take time, but I think being here could help her learn that.

We come to one of the large floor-to-ceiling windows in the hallway, and I slide it open as I stand in front of it.

"Shift and fly with me?" I ask.

Her eyes widen in terror, but she steps to the window and shifts into her white ice dragon form. I step out of the window and shift before I fall to my death on the craggy rocks below. I love being a dragon.

We take to the skies and fly away from Ashgrave. The wind is glorious as it flows around my wings and my body hums with happiness as I enjoy the freedom of flying. After soaring through the air for a while, I bank to the left and she follows.

Jade rushes ahead of me, and I recognize the joy in her dragon eyes as we rise into the clouds and then dip to land. I come to rest on a mountain peak overlooking the valley. In the distance, I spot Ash Town. From here, the village looks like an ant farm. Jade lands next to me with a thump and our wings touch. The connection is instant, and I use this moment while her defenses are down to encourage her. To tell her the things I wished someone would have told me, so that I could let go of my Spectre family... of Zurie.

Jade, you are a force to be reckoned with. A badass fighter, and you would make a powerful ally to anyone you choose to stand with.

She nods her head but refuses to look at me. She

stares at the beauty of the nature that stretches out before us.

Not just that, I continue, *but you are also a fierce dragon. Your abilities exceed most. And the fact that you are here and had the strength to walk away from someone who is family because you knew it was the right thing to do—that takes balls, Jade.*

She cocks her head toward me and I laugh.

You're strong. Stronger than you give yourself credit for, and I would be proud to call you friend, if you can put the past behind us.

Her large white body shakes slightly, and Jade looks at me as a tear trails down her scaled face.

No one has ever been this kind to me, she says, fighting to keep her voice steady through our connection. *Thank you, but I don't deserve it.*

You do deserve it, damn it. Don't let the nagging voice in your head tell you that you aren't good enough or that you failed. You've succeeded far beyond anything Aki could have done or ever will do. You made a conscious choice for yourself and got out from under the rule of someone who was trying to control you. Do you know what that takes? What you have to give up for that kind of freedom?

Jade's dragon shoulders shrug as she gives a slight nod.

I've never had anyone say anything like this to me before. The statement is flat, and it cuts through me like a knife. I see myself in her. I feel her emotions through our connection, and I lock mine down. I can't share how deep this girl's words cut me.

Jade, I will never lie to you. Why would I need to? I don't want anything from you. All I need is for you to be here. Allow yourself the time you need to heal. I only have one rule.

The large white ice dragon stares at me with shiny black eyes and listens to my next statement.

Don't ever sell me or my men out. If you do... you'll fail—and then I'll have to kill you. I let the heaviness of those words boom through our link.

Never, she promises as her eyes widen slightly. I feel her fear and respect as she state the word.

Then you are welcome here for as long as you want to stay.

Thank you, Rory.

I give Jade a nod and we take to the skies. I lead the way back to Ashgrave, and we enter through the large open window that we exited from. We shift back to our human forms and land on our feet. Shifting is as easy as breathing for me now.

"Clothes please, Ashgrave," I say.

"YES, MY QUEEN."

Blue magic and material wraps around me and Jade. When the magic fades, Jade is dressed in a beautiful white dress. The gown has a sheer iridescent chiffon cover over a thin, white silk tank dress that floats over the floor. Her smile is so big that it comes up to her beautiful dark eyes.

I look down at the gown I'm wearing, and it is just as beautiful as Jade's. I'm wearing a sexy, golden sleeveless dress with a slip up to my hip on the left side and flows as I walk. When I move, it shimmers like the sun throwing golden rays of light onto the surfaces of the hallway.

"I don't think I've ever had something this beautiful. Thank you, Rory," Jade says as she steps up to a floor-to-ceiling mirror in the corridor, admiring the gown.

"Thank Ashgrave. He made it."

"Thank you, Ashgrave," she says.

"NO NEED TO THANK ME, MISS JADE. IT IS MY HAPPINESS TO SERVE MY QUEEN."

"Does he always talk that loud?" Jade asks me, laughing.

"Yes," I say with a chuckle.

"Thank you, Rory. I mean it."

I smile and lean in to give her a hug.

"I know you're going to meet with the Andusk, do you need back up?"

The fierce determination in her eyes tells me that she wants to prove herself. But I'm not ready to put her in harm's way yet, even though I appreciate her eagerness.

"No, I already have a plan, but you can stay here and help Brett with surveillance."

She nods with a smile.

"Brett used to be a Knight. He's reformed—well, sort of," I add. "He's still an asshole though."

"I think I can handle him," Jade laughs.

We make our way back to the dining hall, and I narrow my eyes at Brett.

What?" Brett asks.

"Jade's going to help you run surveillance, so don't be a dick," I say as I glare at him.

"I get it, Rory. I'll be nice," the ex-Knight says with a shake of his head.

"Good."

Levi is sitting in a chair looking out the window. I can tell he's been waiting for me to return.

"Are you ready to leave?" my ice dragon asks.

I nod. "Is everyone clear on what they're supposed to do?"

My men all nod as they join me at the table, and Brett and Jade leave the room.

"We already know this meeting is a trap," I say. "Levi and Tucker, you both and Ashgrave will keep your eyes open for Spectres outside. Jace and Drew, you're going to stick with me for the entire meeting."

"I love it when you're bossy, babe," Tucker pipes up.

"Everyone stay safe," Levi adds.

"Ashgrave, it's time to leave," I say.

Ashgrave's little metallic dragon body appears on the table in front of me. He's barely bigger than a cat, but I'm not worried. My bloodthirsty castle is fierce, no matter which form he's in.

We've decided to take the chopper so that we can stay together. Mentally, we've only had two days to prepare. But we're all masters in the art of preparation.

CHAPTER EIGHT

As Tucker pilots the chopper through the mountain range that surrounds Ashgrave, we fly over Ash Town. A faint nagging that I have responsibilities toward the people of the little town grows unbearably loud in my brain.

I've tried not to think about being a ruler—Boss—or queen, but Drew brings it up every chance he gets. As we fly over the village, he brings it up again.

"Have you given any more thought to—"

"Don't say it, Drew," I interrupt him.

I'm not angry. I'm just not ready to be anyone's queen. Even if my fire dragon and the people of Ash Town want me to.

"Rory, you can do this. You can be a Boss," Jace encourages me.

"Great. You want me to be a queen too." I raise a questioning brow at my mate.

"I've always believed in your strength and ability to lead, Rory. It's what drew me to you in the first place, remember?"

I can't bring myself to look Jace in the eyes. It's not that I don't want the responsibility, I just don't feel worthy of it. Having the trust of so many people placed in me, to keep them safe, feels like a train wreck waiting to happen. Or maybe it's Zurie's voice inside my head, telling me that I'm not worthy, that still has some kind of pull. But when I look at my men, I know that Zurie no longer rules my life. My love for them does.

"What about you, Levi?" I ask over the chopper's headset, hoping he will become the voice of reason.

"I say these people need a queen. They need leadership, and if that's you? Well, they could do a lot worse," he says.

"You're no help."

"I think that you being a queen is pretty hot," Tucker adds.

"Be quiet, Tucker!" I laugh.

"Am I the only one that's imagined her wearing the crown and nothing else?" Jace asks.

Really, guys?" I ask, folding my arms over my chest.

"Honestly, Rory, we believe in you. In your abilities. You are the dragon vessel, and you hold the power of the gods inside your body. I don't think anyone is more suited to lead than you." Drew's tone is serious as his eyes look into mine.

Having my men encourage me to lead should reassure me, but it doesn't.

Not after the vision I had last night. And definitely not after the power surge that happened at the Vaer facility. The fact that something like that could happen again and possibly harm the people I'm trying to protect leads me to believe that I shouldn't become queen.

My phone buzzing in my pocket interrupts my thoughts, and I pull it out. It's Harper. I plug the auxiliary cord of my phone into the headset.

"Hey," I tell Harper.

"Rory, I hear you're on your way to meet with Elizabeth?" My friend growls into the phone.

"Well hello to you too, Harper," I say. "And yes, Elizabeth says she has something that could be of great value to me. We already figure it's a trap."

"Good, but don't go in with guns blazing. She doesn't need to know you don't trust her."

"Harper, are you forgetting who you're talking to?" I ask.

"That was more for Tucker. I'm not worried about you," she says correcting herself.

"Yeah, well, Tucker knows better than to piss me off."

Tucker chuckles under his breath but keeps his comment to himself. He may be an adorable goofball, but he's a smart goofball.

The phone goes silent and I wonder if we lost the connection.

"Do you think there's any chance she will join our side?" I ask the Fairfax Boss.

"It's worth a try, as long as she doesn't try to capture you. What would really be the game changer is getting the Nabal or Darrington on our side."

"I doubt that's going to happen," I laugh. "Considering I have both of their heirs living in my castle and neither of them are on their parents' good side. Could you imagine if Jett and Aki came to stay at my castle? Ashgrave would have his hands full."

"He already has his hands full," Tucker chimes in.

As my gaze roams over the four strong, gorgeous men in the chopper, I have to agree. Ashgrave does have his hands full. My lips pull up into a smile as I watch Ashgrave in his steam punk dragon body, looking at the world whizzing by below us with the same sense of wonder he had when he first made his trip out of the castle.

"Be safe and update me when you can."

"I will," I assure her.

"And Rory, not that you need it, but good luck."

"Thanks," I say as I smile into the phone.

The call ends, and I slip my phone back into my pocket. I'm grateful that I changed out of the gorgeous golden gown and into a pair of jeans and a long-sleeved black Henley. My eyes drift to the scenery outside as we fly to Reggie's castle.

The thought of Harper being on my side brings a smile to my face. She is a force to be reckoned with when she wants to be.

The thought of one of the missing orbs being in France has me making a checklist in my mind.

Step one. Get more allies for the war against Kinsley. We have the Palarne, but I can't say anything until they approach us. We don't want our new ally to know we have their capital bugged. And we're meeting with the Andusk in a little while to try to sway them to our side.

Step two. Find the missing orbs and return Ashgrave to his full power. We have a lead that one is in Reims, France, and we're heading there when we finish negotiations with the Andusk. We know it's not cursed, but we don't know who is guarding it and if retrieving it will be dangerous.

Step three. Find the other two Astor Diaries so I can learn more about my magic. I need to know how to control it if I'm going to use it to defeat Kinsley and Diesel.

My shoulders grow tense and I feel the weight of eyes on me. As I look around the inside of the chopper, my gaze meets Jace's, who is watching me intently.

"What's the matter?" I ask my mate.

"I was thinking about the attack on the Darrington warehouse," he answers.

"It's a pretty bold move. I mean you'd have to be desperate to hit a Darrington warehouse. It makes me wonder—"

"Who Diesel is working with?" Jace finishes, and I nod my head.

"I agree. If he's brave enough to knock over the Darringtons, that means he's preparing for war—with the backing of someone powerful."

"I wonder if he's preparing for something bigger than war," Drew adds.

"Or he stole the weapons to knock over Kinsley's

laboratory so he could get his hands on her new bio-weapon?" Levi asks.

The idea hangs in the air like heavy fog on an early morning as we fly over Reggie's castle. If Levi's right, that means Diesel and Kinsley aren't working together. That should be comforting, but it's not.

As we approach the helipad at Reggie's castle, we spot a large group of humans being held back by a makeshift orange fence.

Damn it. Do they know I'm here? A pang of dread settles in my stomach.

"Rory, you look like you've seen a ghost. Stop worrying, those signs say, 'We love Rory,' read them," Tucker encourages me through the headset. He's the only one who can read right through me when it comes to humans. As we land the chopper, their cheers rise in unison. Some are clapping while others are chanting my name. They all look happy to see me.

"How did they know we were going to be here?" I ask.

"Brett is right about those followers of yours," Drew says. "They haunt the places you've been and rush to the areas where people swear they've seen you."

I wonder if this is how movie stars feel when the

paparazzi show up. The chopper lands with its
blades whirring overhead as the door opens. Jace
lowers the steps for me and I duck down and step
out. Reggie is already approaching.

"Rory," Reggie says with a smile on his pudgy,
whiskered face.

He wraps his arms around me and kisses both of
my cheeks in greeting.

"Reggie, thank you for allowing us to meet here."

He gives me a gentlemanly nod. The man may
seem easy going, but I know he'd kick the ass of
anyone who dares to threaten the peace of his
neutral zone.

"MISTRESS, SHALL I ACCOMPANY YOU?"
Ashgrave's voice booms, and his metallic wings
make an awkward whirring sound as he hovers next
to me.

Reggie's face turns pale, and I can tell he's still
not comfortable with my castle.

"Ashgrave, please help Levi and Tucker patrol the
surrounding area."

"AS YOU WISH, MY QUEEN."

Reggie ushers me into the castle as Drew and Jace
walk on either side of me. The ever gracious host
offers us drinks.

"No thank you, Reggie," I say. "I really just want to hear what Elizabeth has to say."

"Very well," Reggie says with a nod of his head. "I do hope that one day you will be able to visit under less pressing circumstances."

"I'd like that, Reggie."

He leads us into a small meeting room where Elizabeth is already waiting to speak to us. My muscles tense, ready for battle as I enter the room. My eyes search for anything out of place or signs of foul play. I swore to myself that I'd hear her out, but if she makes one wrong move, I'll shut her down.

My fists hang at my side—they're ready for a fight.

Let's do this.

CHAPTER NINE

Elizabeth is sitting with her back to the only window in the room at an ornate round table that seats six. The Andusk Boss doesn't have a hair out of place as she looks down her nose at me. Her fair complexion is flawless, and her large brown eyes have perfect lashes that hang over them. She wears a tailored dress that fits her hour glass figure perfectly. She's trying to shake my confidence with her looks, but she will never intimidate me. I've seen fear in her eyes before, and if she tries anything, I'll see it again.

She sits in her seat and waves me over with her manicured fingers. My face shows no emotion as my men and I stay near the door. She thinks she has sway here, but it's up to us to set the rules.

"Jace, Drew…" she purrs their names, and I know she's trying to get their attention.

Neither of them look her way as they search the room.

"Rory, nice to see you," she adds as an afterthought.

I nod at her before I take the seat near the door. Drew pulls out the plush chair to my right and sits in it. Jace remains standing at my back with his arms crossed over his chest. I turn to look at him, and he winks at me while mouthing "You've got this."

His words of encouragement make me want to smile, but I can't show emotion in front of Elizabeth. The light glints off Jace's lapel comm, and the tension in my shoulders loosens. If anything goes wrong, we have more than enough backup.

I turn my attention back to the Andusk Boss. As I expected, Elizabeth has a man at her side. He's almost as tall as Drew, with black hair and black eyes. But the new guy isn't as built as my fire dragon. He must be Elizabeth's man of the week.

"It is so kind of you to accept this meeting," the Andusk Boss says as she flashes me a fake smile. "This is my associate, Talon Baker." She points to the man at her side.

"We're here, Elizabeth. Can we see the artifact?" I ask coldly.

The Boss checks her manicure like she's bored, and she looks at Talon and rolls her eyes. She's stalling, but I sit perfectly still and keep my face free from any emotion.

"Do you believe the dragon gods will return for their magic?" the Andusk Boss calmly asks.

So this is her game—one I refuse to play.

"Let me guess, Elizabeth... you do?"

She nods her head, making her long brown curls bounce against her shoulders.

Elizabeth turns around in her chair and grabs a brown leather messenger bag from the floor by her feet. She places the bag on the table and opens it, sliding it over to Talon. He reaches into the bag and pulls out an old book. The book looks like... an Astor Diary.

"Are you sure you want her to have it?" Talon asks Elizabeth.

"I'm not sure, to be honest," the Andusk Boss replies.

Talon laughs in response. The sound is like nails on a chalkboard and has me cringing inside.

"I don't think she's worthy of this book. But we did come all this way," he says.

My heart skips a beat at the thought of not accessing the knowledge in that book. But my face is frozen in a mask of disinterest.

"You did come all this way. The least you can do is let me see it," I say. "As a sign of good will for the negotiation."

I steal a look at Jace from the corner of my eye, and my mate hasn't moved an inch. His arms are still crossed over his chest. Drew sits next to me with his hands folded in his lap. My men are ready for war. *Good.*

Elizabeth flashes me a smirk. She thinks she has me where she wants me, but we will see about that.

Talon walks around the table with the diary and hands me the book.

As I trace the binding and study the diary's cover, I determine that it's already passed my first test—no visible booby traps. I open the book and start reading through it. My magic doesn't respond to it in the slightest. It's a fake. But Elizabeth doesn't need to know that. The events in this book don't add up with the timeline written in Clara's diary. I've memorized the Astor Diary I have at home in my treasury. With every five pages or so that I read, there's a page that does match. These pages could have been copied from one of the missing Astor

Diaries. Whoever made this fake wanted it to match the real ones.

"Uh-huh," I say to allow Elizabeth to believe she has something that I want.

When I'm finished memorizing the few pages of the book that I can use, I carefully close it and hand it back to Talon. I watch as he makes his way back to the messenger bag that lies on the table. The dark-haired shifter places the book back in the bag then turns around and stares me down.

"Are you interested in joining with the Fairfax?" I ask Elizabeth.

She doesn't answer.

"Let's take a walk. Just you and I, Rory," the Andusk Boss says with a smirk that makes my dragon angry.

Talon walks over to the window and opens it. Outside, the humans are chanting my name so loudly that the window pane shakes.

"Must be nice to be adored," Elizabeth utters.

"I'm not taking a walk anywhere with you."

"Jace—" Tucker's voice comes over the comm and then it goes silent.

"I brought you the diary. If you don't want it, fine. You'll be begging for my help before this is all over, Rory."

Something explodes outside the open window, and I jump up from my seat.

Jace motions for me to stay back as he hurries to the window. There shouldn't be gun fire here, not in a neutral zone. Humans are becoming bolder since Kinsley's attack on the city. There was a chance that Reggie's place wouldn't be completely safe, but it's safer than any of the other neutral zones.

Drew puts his hand on the small of my back as Jace stands with his body behind the wall next to the window and looks outside. Meanwhile, Elizabeth's lips are turned up in a devious smile.

I watch as Talon peels some kind of transparent film from his hands. My eyes bounce from Elizabeth to her man of the week and back again. My mind is foggy, but I start to piece together what they have done. The fake Astor Diary is poisoned.

I'm instantly back in Zurie's dungeon reliving my training on poisons. Zurie often used deadly concoctions to take down our targets.

The ground starts to tilt under my feet and black spots dot my vision.

"Rory, we have to help the others!" Drew shouts.

I want to ask why, but I can barely stand up.

"Those humans have weapons," Jace adds.

My hazy brain thinks about Tucker, Levi, and Ashgrave.

Shit.

I try to focus my magic into my palms, but I can't. Something is wrong. I can't summon my magic, and my brain is trying to turn itself off. Drew wraps me in his strong, muscular arms before I fall to the floor. Damn it. I want to wipe the smug looks off Elizabeth's and Talon's faces, but I can't even stand on my own. If I didn't have my fire dragon's arms around me, I'd be on the flashy oriental carpet. It's taking all of my energy to stay conscious.

"I found that book on one of my expeditions," Elizabeth says. "I'm not stupid though. I sent one of my best men to pick it up, and within minutes he was out cold. I'm surprised that you're still on your feet."

My head rolls to the side and the world tilts.

"If you'll be so kind as to hand the dragon vessel over to us, we will be on our way," Talon says with a smirk.

"Why the hell would we do something that stupid?" asks Jace.

"Because we're the only ones with the antidote," Elizabeth says matter of factly.

"What makes you think you're going to leave this room alive?" I ask as Drew's body tenses.

I know that Drew and Jace will attack at a moment's notice.

A thunderbird crashes through the window, knocking Jace backward. The dragon's body is covered in silver electricity, and he has a silver stripe that flows from the middle of his eyes to the end of his tail.

"Flynn! Do it, now!" Elizabeth commands.

But before Jace can attack him, he blasts Talon with his silvery magic. I'm barely conscious, but the surprise attack on Elizabeth's man has me shaking some of the fogginess from my brain.

"What the hell are you doing, idiot? Get the dragon vessel. Get Rory, now!" The Andusk Boss motions toward me, and Drew pulls me into his mountainous chest.

Flynn's scales flash brilliantly in the lamp light as he winks at me and shakes his head at Elizabeth.

"Now, you moron," she orders the thunderbird in front of her.

A large ball of thunderbird magic roars through the room, heading straight for the Andusk Boss. The magic hits her in the chest and she flies backward and hits the wall.

The thunderbird holds out the tip of his wing toward me, touching my arm. Even though my head is numb, he presses his thoughts through our connection.

Name's Flynn Blackwell, dragon rebel leader. How do you do, Ms. Quinn?

Thanks to our new ally, my magic responds. My dragon is nudging me. Urging me to keep fighting.

Elizabeth is stumbling out of the hole in the wall that her body made while Talon is on his feet and going after Flynn.

My hands start to shimmer with my blue magic— it's slow at first. But then, the magic is covering my arms. I hold my palms out flat in front of me and call my magic battle axe. The curved handle in my hand is comforting. Drew steps back to let me stand on my own as Jace steps closer to us and takes a fighting stance with his feet shoulder width apart. His fists are up and ready to rip the Andusk Boss's head off.

Flynn urges us toward the door that leads into the hall with his large head. I think I'm going to like this guy.

"Drew, wait! Jace, stop! Why are you helping us, Flynn?"

The thunderbird's eyes bore into mine, but he takes the time to press his head against my forehead.

I want protection for my rebels. A place where we can be safe. Since I turned on her, Elizabeth won't allow me to live if I stay with my family. I have the antidote for you, but you have to agree to my terms.

When it comes to trust, I don't give it easily. But, he did just risk his life for us. And for some reason, my dragon likes him. She's encouraging me to accept his offer.

You need to give me time. Time to think before I can agree to anything. You can call this a temporary agreement, I tell him through the connection.

Flynn gives me a toothy dragon smile and I smirk

As I make my way to the door, I lock gazes with Drew and Jace, who flank me on either side. Flynn blasts an arc of his thunderbird magic toward Elizabeth and Talon. It flashes across the room and forms a shield to hold them off.

We rush down the hallway and exit the castle, making our way to the chopper. Drew grabs my arm and helps me up into the chopper, and I let my magic axe disappear. Jace waits for Tucker, Levi, and Ashgrave to join us. Over the comm, Tucker informs us that the humans confessed that they were hired by the Andusk as a diversion. When the Boss didn't leave the castle with me, they dropped their weapons and started to scatter.

Tucker runs up the steps and takes his seat. He puts on his headset as Jace and Levi buckle up, and Ashgrave sits near my feet. The chopper blades start spinning, and within minutes we're airborne. Flynn follows behind us at a safe distance.

"Guess we can cross the Andusk off our list as possible allies," Drew says.

I try to nod, but my head starts to get foggy again. "I'm trying to get Harper allies, but this is starting to be a pain in the ass."

Jace nods at me, and I look past him out the chopper window and spy the thunderbird who helped us escape. I fall into Drew's arms as the world around me goes dark.

CHAPTER TEN

As Flynn and I sit across from each other at the ornate mahogany table in the main dining hall of Ashgrave, I'm thankful. The antidote Flynn gave me has me feeling better. My head is clear, and the dizziness is gone.

"Thank you for giving me the antidote, Flynn." I croak out.

Ashgrave has prepared a breakfast of fresh fruits and coffee, but his metallic dragon form hasn't left my side since I woke up this morning.

Flynn gives me a silent nod. I summoned the rebel leader and asked for him not to say a word. He's obedient. Good.

I wonder how many fake Astor Diaries are floating around. No doubt Elizabeth won't be the last Boss to try to lure me out with one of them. I sure as hell won't be making that mistake again.

As I sit back in my chair, I'm comforted by the plush high-rise back that supports my spine. Even though my body is almost back to normal, it still feels loose and slow to respond. I take a sip of my coffee as I watch Flynn shift uncomfortably in his chair. He's waiting for me to say something about our temporary agreement—but I'm not ready.

I need to learn who he is and where the hell he came from. Until I do, Flynn can just sit and be uncomfortable.

I replay in my mind the image of Elizabeth and her smug look when she revealed that she knew the book was poisoned. My eyes searched every inch of that meeting room, looking for cameras, wires, or anything out of the ordinary. I should have been watching Talon for any tells, but seeing him handle the book first made me assume that it was safe. And that assumption almost cost me *big time.*

Flynn clears his throat. "How are you feeling?"

"Obviously, the antidote worked."

He flashes me a confident grin and rubs the back of his neck. I can tell his nerves are getting the best of him.

"Why did you decide to help me, Flynn?" I ask the rebel leader.

He examines the wall for a moment, and his eyes drift in and out of focus.

"It was me—I was the guy Elizabeth sent to get the diary. The poison on the book almost killed me. You should've seen the look on her face when she reluctantly gave me the antidote from her supplies. I knew that the Andusk Boss was aware the diary was cursed and didn't care. She sent me to retrieve it anyway." He clears his throat again and is unable to meet my eyes. "Elizabeth is as proud as she is vain, and equally as cruel. She constantly punishes me or demeans me when I won't bend to her every whim."

Damn it. I recognize the look on his face, because I've seen it before on Jade's face. It's the look of someone who's been tormented and betrayed by someone they care about. Flynn keeps talking, and his eyes glaze over as if he's forgotten where he is and who he's talking to.

"I'm the only thunderbird in the family, which means, according to Elizabeth, I'm supposed to be displayed and shown off whenever she wants." He shakes his head like he's trying to shake the memories from his mind. "But I'm too damn stubborn to go along with it, and she hates me for it."

I hold my coffee cup with both hands and force the rising anger within me down. "I can't imagine what that must have been like for you."

He takes a deep calming breath and continues. "This one time, when I was younger, Elizabeth had me strung upside down by my ankles to a tree branch and left me there. I tried for hours to get myself down. Eventually a stranger—a damn stranger—cut me down. When I hit the ground, I just stayed there for the night. I was so dizzy that I couldn't stand."

"Why?"

"Because I questioned her, and I can't even remember what it was about."

"Damn," I say as the hundreds of times I suffered from Zurie's cruelty flash through my mind.

No. This isn't the same thing—you don't know him, I remind myself.

"It's funny," he says, "no matter how much wealth we acquired or how prestigious we became, my family was never willing to give me the one thing I wanted."

"What is it that you want?" I put my mug on the table in front of me.

"Freedom. All I want is freedom. The freedom to make my own choices and to be my own man."

Flynn scoots his chair away from the table and begins pacing the wall across from me. He watches the ground and is unable to look me in the eyes. His hand continues to rub his neck like he's nervous.

"I just want to do what is right according to my conscience. Everyone else gets to make their own choices and do what the hell they want, why can't I? Why can't I choose my own destiny? According to Elizabeth, I was just a trophy. Something for her to show off. But because I wouldn't obey, they kept me hidden… like some kind of shameful secret. They kept demeaning me like they wanted to break my will before they could send me off into the world. The way my family treated me was wrong. It was bullshit!"

"It was wrong. You're right," I say softly.

"Rory, I need your help. I have hundreds of rebels —dragon shifters—who want to fight. They don't want to be told what to do or who to be anymore. They're willing to fight for you, if you'll have them."

His eyes plead with me as he gazes into mine. My mind swims with what accepting his offer could mean. If his rebels become allies, it could turn the tide of the brewing war in our favor. I shake the thought away. If they're coming here, I'll keep them safe. I won't ask them to fight for me.

I look down at my folded hands and nod my head. "Of course they're welcome here, Flynn."

Flynn drops the hand he was rubbing his neck with to his side as his shoulders relax. It's as if a weight has been lifted from his body, and he flashes me a grateful smile. He opens his mouth to speak and is interrupted by Drew's heavy footsteps.

My fire dragon storms into the dining hall with his jaw tight and his shoulders hunched forward. He's pissed, and I don't really want to ask why. Brett and Jade follow on his heels with blank faces and wide eyes.

"What happened?" I ask, knowing I'm not going to like what they have to say.

Drew says nothing as he makes his way to the large television on the wall and turns it on. Images start to fill the screen as my mind tries to make sense of what I'm seeing. Dead bodies and blood—it's horrifying. The broken voice of a newscaster floods the room.

"In breaking news, over eighty-seven men, women, and children are dead because of an unprecedented attack. Our sources are saying the attackers are followers of the infamous Rory Quinn, the dragon vessel, who recently publicly battled the dragon shifter, Kinsley Vaer. Neither Ms. Vaer's nor

Ms. Quinn's whereabouts are known at this time. Anyone with any information on—"

My fire dragon turns down the television and runs his hand through his hair as he paces the length of the room.

"Son-of-a-bitch!" he shouts furiously. "We were right there, Rory. Our hack was supposed to catch shit like this and instead... we missed it."

"But we've been going through the intel and we didn't see anything in the stored information related to this." I gesture toward the television, but Drew is already typing and swiping at his tablet furiously. "Are you sure you missed it?"

"I see it here, but it's encrypted and it didn't get decoded until now." His gorgeous lips pull down and his face turns red. "We had the info, it was right here, but we found it too late."

"Didn't we break into the Vaer facility to stop this kind of thing?" I ask as the death toll keeps replaying in my head. Eighty-seven, eighty-seven...

Drew gives me a small nod with his shoulders slumped forward and his head hanging toward his chest. "I'm sorry, Rory."

"I don't blame you, Drew. I'm pissed that I wasted time with Elizabeth. If I would have turned her down, we could have helped those people. We could have been going through the intel together and caught the encrypted message. I could have stopped these people from dying, especially since they're trying to blame me and my so-called followers for this."

My blood is boiling, and I have to pace. I have to figure out a way to make some good come from this. Flynn has taken his seat at the table and is being still as stone, while Brett and Jade hang their heads and refuse to look at me.

"Rory… " Drew's husky voice interrupts my thoughts and I stop pacing to gaze at him. "You can't be everywhere at once. I know that if you could have, you would've saved those people."

"Damn it!" Brett shouts and his outburst has everyone in the room looking at the large television he's pointing at.

Pictures of me and Irena are on the screen, and Brett walks over to turn up the volume as the newscaster's voice booms through the room.

"…our updated sources indicate that Rory Quinn *and* her sister Irena are responsible for the recent death toll."

Brett flips to another channel and there are two reporters talking to each other on the screen. The first reporter is a pretty, young woman with a fair complexion who's talking with a large dark-skinned man who is frowning.

"What do you have to say about the recent allegations against Rory Quinn and her sister Irena?" The woman asks.

"Well, at this point we can only speculate, but many are saying that it is the sisters' actions that are provoking the dragon violence," the man replies.

Drew growls and rushes to turn it off, but I grab his arm.

"No. I want to hear what they say."

Brett changes the channel again.

"…Dragon sympathizers are responsible for the humans' rising death toll."

Each channel seems to get worse with marches, protests, and people screaming for the military to intervene.

"The Quinn sisters are enemies of the people," says another news reporter.

My rage boils and my dragon is pushing against me to do something.

"It gets worse, Rory," Brett says with sadness swimming in his eyes as he looks at me.

"How?" I ask.

"Apparently," Drew says as he reads something

from his tablet, "the Vaer are lobbying for you and Irena to be banned from international travel."

"Is that even legal?"

Brett shrugs his shoulders.

"The Polish government has already placed you and Irena on their 'No Fly' list, and the rest of Europe will probably follow their lead.

"That's bullshit."

"Don't worry, I'll take care of this," Brett promises.

My public relations expert grabs his phone from his pocket and starts dialing. He growls into the phone and walks out of the room.

"I believe in you, Rory," Jade says as she walks up to me and places a hand on my arm. "No matter what they accuse you of. I know you couldn't do any of those things."

She takes her hand off my arm and flashes me a genuine smile as she walks off to join Brett.

My phone rings. It's an unknown number. I hit the answer button and wait for the caller to say something.

"Have you heard what they're saying about us?" My sister's voice growls over the line.

"Yes," I answer as I keep in mind that Diesel is

constantly hacking Irena's phones, so I can't say anything about the Vaer intel.

"Kinsley is going to pay for this," Irena says.

"Leave Kinsley to me. Just keep tracking Diesel."

Now he knows we're trying to find him. That will either force him to make another move, or it will cause him to go into hiding.

"Have you found out anything about the bio-weapon?" I ask.

"No. Not yet."

"If Diesel finds it and uses it on people, it will make matters worse."

"You're right. I'll keep tracking him, and I'll stop by soon. I need some sister time. Don't die, baby sister."

"Thanks. Take care of yourself, Irena," I say, and the line goes dead.

I hope this conversation will force Diesel's hand and lead us right to him.

I slide my phone back into my pocket and shake my head.

Even as a Spectre, I've never been labelled an Enemy of the People. Never. And I'll be damned if it happens now. Kinsley Vaer is not going to determine how history will remember me.

CHAPTER ELEVEN

I press my face deeper into my pillow and pull the thick quilt tight around my neck. Images of humans dying and angry people shouting and yelling spring into my mind. News reports play over and over. Irena. Me. Humans picketing—demanding we be held accountable for the rising death toll.

Groaning, I reach out my hand, searching for my sexy fire dragon. Drew's gone. My dragon and I pout. We're both in the mood to play this morning.

"MY QUEEN, A WOMAN APPROACHES." Ashgrave's voice cuts through the silent morning like a heavy battle axe, startling me. I fall to the floor, banging my knee on the bedside table.

"Damn it, Ashgrave," I whisper as I stand up, brush myself off, and run my fingers through my tangled hair. I immediately jump into action, getting dressed, brushing my teeth, and running a comb through my dark brown hair.

My dragon snarls, ready to use our magic on whoever is trying to sneak up on us. We both think it could be Elizabeth, and we think she's trying to lure us out again. I estimate Irena won't be here for another day, unless this is *really* important and she expedited her trip.

"Ashgrave, can you identify the woman?" I ask.

"IT IS YOUR SISTER IRENA, MISTRESS. SHALL I CHASTISE HER FOR WAKING YOU?"

"No, Ashgrave. That's not worth a smiting." I shake my head at my murderous castle.

I stretch out my arms and relax my shoulders.

"WOULD YOU LIKE ME TO MAKE YOU A GOWN, MY QUEEN?"

"No, thank you. What I'm wearing is fine." I look down at my jeans and V-neck, long sleeved T-shirt and head out into the hallway.

"Hey," Levi breathes as he almost runs into me.

"Hey." I smile, surprised to see him outside my door.

My ice dragon must have been coming to check on me as I stepped out of my room. The heat in his ice blue eyes tells me he wanted to do more than just see how I'm doing, but my sister's visit just threw a wrench into his plans.

Levi wraps his warm arms around me and holds me close to him while he plants a searing kiss on my lips. Oh *Levi*. As much as I'd love to slip back into my bed with the sexy shifter in my arms, I can't. Irena's here. I pull away from him and kiss him on the cheek.

"Are you regretting stepping out of the shadows?" he asks with a smirk.

I smack his arm playfully. "I'm getting ready to meet with Irena."

My master of stealth shrugs his shoulders and gives me a wink—then blows me a kiss as he steps aside for me to walk in front of him. That's the Levi I know and love. He's always watching my back. I head for the throne room with my silent guard following behind me.

"HOW SHALL I ANNOUNCE YOU, MY QUEEN?"

"Say whatever you want," I tell him, not wanting to argue with a centuries-old castle.

As I follow the passageway to the stairwell that leads to the main hall just outside the throne room, I look over my shoulder at Levi, and he gives me a bright smile. I'm so grateful for him. For all of my men.

'THE ONE TRUE QUEEN OF ASHGRAVE APPROACHES. ALL HAIL THE QUEEN OF CHAOS AND ALL MAGIC," Ashgrave's booms as the large, ornate double doors open to the throne room and I walk through.

"Hey, little sister," Irena says with a smile as she wraps me in a tight hug. "I come bearing gifts. I know these won't solve all of our problems, but they should help."

"Thank you," I say as I look over the items she has displayed on a side table—Spectre tech which includes bugs, mini cameras, wire taps, and more voids. "These will come in handy."

Levi flashes me a smile and then excuses himself so my sister and I can have some alone time. He knows I'm safe, and he and Tucker are trying to get some maintenance done on the chopper and jet.

"The truth is," Irena adds when the doors close behind my ice dragon, "I have an ulterior motive for visiting you."

"I figured," I say with a knowing grin. "Diesel still has your phone hacked?"

She nods. "I don't think there's a way to get around it. I bought a burner phone, but he hacked that too. The new Ghost is a persistent asshole. I'll give him that."

"Do you know where he is?"

Irena shakes her head. "I was hoping you might help me with tracking him. I figure with Drew's back channels and network, he might be able to find out something. Everything I've tried isn't working."

"Ashgrave, ask Drew to come to the throne room."

"RIGHT AWAY, MY QUEEN."

I pick up one of the bugs and turn it over in my hand. It's hard to believe that because of one of these little pieces of Spectre tech, we now have an ally in the Palarne.

The doors open, and I turn to see my fire dragon walk in.

"Drew," I whisper as my mind is flooded with the heated moments we shared last night.

I bite the inside of my bottom lip, and Drew winks as his eyes trail over my curves. He looks hot as hell in his tight black shirt and jeans.

"What can I do for you?" He quirks a questioning brow.

Heat flushes up my neck as I remember everything he did for me last night, and I clear my throat. I turn my attention back to my sister, who's watching us with her lips turned up and a spark in her eyes.

"Irena needs to know if you can find out where Diesel is. He still has a hack on her phone, and she thinks he hacked her new burner too."

"If he hacked her phone, there should be a way to trace that. I'll get to the bottom of it. Give me a few minutes, and I'll be right back, I'm going to 'clone' your phone so that I can trace Diesel's hack." Drew says with a wink and he rushes out the door.

"How have you been since the news reports started calling us Enemies of the People?" I ask my sister.

"You know I stick to the shadows. I did it when Zurie's death plan plastered our pictures all over the place, and I'm doing it now." Irena smirks. "How about you, how are you doing with all of the craziness?"

"I won't lie to you, it's not easy," I admit. "Especially since I work so hard trying to keep people safe. I do know that Kinsley and Diesel need to die over all of this though."

"They will, little sister."

Drew opens the door and steps in. "There's a bio-weapon delivery going out from one of the Vaer labs next week. It is being shipped to someone by the name of 'Overlord.' Does that code name mean anything to either of you?"

"Diesel," Irena sighs. "Now we know for sure that he's going after the bio-weapon," she says while shaking her head.

"They're just going to *give* it to him?" I ask in a doubtful tone. "That doesn't sound right."

I thought Diesel was breaking into the Vaer lab like he did the Darrington warehouse. My blood boils as the pieces slide together like a jigsaw puzzle in my mind. Diesel and Kinsley are working together in some capacity. They have to be.

"This is horrible news." Irena rubs the back of her neck.

"Unless," I say, "we find out where it's being dropped off at and we take the bio-weapon before Diesel gets his greasy hands on it."

"That's a great idea, sis!" Irena says with a toothy grin, as Drew hands Irena's phone to her.

"From the intel I've gathered, Diesel or this 'Overlord' is making deals with a few different human factions. He has his hands in dealings with the black market and is loading up on anti-dragon and anti-magic weapons. Because of the attacks on humans, the weapons are in higher demand. We have to be careful, especially if the Spectres and the

Vaer are working together. I've got a trace going so we can track Diesel."

"The orb in Reims—is it real?" I ask, trying to piece together a plan.

Drew nods. "My sources confirm it is, though we will know for certain once we see it for ourselves. I figure I'll put together a small team and take them to get it for you. I think between Jace and I—"

I interrupt my fire dragon. "No. If you're going, I'm going. Period. We're a team. We all go, or no one goes."

"Fine," Drew says shaking his head with a flirty grin.

Irena is watching us with a smile on her face and doing a bad job of hiding her chuckle behind a fake cough. I want to ask her what's so funny, but Ashgrave interrupts.

"FLYNN BLACKWELL IS ENTERING YOUR THRONE ROOM UNINVITED, MY QUEEN. SHALL I SMITE HIM?"

I turn and watch as the normally confident guy jumps at the fact that my castle just implied he could be killed for interrupting me, and I can't help but let out a little chuckle.

Flynn starts walking toward us as he shakes his head. "Rory," he says with a bow.

Is the rebel leader being serious? Drew smirks at the action, and I know exactly what his smile means —my queen. I wonder if Drew has talked with Flynn about me being a queen. Fan-freaking-tastic. They're all in on it.

Irena has gleam in her eyes and a quirked brow as Flynn approaches. She looks him over.

"Rory, my rebel group will reach Ash Town soon. We are respectfully awaiting further orders."

"YOUR HIGHNESS, A GROUP OF FIVE HUNDRED DRAGONS ARE APPROACHING THE BORDERING VILLAGE. ARE THEY PERMITTED TO LAND? OR SHALL I DESTROY THEM?"

The people of Ash Town are probably afraid with that many dragons flying toward their small village.

"Ashgrave, please inform the group of dragons to come here instead of landing in the village. We have more than enough room, and as long as they're here, they'll be under our protection."

This way, if any of the rebels tries anything, my murderous castle will happily smite all five hundred of them.

"YES, MY QUEEN."

"Flynn, tell me about your rebel group."

The rebel leader puffs out his chest and lifts his

chin. "I've been building this group for years by connecting with like-minded dragons who are unhappy with Elizabeth's leadership or who've suffered her wrath. Over time, we refused to pay taxes to the Andusk Boss and refused to do her bidding. Her requests are often unnecessarily cruel."

I nod as I watch Flynn's facial expressions. He lowers his gaze and his head hangs slightly. The rebel leader's stance tells me he's done things he's not proud of because he was ordered to. I know that feeling.

"You did a brave and dangerous thing by helping us back at Reggie's. I appreciate it."

"And I'm grateful to you, Rory. You're giving my rebel group a place to be safe and free. If there's ever anything I can do to repay you, just ask."

A shuffling of feet has me watching Drew out of the corner of my eye. He's watching us with a raised eyebrow. Is he… could he be jealous?

The corner of my lip turns upward. That's kinda hot, but he has nothing to be jealous of. Flynn has lived the same kind of life I have, and he's done horrible things to others because he was ordered to, even though he didn't want to—and so has Jade.

"I do have something you can do, if you're interested?" I ask Flynn. "Are you up for joining us on a little adventure? There's an artifact in France that we need to retrieve. We could use some back up."

"Hell yes!" he says and pumps his fist in the air.

"I hate to interrupt," Irena interjects, "but I've gotta go. I have my own group of rebels to lead."

Flynn faces Irena and extends a hand toward her as his eyes roam over her curves. My big sister's cheeks turn pink. "I don't think I've introduced myself. I'm Flynn Blackwell," he says with a smile that lights up his face.

"Yeah, I heard. Ashgrave is loud as hell," she says as she gives a quick shake of his hand, careful not to let her eyes linger on his. "Rory, when it's time to get the bio-weapon, I'll be there."

"I know." I wrap my sister in my arms before she leaves.

When Irena says she's going to be somewhere and do something, nothing on the face of the earth can stop her.

CHAPTER TWELVE

As I watch the sun set through the treasury windows, I take Clara Astor's Diary off its pedestal and sit in the corner of the room on the floor. I flip through the familiar pages as my eyes search for new information—anything I might have overlooked.

"Ashgrave," I call out.

"YES, MY QUEEN."

"You mentioned that one of the orbs might have been destroyed."

"I DID, MISTRESS."

As I re-read over my notes, a thought forms in my mind. "Is it possible to reconstruct a destroyed orb?"

Ashgrave doesn't speak for a while, and I wonder if I've insulted him. I know the orbs are made of the same magic that he is. They're part of him. We need the orbs to bring every piece of my castle back to life.

"I BELIEVE IT TO BE POSSIBLE, MY QUEEN. THOUGH UNDER MORGANA'S REIGN, IT WAS NOT NECESSARY."

Humph. Morgana. Her name is like nails on a chalkboard and has me cringing. I wonder who he would choose if a choice had to be made. Me or Morgana?

"Is there a way to find out?" I ask.

"YOU MUST FIND ESMERALDA'S DIARY."

Shit. That's not the answer I wanted.

I close the ancient book and put it back on its pedestal. I have no idea where the other diaries are or how to get them back. If handling a fake can poison someone, then I need to be prepared for the possibility of running into more dangerous traps.

My head pounds in time to my pulse, and I know I need sleep.

"Ashgrave, take me to my room, please."

"AS YOU WISH, MISTRESS. WOULD YOU CARE TO WEAR YOUR CROWN?"

"What?" I shake my head. Damn it, first my men and now my castle. They're all pushing me to be queen. "No, Ashgrave. I'm going to sleep. I don't need a crown to sleep."

I laugh silently to myself. This castle is so pushy.

I step out into the hallway and one of Ashgrave's private tunnels opens in the wall in front of me. If he can do this with two orbs in place, I can only imagine what other powers he will have when we replace the missing ones. My pulse quickens as I think about the metal dragon army coming online. Based on what's happening around us, we will be needing that army soon.

The more I think about it, the more Reims, France is looking better and better. But first, I need to sleep to clear my head.

As the wall of the private tunnel opens into my room, I step through and start taking my clothes off, throwing them in a pile in the corner. I grab my nightgown from the back of my chair and pull it over my head. I admire the way the moonlight reflects off the baby blue silk. I finally crawl into the comfort of my bed. I might not be a real queen, but I feel like one living here. My head pounds as I drift off to sleep.

The morning sun shines through the windows of my room, and I'm thankful that a good night's sleep has made my headache go away. I quickly take a pair of jeans and a sweatshirt from my closet and get dressed before hurrying downstairs to the kitchen for breakfast.

Giggling comes from the kitchen, and I stop in my tracks. As I silently stalk to the doorway, I spy Jade and Brett sitting at the breakfast nook in the corner of the room. Jade was the one laughing, and it makes my heart swell that she is happy. I can't hear what they're saying, but Jade has a smile that warms her face and has her eyes sparkling with joy.

Brett leans toward her and says something, and Jade laughs again. Her hand reaches for his, and they both just stare into each other's eyes.

I'm hungry, but I don't want to interrupt their time together. I lean against the wall opposite the doorway of the kitchen and watch them. I notice a small downward glance of Jade's eyes. She's more relaxed here—sure. But she still misses her father.

I wonder if Aki would be open to talking with Jade, or if it's even something she would want. I turn away from the kitchen. Breakfast can wait.

I have some questions for Drew anyway, and I head for the stairs that lead to the surveillance room.

I open the door and notice he's on one of the computers and watching both of the screens while familiar voices flood the room.

"You're up early," I say as I watch his muscles tense under his tight T-shirt. Drew turns his head and gazes at me with his sexy black eyes as he relaxes.

"Yeah, I had a restless night," he says as he turns back to the monitors with a scowl.

I walk up behind him and massage his shoulders. "Is there anything I can do?"

"Well," he says, turning his chair around and planting a kiss on my cheek before turning back to his computer.

"Work first, play later," I retort, rolling my eyes.

"That's Jace's motto. Not mine."

I watch my fire dragon's back and think of all the fun things I'd like to do to him. My dragon is doing somersaults and licking her lips at the thought of playing with Drew. She's as hungry for him as I am.

"I have some intel for you," he says. Damn it. He's in work mode, not play mode.

"Really?" I walk around the chair and stand on his right side so I can see the screens.

"I've got a time and a location for the bio-weapon delivery."

5564OLIVIA ASH

"When?" Diesel, we've got you now, you son-of-a-bitch.

"We've got two days. There's a Vaer owned restaurant in L.A.—Chinatown—and the delivery will be at 10 p.m. looks a little suspicious if you ask me," he says with a shake of his head.

My fire dragon is wary, and so am I.

"It does seem suspicious, but Diesel doesn't know we're tracking him, and the Vaer still don't know we've hacked their network. That at least puts us at an advantage. We just need to go into Los Angeles prepared. We *need* to take out this asshole and stop the spread of Kinsley's new bio-weapon."

I start making plans in my mind as the voices that echo in the room become unfamiliar.

"Who are you listening to?"

"The Darrington bug," he says as he looks down at his lap.

"Are you spying, or are you listening in on your family for you?" I know that some part of him must be missing his brother and father, even if he hasn't talked about them. Drew doesn't answer, and I don't push him. We all have to deal with change in our own ways and we've all lost someone. Loss doesn't get easier, and sometimes it gets harder.

"Any updates? Or does Jett still want to kidnap me?" I ask with a smirk.

He wraps his arm around my waist and pulls me onto his lap. Drew studies my face and leans in, pressing his soft warm lips against mine. "Milo has changed. He stopped blaming others for his actions and doesn't whine about everything. He's starting to step up to the duties of being a leader."

I run my fingers through my fire dragon's black hair then look into his large black eyes. "Does that bother you? Jett really wanted you to be his heir. We both know that."

Drew closes his eyes and lets out a heavy sigh.

"No. I just wish Milo would put all of his newfound dedication toward something good. Toward making a change that matters."

"There's still time. Don't forget that he covered for the Farifax with your father. That was good."

"Yeah, he did," Drew says with his eyes closed. I plant a gentle kiss on his scruffy chin and lean against his strong chest.

"I hope he makes better choices for your sake, and that he will never cross us again."

"I hope so too, Rory. But if he ever messes with us again, I'll end him. I won't have a choice." The pain in his voice has me trembling inside. My fire dragon tries to hide how much it would hurt him to end his brother, but I feel his pain.

"If we even run into your brother again," I say, "I'm confident it will be on better terms." Because if it isn't, gods help Milo Darrington.

CHAPTER THIRTEEN

The sun shines through my bedroom window, making me grumble against the new day. I couldn't sleep last night. I spent most of the night walking the hallways of Ashgrave, admiring the beautiful paintings that were put here by someone who came before me. Maybe Morgana? I'm not sure. I don't really want to think about her since I have a busy day ahead of me. My men and I will be preparing for our trip to L.A. tomorrow night.

I know what needs to be done, but there are so many unknowns that I can't prepare for.

Retrieve the bio-weapon before Diesel or his men.

Find Esmeralda Astor's diary.

Restore the destroyed orb, if we can get our hands on its pieces.

These all seem easy enough to do, considering what my men and I have been through, but it's the things I can't prepare for, the things I can't control that bother me. Like, how many men will Diesel have with him at the bio-weapon delivery? Will Diesel's men be prepared for an outside attack? Is Esmeralda's diary protected or enchanted with some kind of magic? And... this is a huge one, is it even possible to restore the orb Ashgrave believes is destroyed?

He says it is, and I wonder what it will take to repair it. Even as my magic flows through me, I have to wonder if the gods' magic will be enough. Especially with the power surges I've been having lately. There are too many unknowns.

I get dressed and step out into the hallways, the light streams through the elegant windows, bouncing off the golden threads in the beautiful floor-to-ceiling draperies. All of my men will be up soon. As I walk the long way to the kitchen, my eyes take in the lovely sloping hills and mountains that surround the castle grounds. I love my home. I love my men. I care for the people who are seeking refuge here, and by the gods'—I'll do anything to protect them.

I take the winding stone staircase down to the main hallway. My first stop is the surveillance room. I peek in and see Drew pacing the room, talking on the phone and making plans for our trip to Los Angeles tomorrow. My fire dragon gives me a wink as he continues his conversation.

"Good morning," I mouth, before I leave to grab some coffee.

To my surprise, there are no voices coming from the kitchen, and it's empty except for a plate of fresh rolls and jelly, and a couple of half empty glasses of orange juice that sit on the counter. Wherever they are now, they're probably off preparing for our trip. I pour myself a cup of steaming hot coffee and grab a roll.

"Ashgrave, locate Tucker, please?"

"YES MISTRESS—TUCKER IS SORTING WEAPONS IN THE ARMORY."

"Thank you, Ashgrave."

"IT IS MY PLEASURE, MY QUEEN."

While I drink my coffee and eat my roll, I walk the long way to the armory. When I arrive at the door, I peek in and see Tucker's back to me. He's tapping a pencil against his head and then writes something down on a small notepad. I figure he's trying to decide what we're going to need and how much ammo to take. I want to laugh at how focused he is, but I don't.

I think about interrupting him by running my fingers through his messy brown hair, but I resist the urge. Instead, I back away silently and head back toward the kitchen.

I need to call Irena.

Damn it. Diesel still has her phone hacked. This is going to be tricky.

I pull my phone out to call her and it goes straight to voicemail.

"Hey sis, just wanted to see if you'd like to get some Chinese take-out with me. I really need some sister time. Call me back."

That should be coded enough for her to know that she can meet up with us in Chinatown. And she already knows that "sister time" means I want to see her in person because we have work to do. Damn Diesel and his hack. I know that my men and I can handle him if he finds out that we're going to be there. My main concern is that they'll move the drop to a different time and location, and we won't be able to get to it in time to intercept it.

There's a shuffle of footsteps down the hallway

behind me as I put my phone in my back pocket. I turn around to see Brett walking toward me.

"Rory! I've been looking for you."

"What's up, Brett?"

"Actually, I need you to do something—and I already know you aren't going to like it," he says.

Gods. He probably wants me to do some publicity thing like make a video. I hate that.

"What now?" I ask as he motions for me to follow him.

"I think it'd be a good idea for you to make a video condemning the attacks that are killing humans, you know—for damage control."

I look down at the plush carpet in the hallway and shake my head. I was right, another video. Damn it. "Brett, do you really think a video will make a difference? When are you going to let my actions speak for themselves? When I take Kinsley and Diesel down and these attacks stop, people will know the truth."

"I know that, Rory. But the people of the world don't, and the longer you say nothing, the more riots and lies will spread, and the more your image is tainted and twisted by others. When it comes time to fight, we want as many people on our side as possible."

He's got a point, but I'm not happy about it. We walk past the surveillance room and Brett takes me to the room next door. A large table sits in the center of the room, surrounded by oversized, cushioned velvet chairs. Brett has a video camera, large ring lights, and a microphone already set up in front of a small desk in the corner of the room. Brett prepares the video camera and points his finger, directing me to sit behind the desk.

"Just give me something quick, Rory. Okay? Something to let people know that you are not behind the attacks and that the people who are doing them are not your followers. Let them know that you stand for peace not war and death. Your real followers already know that, but this smear campaign against you and Irena has turned a lot of neutral parties against you. This is just to turn the tides back in our favor."

I'm pissed off, but I take my seat. The moment Brett points at me, telling me to go ahead, I talk. "I know what you're seeing on the news and on the internet, and I know what you're hearing. Those who truly know me understand that I don't stand for any of that. I would never condone violence against humans or any race or species." This never gets any easier—I hate being on camera. "I don't know what to tell you except that I believe we can all live in peace. The day will come when we can, and the violence you're seeing, it doesn't come from me or those who are on my..."

My tongue feels stuck to the roof of my mouth.

I have to stop. This whole thing feels forced.

"I'm sorry, Brett. You have to stop filming. This seems... almost robotic." I shake my head. "It's not me at all."

"I understand, Rory. I do. You have to understand though, that right now we're fighting an opinion war. Which in most cases are just as important as the actual war."

I walk away from the video set-up and run my finger along the large table in the center of the room. I don't like this at all.

"Rory," he continues, "it's important. Three more countries have declared you and Irena terrorists because of the nonsense in the media."

I whip my head around to stare at him. "Are you kidding me?"

"No, I wish I was, but I'm not. Look, can I at least use a little of the footage that we have?"

"It's just dry. It's not my style," I tell him, but his determination isn't shaken. "Fine," I sigh. "Just don't make me look dumb or I'll break every bone in your body, got it?"

"Fair enough."

I need to let off some steam. The moment he starts messing with the camera, I rush out the door. I need Jace. Now.

"Ashgrave, where's Jace?"

"IN HIS ROOM, MISTRESS. WOULD YOU LIKE ME TO BRING HIM TO YOU?"

The image of my castle picking Jace up by the back of his neck with his mechanical arms and forcefully dropping my mate at my feet has me laughing.

"No, that's okay. Can you have him meet me in the west mountain range where we trained a few days ago?"

"YES, MY QUEEN."

I run down the hallway, nodding hello to the unfamiliar faces I pass. The shifters smile back at me, and I'm thankful that the large castle is hosting Flynn's rebels. It feels like my castle is getting much needed use out of its rooms. I'm sure Ashgrave appreciates being kept busy.

I reach the floor-to-ceiling windows near the kitchen and open them. As I look around to be sure I'm alone, I shrug off my clothes, folding them neatly, and placing them in the corner, out of sight. I step out into the air and shift, as I catch the wind and glide over the beautiful snowcapped mountains. When I've gained height, I bank to the left and head for the mountain range that's farthest away from Ash Town. This is where Jace and I usually work on my magic.

As I tuck my wings into my side, my elegant tail whips around, the gold stripe glittering in the sun as I land gracefully. I'm still not used to the stripe yet, but it is beautiful.

I calm my nerves and sigh as I think about the images of blood and death that have been playing across the news over the past few days. It never gets easier to see. I had hoped to address the issue after revealing that Kinsley was responsible for killing the humans. It was not my doing, and definitely not Irena's.

Actions, not words—that's how I like to do things.

The gentle pounding of wings against the wind lets me know that Jace is approaching. And, of course, Ashgrave is accompanying him in his little metallic body. Ashgrave rushes ahead of the thunderbird and lands gracefully on a boulder a few feet away from me.

Jace shifts to his human form, and my dragon purrs. I roll my eyes at her. We need to work, not play.

"Ashgrave, clothes for me and Jace, please. And be sure to make me pants and a shirt, because we're going to train."

"AT ONCE, MISTRESS." Ashgrave's metallic body makes a whirring sound as he flies around us and dresses us in magical clothes.

"You know we should be preparing for the capture of the bio-weapon, right?" he says casually.

"This *is* how I'm preparing," I counter. "I'm sparring with you so that I'm ready for tomorrow night, in case Diesel picks up on the fact that we're going to be there."

He shrugs. "Sounds good. Let's work on your magic weapon shifting."

I nod and hold my palms out. I feel the energy rush through me, and I close my eyes to embrace it. This is who I am now—I don't have to look at my hand to know the dagger is resting in it, perfectly poised to be used. Calling on my magic weapons is getting easier.

"WELL DONE, MISTRESS," Ashgrave encourages me with a hint of excitement brewing in his booming voice.

"That was quick. Now, try the axe, and then the mace… "

My magic is already forming the axe before he even finishes his sentence. I smoothly switch over to the mace. The handle of the mace is metal and topped with a large steel ball that's covered in spikes. I expect it to be heavier than it is, but it's surprisingly light. I figure it's just a benefit of the magic weapons. I swing the ball of the mace in a circle above my head. Jace jumps back.

"Woah. Easy there." He offers a teasing smile and I return it, allowing my weapon to fall to my side and disappear.

"I just can't believe how light they are," I say.

"Maybe I should hand you a weapon that's harder to handle," he says with a raised eyebrow.

"I can handle anything you throw at me," I say, biting my lower lip.

"Damn woman," he whispers, taking the bait. He stalks toward me, and my dragon is jumping up and down with excitement. But, I'm not ready to play just yet. His guard is down, and I use this rare moment to summon a ball of magic light and fling it at him. Jace is quick though, and he dodges it by somersaulting forward and flying to his feet. His face is inches away from mine. Good. Our sparring session will be hand-to-hand combat.

I clench my hand into a tight fist and aim it for his chin, but his strong and steady palm stops the impact. He grabs my hand, bending my arm behind my back before I can pull my hand away. My free hand grabs his wrist, trying to pry my captured hand from his grip, but he's anticipated my move, and in the next second he has both of my hands pinned behind my back.

His lips are within kissing distance, and he leans in to whisper in my ear. "You're gonna have to be faster than that, love." His voice sends a tingle up my spine.

Oh gods, his body is so warm it feels like he's trying to light me on fire. My dragon is hungry for him, pacing back and forth with anticipation. Craving even his slightest touch.

But I have work to do, so I lean in closer to my mate. "Oh, I am."

I pull my knee up quickly between us, using the force of it to press into his stomach and knock him on his ass. With my hands free and Jace on the ground, I do a forward roll and end up on my knees. I crawl over to him and straddle him. I put my hands on my hips and look down at him with a smirk.

He reaches up, grabbing my waist as he pulls me down onto his hardened body. Jace rolls on top of me and pins my wrists to the ground.

He flashes me a tender smile, and I'm caught up in the moment. I can't believe this strong, sexy man is mine. My *mate*. My dragon sighs with happiness.

He leans over and kisses me. Gently at first, then with more passion. I want to lose myself in him. To take advantage of the warm sun on our skin. Unfortunately, we don't have time.

I summon my magic, focusing it into my wrists. I picture them burning like fire, but I don't let Jace know what I'm doing. He continues to kiss me, and I raise my knees up a little, squeezing him as he presses his body harder into mine.

Damn, I want him bad. But I have to focus on my magic.

He suddenly lets go of my wrists. "Shit! That's hot. He scrambles quickly to his feet and looks down at me with a confused expression. "What the hell, Rory?"

I stand up and brush myself off, chuckling. "You okay?" I tease, as I summon my dagger and take a defensive stance.

He looks over his hands, both the front and the

back, making sure they're not burnt. "It felt like my hands were on fire. Did you do that?"

I let out another chuckle. "I wouldn't actually burn you," I say, watching his expression. He doesn't speak for a moment as he studies his hands.

"I'm not going easy on you after that," he finally says while taking a fighting stance.

"I don't expect you to," I tease.

For the next few hours, we fight like we used to. Hand-to-hand and then magic against magic. It's as easy as breathing, when I train with Jace. Even when I get knocked down, he presses me to fight harder. I love the way my mate pushes me to be the best fighter I can be.

"I'm going to do a jump kick attack, and I want you to summon your magic. Use your magical weapons to deflect me."

"Are you sure?" I ask with a quirked brow.

"The point is, we need to test your limits and see what else you can do. Your magic is growing —changing."

Use my weapons to divert his attack? I'll have to move quickly. Maybe I can summon two at a time. There's definitely a benefit to learning something like that. I plant my feet shoulder width apart, settling into a slight squat before holding my hands out in front of me with my palms facing the blue sky. I picture the weapons I've learned to create with my magic. Easy. I can do this. Jace puts some space between us so that he can have a running start.

He runs toward me, and I feel like he's going to run right through me, but then he jumps into the air, and I have a second to react. I summon my mace in one hand and my sword in the other. I make a figure eight in front of me with my mace, making it impossible for him to kick me. I'm prepared to strike at him with my sword, but I feel a sudden surge of power. The sword pulses with brilliant light.

Shit.

I can't stop it.

His foot hits the swinging mace, which acts like an energy conductor. It shines brighter than the sun, and I'm temporarily blinded. Jace flies backward and he hits the ground so hard that the force causes him to roll backward.

I run to him to make sure he isn't hurt.

He immediately sits up, shaking his head. "That packed a hell of a punch."

I kneel next to him, looking him over for injuries as I force the stirrings of another power surge back down inside.

"I'm okay, but I'd say that was another surge." His

fingers gently trace my chin as he searches my face for the truth.

Good thing I've been trained to lie with a straight face. "I think I just lost focus. I'm tired—we've been at this for hours."

"I know that was a power surge, Rory. Maybe we should slow down." He lifts my chin and challenges me with his eyes.

"I'm fine. I'm pretty sure this has to do with my dragon growing inside of me. I can feel her getting stronger—maturing." I look away from him, frustrated. Everything is under control. It has to be.

"Fine." He releases my chin. "Just let me know if something weird happens or if it gets out of hand."

I nod. "You'll be the first to know."

"Good," he says, standing up and extending his hand to help me to my feet.

I wink at him, grinning from ear to ear as I walk away and sway my hips.

I turn around and his eyes blaze with lust. I love knowing he desires me as much as I desire him.

CHAPTER FOURTEEN

My time in the mountains training with Jace has made me happy and exhausted, and while my mate is content to head off to sleep after sparring, I need time to wind down before I can head to bed. We fly together toward the castle with Ashgrave's little body hovering behind us. Even though the sun has set and I should be winding down, my mind is still racing with the millions of 'what-if's' that could go wrong tomorrow. I hope Diesel hasn't picked up on the fact that we're intercepting his delivery of the bio-weapon.

Hopefully his hack on Irena's phone gave him nothing, since we've been careful to speak in our code language or meet in person. I'm concerned anyway, because we were all trained by Zurie. She taught us not to rely on one source of information, because people lie.

My clothes are folded neatly in the corner near the large windows where I left them. I dress quickly and hurry to the surveillance room.

"Drew?" I call out as I step into the room. Damn. He's not here.

That's fine. I can do this alone. Nothing like spying on the Vaer to wind down for the night. I sit in the high-backed office chair and settle into the comfort of the thickly padded seat.

I turn on the dual monitors, plug in the headphones, and slide them over my head. I switch between channels, looking specifically for intel from the Vaer intelligence network. Unfamiliar voices talk about the Vaer's usual dealings of trafficking and drugs, then a familiar voice comes over the line. His tone is dark but smooth as silk. I thought I killed him. Kinsley's young commander. He's being manipulated. Kinsley's lap dog is relaying some orders on tightening up security.

My eyelids grow heavy as I listen to the chatter, but I'm not ready to call it quits for the night. Knowing the Vaer's security plans in advance will help me and my team a great deal. I need an energy boost. I'll jot down the security info now and rest later. I'm getting some pretty important information from the bug. I can't take any chances. I can sleep later.

"Ashgrave, can you please make me some coffee?" He's been able to do everything else. I figure there's no limit to what his robotic dragon form can do. It would be funny to see little robot Ashgraves with bow ties bringing me coffee and cookies. I chuckle at the thought.

"Harrumph," a muffled grumble comes from behind me, and I turn to see Tucker dressed in pajama pants with a toothbrush hanging out of his mouth and an irritated look on his face.

"YOU WILL MAKE COFFEE FOR MY QUEEN," Ashgrave's voice booms. "MISTRESS, WOULD YOU LIKE CREAM AND SUGAR?"

That's not what I thought would happen. "Never mind," I tell Ashgrave. "I'm sorry, Tucker. I didn't know he would have you make it."

Tucker opens his mouth, toothbrush still hanging out, and I can tell he has a few obscenities that he would like to share with my castle. But before he can say a word, Ashgrave's metallic hand emerges from the floor and whisks him away. Great. Now my castle is waging a joke war against my weapons expert. I wonder if Ashgrave understands the hell he's unleashing.

Turning my attention back to the screens and the voices on the headset, I can tell much of the chatter is dying down. It seems to be getting too late to pick up anything new. Using the hacking software, I enter my password and get into the Vaer's computer files. I look through documents, emails, anything that looks like it might hold any new information. While reading the list of sent emails, I notice one of them has an encoded recipient, and it's from the Commander. I open it.

As I read through the email, my heart pounds as I realize just who this is directed toward. In fact, it looks like there's been some back and forth between the sender and recipient for a while. The email is between the Nabal and the Vaer. There are offers of power, of riches from the Vaer, and demands from the Nabal in the emails. The Vaer are courting them as an ally, and whoever is responding on behalf of the Nabal seems to be warming up to the idea.

Fan-freaking-tastic.

I wonder if this alliance is already completed. I know Aki has it out for me. He didn't like me to begin with, and now that his daughter has turned her back on him to follow me? He probably wants to burn me at the stake.

Gods. I wonder what Jade will do. If her father does side with the Vaer—would she betray me in an effort to prove herself one last time? She seemed genuine during our moment on the mountain top. And she did step between me and Aki when it mattered. But given how sad she's been since coming to live here, I can't completely rely on her loyalty. It would be stupid to do so. And I am definitely not stupid.

I lean back in my chair and think about everything I read in the emails.

I wonder if Jade regrets her choice of abandoning her father, her inheritance—her identity. If she does, that could mean allowing her to stay here is dangerous.

There has to be a way to prove where her allegiance lies. I don't like it, but I have to find out.

I slide my phone out of my pocket.

The phone rings once and Brett answers. "Yeah, Boss. What can I do for you?"

Please let's not add Boss to the list of titles my men want to put on me.

"Hey Brett, do me a favor and take Jade to the

war room and set up a video call to her father for me. Don't tell Jade I asked, understand?"

"Sure, Rory. Anything you say."

"Thanks." I end the call and switch the video views to the cameras set up in the war room. It's my job to look after everyone in my castle. I didn't tell Jade that Aki's last parting words to her were that she was dead to him. I wonder if he will even accept a call from her.

Their voices come over the headset before they even enter the war room.

"…impressed with you," Brett says, opening the door and ushering her inside.

"Thank you," Jade responds as she takes a seat at the large table.

Brett seems genuine, and I can tell by the smile on her face that he's just given her a compliment.

"I'm just unhappy that the relationship with your father seems unresolved." He gazes at her with a look that reveals his concern and affection for her.

Jade's smile falls as the sadness returns to her eyes. I've seen the same look in the mirror too many times to count.

"I agree, Brett. I wish I could have the chance to explain why I chose this, even if he doesn't accept it. I just need for him to know why."

"I understand." He reaches out to gently touch her shoulder in reassurance. I can't help but wonder if they've talked about this before.

"I don't mean to seem ungrateful... " She looks up at him.

"I know you miss him. And believe me, I know that standing up to your father, or any father figure —is difficult. Maybe this call will finally give you the closure you need. You know, so that you can move on."

Her eyes go in and out of focus. She lowers her head to look at the floor.

"If it doesn't go as you hope, I'm still here for you, okay?"

She nods but doesn't say a word.

"Do you want me to stay or go?" he asks, releasing her shoulder.

"I'd like to be alone, if that's okay?" she says softly. He nods and brushes a stray strand of black hair from her face. Brett sets up the video call then leaves the room—but if I know Brett, he hasn't gone far.

It seems like time is standing still, and then Aki answers.

"Father, I've missed you." Jade's voice wavers.

"What do you want, *child?* I've got an empire to

run and men awaiting my orders. Men who are *obedient* and who do not *fail*."

What an asshole. I fight the urge to storm into the room and tell him just where he can shove his obedient men. But I can't. I have to see where Jade takes this test. I have to see how Jade reacts to her father and the way he treats her. I told her what would happen if she ever sold me out, and now is the moment of truth.

"I'm calling because... I need you to know that you're still my family, but I can't kill Rory. It just isn't in me," she says, despite his comment.

"Well, my child," his voice softens like a slithering snake. "I may be able to forgive you if you give me intel on Rory and her castle. Did you think I wouldn't know where you're calling from?"

"I can't do that," Jade responds. My nerves are on edge. If she tells him anything, it will put us all at risk.

"Come now, my daughter. Just a little insight into her weaknesses, her defenses... you'll be welcomed home with open arms."

I'd love to throttle this guy.

"No. I refuse." She's silent for a moment before she speaks again with resolve. "Rory is everything you're not. Where you have failed me, Rory has shown kindness and compassion. Where you exert dominance and demand obedience—Rory gives grace. I don't need or want your forgiveness. I just wanted you to know why I refused to kill Rory and stood between the two of you, and to have you understand that I am my own person now. When it comes down to it, I will choose Rory and the team, her family, over you." She presses a button and the screen goes black before Aki can let loose his string of abusive words.

Her small shoulders tremble as her eyes swim with tears. I jump out of my chair.

"Ashgrave, take me to the war room, now."

The wall opens and I enter his magical tunnel. I am extremely grateful for this gift that he has. The tunnel takes me to the hallway outside the war room. I was right—Brett is standing in the hall just outside of the war room.

"Just give me a few minutes with her," I tell him, and he nods. I rush into the room and wrap my arms around her. I don't say a word as I let her cry for a few moments into my shoulder. When her sobbing slows, she looks up at me.

"I can't believe I did that," she says, her voice breaking and her eyes red from crying.

"Jade, you are so strong. I'm proud of you." I beam at her.

I know what it takes to say those things and the kind of strength you need to finally stand up for yourself against the people who push you down.

"I think there's someone outside waiting to see you." I release her and walk to the door, opening it and then nodding to Brett who's still standing outside. "Thank you, Brett."

He gives me a curt nod before shaking his head and slipping inside the war room.

I know he's upset with me. But I'm not sure if it's because I asked him to play a part in this tragic call, or because I spied on her.

I got the proof of loyalty that I was looking for. I'm so damn proud of Jade.

Now to get some sleep, because tomorrow is coming with its own challenges.

CHAPTER FIFTEEN

"Flynn, if you or any of your dragon rebels get out of hand while I'm away, Ashgrave will burn you to ash."

Flynn has a half-smile on his face as he tries to figure out if I'm teasing him. I smirk, and he instantly relaxes.

He gives me a flourishing bow. "I'll make sure the castle remains in one piece until you return."

"Ashgrave will leave you in pieces if you mess with him," I say with a playful smile. "We should be back in a couple of days. My home is your home, but remember, Ashgrave is murderous by nature. Be respectful and enjoy it—it's one of the most beautiful places I've ever seen."

"I agree," the rebel leader replies. "Don't worry, my people are trustworthy."

"Brett and Jade are here if you need anything."

He nods. "We will be okay."

I want to give Flynn a list of do's and don'ts, but I'm out of time. My men are waiting for me in the kitchen so we can go over last minute details before we leave.

As I head for the kitchen, I give Ashgrave orders to take care of the dragon rebels. I'm not worried about my castle—he can take care of himself. If any of the rebels tries anything, his dragon form will let me know right away. There's not a chance in hell I'd leave Ashgrave's metallic dragon form behind while I travel to the States. Having his portable form online gives me the chance to keep an eye on my castle while I travel.

"Good morning, babe." Tucker's grin greets me as I enter the kitchen.

"Good morning," I respond, giving him a kiss on the cheek.

Drew, Levi, and Jace enter at the same time, and I wonder what they've been up to.

"Are you guys ready?" I ask with a quirked eyebrow.

They nod in unison. These men of mine are up to

something. I can't help but smile. If we're going to war, I'm glad I have them by my side.

"So," Tucker says grabbing my attention, showing me the list of guns and ammo that he was able to pack into the chopper. I know he's a weapons expert, but I'm impressed by the sheer number of items he managed to load into his flying toy.

Drew chimes in. "And if that's not enough fire power, a few of my contacts will meet us in LA. I've arranged for them to bring us some assault rifles and extra ammo. Two armored cars will take us to a drop off point, and there's a hotel where Tucker can check in and get set up.

"Is the hotel owned by someone in your network?"

Drew nods. I swear he has secret allies all over the globe.

"And Brett?" I ask.

"Brett is in the surveillance room. He's going to keep us informed of any changes the Vaer make."

"Let's head out," Jace says.

He always gets bossy when we have a mission.

We all load into the chopper, and Tucker gets into the pilot seat and starts flipping switches and turning knobs to get the chopper ready for takeoff. Ashgrave's metallic body flitters up into the chopper before Drew closes the door, and the blades whir to life. Within minutes, we're flying through the air.

I'd love to fly in my dragon form, especially since I've gotten better at it, but that wouldn't go over well. Kinsley's made it hard for dragons by unleashing her fury on a human city. Descending on Los Angeles as my diamond dragon won't help.

Ashgrave's cat-sized dragon body sits next to my feet on the floor. His metallic head tilts slightly as he watches the snow covered land below. I smile at the idea of him traveling with me so far from home. Levi sits next to me while Drew and Jace sit together, looking at a tablet that Drew's holding.

After hours of flying, we finally approach a small airport with a private terminal just outside of LA. I slide my tablet out of my bag and pull up the layout of the restaurant on my screen. Drew has arranged for Tucker to stay across from the restaurant at a stylish hotel with roof access. Tucker will watch over the whole mission with a sniper rifle. Drew and I have reservations at 9 p.m., and we've asked to be seated in a private booth. I brush the blonde hairs of my wig out of my face and smirk. This should be fun.

My phone hasn't buzzed once during our flight. I

suppose that no news is good news, but I really want confirmation that Irena will be there tonight.

I call my sister again. "Hey Irena, I missed you yesterday. I really want some sister time. Chinese food tonight?" I say cheerfully. I know Diesel's not stupid, and I can only hope he isn't onto us.

I'm not nervous that Irena hasn't called me back. She knows Diesel is monitoring her phone. Knowing my sister, she's waiting to contact me until it's safe.

My thoughts go to the new bio-weapon. I shudder at the memory of how Kinsley's first one almost killed Irena. Her eyes are forever bright green, and she has some dragonish tendencies because of it. If the new one is worse, it could kill hundreds of thousands of people, or make the Vaer a massive army of manufactured dragons.

And if Diesel gets his hands on it, there's no telling who he would unleash it on. Dragons, humans—men, women, and children. He doesn't care.

Even if we get the bio-weapon tonight and are able to destroy it safely, we will still have to find the laboratory that created it and burn it to the ground. We have to end the threat once and for all.

As the lights of the city shine through the front

window of the chopper, Tucker turns around to look at me.

"Can I get you a coffee, Rory?" he jokes over the headset.

"I'm good. Thanks, Tucker."

Adorable goofball. Even with my nerves on edge, I can't help but chuckle. He turns back to face the front of the chopper and reaches into a satchel that sits next to him on the floor.

"Here babe, I got you a present." He turns and tosses me a small black case. I flick open the locks, and inside are a beautiful set of silver throwing knives, a pearl handled .22 caliber pistol, and an ivory handled dagger. "Take your pick or use it all… whatever." He smiles the grin that I love so much then turns back to flying the chopper.

He sure knows how to treat a girl right. I'll have to reward him later. I grin mischievously at the thought.

Out of the corner of my eye, I notice Levi shift uncomfortably. My gaze catches his ice blue eyes, and they have bruise like shadows under them. Why didn't I notice it earlier?

"Levi?" I say softly, and he turns to face me.

"I'm fine," he assures me, but I don't believe him. I reach out and touch his bare arm.

Levi, really... are you okay?

He stares into my eyes, knowing he can't hide his feelings from me.

I've been having some weird dreams lately.

What happens in these dreams? I press.

In my dreams, I'm feral. His icy blues shoot a feeling of dread through me, and my heart goes out to him. I know that's his worst fear. To lose himself again.

Levi, you've come so far. You and your dragon trust each other, and you can easily shift back and forth. I want to encourage him, but I can't find the words. Instead, I push my love, pride, and encouragement through our bond.

"Heading for the landing strip," Tucker announces into our headsets.

Our private landing strip was arranged by Drew during one of his many calls yesterday. I swear my fire dragon has connections everywhere.

Armed men are waiting on the small landing strip, and I know they're the backup Drew promised.

Levi and I end our secret conversation, and we all hurry to grab our gear and the extra weapons Tucker has tucked into the small storage compartments of the chopper. Ashgrave looks out the window at the four armed men waiting for us.

"SHOULD   I   INCINERATE   THEM,
MISTRESS?" Ashgrave's voice echoes inside the
chopper, startling all of us. My men and I all jump at
the same time.

"No, Ashgrave. Those are Drew's men. They're
here to help." I let out a nervous laugh. "I'll let you
know when I have someone for you to smite."

To be honest, I would've liked to see more than
four men, but I know we're trying to keep a low
profile. More armed men makes us more conspicu-
ous. If Diesel gets word that we're in California, the
bio-weapon drop will be cancelled.

"VERY WELL, MY QUEEN."

Damn little metallic beast. Drew and I exchange
glances, and I roll my eyes.

Our plan is set, and we know what we have to do.
We exit the chopper, loaded with weapons, and
confident and ready to go.

CHAPTER SIXTEEN

Drew's men lead us to the waiting armored cars. I'm thankful for the tinted windows as my men and I split up to travel to Chinatown. Tucker, Jace, and Ashgrave are in the first car. Drew, Levi, and I ride in the second. There are digital billboards along the freeway with various images. Some I recognize, some I don't. There are even a few with images of me and Irena, and to my shock, they're showing us in a positive light.

I spy a still image from the day Brett recorded the video of me with one word on the digital screen. 'Protector.' I wonder how much of the footage he's used to sway people's opinions of me and my sister. I haven't seen the final version, but this seems to show me in a better light.

My new campaign is more honest than Kinsley's smear campaign. Brett has done something right. Maybe he deserves a raise—or a vacation. I chuckle to myself. He's devoted himself to helping me look good in the court of public opinion at every chance he gets.

Not bad.

As we near downtown LA, I start to feel better about the situation—until I spot a group of humans protesting. I struggle to read their signs, and Drew leans into me to look out the window on my side of the SUV. Whoever—whatever they are, they're angry. As some of them pace back and forth, I finally get a glimpse of a few signs.

Crudely drawn stick dragons with big red X's over them. 'Death to all dragons' is written on a couple. 'Dragons are unnatural' says another. There are a few with more obscene and harsh depictions, and it breaks my heart. This protest is obviously put in place by someone who knows nothing about the true nature of dragons. At least those of us dragons who want to live in peace.

Damn it. Every time I take a step forward, my enemies push me two steps back. Traffic is brutally slow, and the smog here makes it hard to breathe.

I'm already missing the beautiful hills and mountains that surround my castle. I can't wait until this is over and we can go home. Home. For once in my life, I feel comfortable thinking that.

The armored cars take us to Chinatown, parking a few blocks away from the hotel where Tucker is supposed to be staying. Drew and Levi stay in the car, and I wear my blonde wig and a pair of black rimmed glasses. I watch as Tucker exits the SUV in front of us, carrying his suitcase and the extra-large duffle bag that holds Ashgrave's metal dragon body. Drew's contacts have handled everything, and there will be no questions asked when Tucker checks in.

My phone beeps with a text message.

You look hot in that wig. If we make it out of here, we can use it during our next naked aerobics session.

A blush creeps up my cheeks and I chuckle, then text Tucker back.

Stop playing around. Let me know when you and Ashgrave get into your room.

It takes a few moments, and he texts back.

You got it, babe.

I message him back.

Make sure to tell Ashgrave that his queen is ordering him not to speak. His loud mouth will give us away.

Tucker responds.

You got it.

I take a pair a binoculars out of my bag and turn in my seat to watch the hotel windows. The minutes feel like hours as I wait for a signal from Tucker.

We're in position.

I peek through the lenses and spot an open window with a rifle's muzzle sitting in it. I know my weapons expert has his sniper rifle lined up for a shot.

We still have about twenty minutes until our reservation, and I'm wondering when Irena will join us.

Drew's hand grabs my knee. "We've got this." I know we do, but him saying it makes me feel better.

Levi opens the car door and gives me a wink as he closes it. Jace exits the other armored car and they both walk across the street toward the back of the restaurant. I know they have weapons, and they're prepared. But I just want to get in and out.

"Ready?" he asks.

I nod and wait for him to open my door.

Drew takes my hand as he escorts me toward the restaurant.

"Might as well pretend we're a real couple," he teases.

"We are a real couple," I respond.

He winks at me, and I smile as we head toward the front door of the restaurant. As we enter, an older man holds the door for us.

The hostess, who wears a name tag that reads 'Cindy,' greets us.

"Party of two, nine o'clock for Mr. and Mrs. Hargrove," Drew tells her.

"Ah yes, Hargrove. Right this way, please. You requested a private table, right?"

Drew nods at her, and she gives him a dazzling smile without even looking my way. Her ruby red lips shimmer under the dim chandelier lights of the restaurant. The young brunette is enraptured by Drew. She can't take her green eyes off him. I watch her, amused. It's not the first time I've been out with one of my men and another woman has noticed them.

I can't stop the smug little smile that plants itself on my lips.

He's mine, I think as she seats us and offers to bring us a drink.

Drew nods and orders us a sweet Moscato. I know we won't be drinking it, since we have to be clear headed and alert.

The one thing that bothers me, more than the woman trying to flirt with Drew, is how empty this place is. From our research, we know this is a popular spot to eat. That's why we made reservations and asked for a private table. Outside of the restaurant, there were people everywhere. It's like LA never sleeps, but in here—crickets. I don't like it. This feels wrong. I tense my jaw and glance at Drew.

He's noticed it too, and his eyes dart around the room. Something isn't right.

Cindy returns with our Moscato, but Drew waves it away. "On second thought, can we please have some coffee?"

I pretend to yawn, as I watch her. "We've been traveling."

"Absolutely," she answers. "Cream and sugar?"

I nod.

We browse our menus, and I pretend to laugh as I peer over my menu at him. "It's too quiet and empty in here," I say, barely whispering, keeping a false smile on my lips. I have to pretend that I don't suspect a thing.

"I agree," he smiles back. "I think it's a trap." He laughs in return, his eyes shine even though it's an act.

"If that's the case, then the Vaer figured it out, or they know about our hack. They could've orchestrated this whole thing."

As if they've been listening in, six men march into the main dining room from the kitchen, shoving Jace and Levi forward with guns pressed into their backs.

The bells chime from the front doors and another ten men enter. They're a mixture of Nabal and Vaer.

Kinsley's young lap dog leads them. "Good to see you again, Rory." His words are as cool as ice. "Kinsley sends her regards," he says as I give him a wide-eyed stare.

"I guess you've got us all figured out," Drew says.

"I've figured out enough." The young Vaer commander moves closer to Levi and Jace. "I knew that if something big was going down, that Queen Rory and her men would try to show up and stop us. You cost us millions in research by taking our test subjects."

The punk brings back his fist then lands it in Levi's stomach with a hard thump. Levi doubles over, groaning. My blood boils. My dragon wants to rip his throat out. I stand suddenly, and everyone around us pulls out their weapons.

"It looks like you've got yourself into a bit of a predicament, haven't you Rory?" the baby faced Vaer taunts. There are less men here than what we faced in the facility, but these men already have their weapons trained on us. They aim their guns at us at the same time, and my intuition tells me not to underestimate them. Not with my men's lives on the line.

"Maybe," I answer.

The punk Vaer commander flashes me a smug smile. "I have some good news. If you come with us, all of your men can leave unharmed."

Yeah, right. I'm the only one he's been told to keep alive. To him, my men are expendable. Why would I believe a word he says? Hell, I thought the asshole was dead until I heard his voice the last night.

"Fine," I say, still searching my surroundings for a better option. "Was there ever a bio-weapon to give to Diesel, or was that made up too?"

"That may be the only part that's true, Rory dear. We're delivering it to him as we speak. And I hope that he kills as many of those sniveling humans as possible," he growls.

"You honestly think that Diesel will stop there?" I question. "Are you serious? That asshole will destroy anyone he needs to just to get what he wants. He won't stop at humans. He will kill dragons. He will kill you."

"I don't care," the young Vaer replies, looking me dead in the eye. "My job is to take you to Kinsley. That's my only concern."

"And if I refuse?" I ask, realizing I'm playing with fire. The fact that they want to kill us is in the eyes of every man in this room.

He shrugs. "She didn't say I had to bring you in all nice and pretty, so it's your choice."

What this young punk doesn't know is that I'm an ex-Spectre who is slick as hell, and while we've been chatting, I've slid a throwing knife into my hand and I'm about to do Tucker proud.

Tucker. No doubt he's exchanging his rifle for something bigger.

I give Kinsley's lap dog a smirk.

Poor kid. Nice and pretty just isn't my style.

CHAPTER SEVENTEEN

I reposition the knife in my hand and leap forward, thrusting the tip toward the young commander's stomach. The little bastard is quicker than I give him credit for, and he manages to dodge my attack.

I pull my arm back, with the intention of thrusting my blade at him again, but he grabs my hair. The blond wig slips off in his hand, luckily, allowing me to free myself from his grasp. I roll forward and jump to my feet. But one of the Vaer soldiers is throwing a punch at my face. I jerk to the right, but his knuckles graze my chin. I return the favor by throwing a fist of my own. I hit him in the temple and he falls to the floor, unconscious. Gunshots erupt from the left side of the room.

As I turn my head to find out what's happening, I'm attacked by three men. One is trying to punch me in the face and the other two are attempting to grab my arms. I head butt one of the soldiers trying to pin my arms as I duck the fist aimed for my face. I grab the hand that was trying to knock me out and pull him into his friend and they collide with a loud *thwack* as they fall to the floor in a heap.

From the corner of my eye, I spot Drew fighting hand-to-hand against a few of the soldiers. Metal flies through the air, and I duck as a chair is thrown into the hostess desk. Guns clatter on the floor as Levi and Jace fight back-to-back against the guards by the door.

The shuffle of footsteps has me turning my head to the right, and the little punk's eyes are shining with his desire to capture me. To use me—my power.

Kinsley's lap dog keeps coming after me like a dog trying to corner a stray cat in his backyard. The Vaer commander charges me and I throat punch him. His unconscious body falls to floor with a thud. But what the punk commander doesn't realize is the only way the Vaer will leave this room will be in body bags.

The click of a gun cocking has me paying closer

attention to the battle. A Vaer guard, with a baby face, gives me a look that could thaw the mountains surrounding Castle Ashgrave. He aims the gun at my head, his finger resting lightly on the trigger with eyes as big as saucers.

"Are you sure you want to do that?" I question, paying attention to his body language.

He doesn't say a word, and to my surprise the young Vaer squirms as droplets of sweat trickle down his forehead. Either this is his first mission, or he's worried about going up against the dragon vessel.

I stalk toward the young guard who is aiming his gun at me. With each footstep I take, the whites of his eyes become larger and larger.

"Hit her, now. We need to get her to Kinsley." The Vaer commander yells from behind me, but the kid in front of me isn't moving. He can't take his dinner-plate sized eyes off me. His gun is rattling as its aim starts to drift toward the floor.

I note his hesitation. "You don't have to do this. Just hand me the gun and get out of here. I'll make sure you escape safely," I promise.

I'm trying to help him, and he seems to know that. The young guard lowers his weapon just as a gunshot rings out. The young man falls to the floor, dead.

"I knew he was weak," Kinsley's lap dog says with a smoking gun in his hand as he watches the pool of blood grow around the dead soldier. "But I'm not." He aims his gun at me.

I summon my magic and take a fighting stance with my palms facing the ceiling. The blue sparks grow in my hands as I start to make my magical mace.

The thunder of a large man's footsteps rushes toward us, and Drew tackles him to the floor. Just before the gun goes flying through the air, it goes off. I throw myself to the ground, yanking a table down with me. Drew is straddling the young commander's chest and pummeling the punk with his fists.

"Drew!" I call out to him. Gunfire echoes around me as soldiers fall to the ground, dead.

Ten more soldiers enter the restaurant through the front door. I grab two of my throwing knives sheathed beneath my blouse, lean around the table, and toss them at a couple of the new guards. My knives hit two of our new visitors in the stomach. Blood pours from their wounds as they search for their attacker.

The young Vaer commander stops moving, and Drew springs to his feet, leaping over the table I'm behind and ducks down next to me. He pulls a gun from his waistband and starts firing at the soldiers who are still standing. I pull out my pretty pearl handled gift from Tucker and do the same. We need to get this chaos a little more organized.

Jace rushes one of the newcomers and punches him in the face, knocking him out. He's so smooth— hot. I'll have to compliment him later.

Levi is surrounded by six unconscious guards as he faces two more. He moves like water, fast and smooth, as he fights with one hand and shoots with the other.

I wonder if Tucker's okay. As if he can read my thoughts, my weapons expert bursts through the front door like a badass. He has a bazooka resting on his shoulder with its strap around his back and he fires it, knocking out five soldiers at once.

Hovering at Tucker's side is Ashgrave, who is burning the Vaer and Nabal to ash, one by one. I figure if a metallic dragon could smile, he would be. Together, Tucker and Ashgrave are an unstoppable force. We're finally starting to get the upper hand.

Nabal soldiers start to pour in from the back of

the restaurant and fill the dining room. Damn it. They just blocked our exit.

My magic pools in my hands, forming two daggers, and I throw them at the men closest to our downed table. Tucker and Ashgrave aim their blasts at the new threat.

"Tucker, do you have a smaller gun, babe? I'd like to escape, not have the roof collapse on our heads," I yell over the table, grinning as I take out a couple more Nabal with more of my daggers.

"How about this, babe?" Tucker tosses the bazooka over his back as he lifts an AR-57 and unleashes a torrent of bullets on the soldiers standing in the dining room.

The young Vaer commander starts to pull himself to his feet, but Jace is at his side before I have a chance to blink. There's a flash of steel as Jace sinks a blade into the punk's gut and the Vaer falls to the floor. The young commander's blood pools around him quickly.

Jace and Levi are battling the remaining Nabal newcomers in hand-to-and combat. Tucker is shooting the Vaer who dare show their faces with his .50 caliber handgun, and my evil butler is smiting anyone dumb enough to try and attack Tucker's back. I can't let my men have all the fun.

I bolt out from behind the table. Something hits me in the middle of my back, and the air is forced out of me.

Hell, that hurt. Feels like someone brought out the anti-dragon weapons.

My dragon is begging to be let out to play.

But, I can't. Shifting in a human zone is against the law. It would turn all of the humans against me— and all dragons—forever.

"Shit, Rory!" Drew runs toward me, but he's shot too. Who in the hell brought anti-dragon guns to a dragon fight?

Ashgrave unleashes his magic on a small group of Vaer soldiers as he tries to get to Tucker. My weapons expert is backed against a wall by three Nabal fighters with guns aimed at him.

I have to do something, quick. I can't lose Tucker. I can't lose any of my men.

The hail of bullets stop, and where we had the upper hand moments ago, fate kicked us in the ass with anti-dragon guns. I can barely breathe, but I'll be damned if any of my men die here tonight.

The young Vaer commander is dead, finally. But another Vaer steps up to take his place. As the new guy approaches me, he aims his anti-dragon weapon

for my back. If I get shot by that gun again, it'll para-
lyze me. I won't be able to escape.

"Are you willing to give up, now?" The new man
asks.

I pull myself up to stand on my feet as I'm
about to stall him, but the loud, high-pitched
squeal of a missile being launched has me and my
men throwing ourselves to the floor. The front of
the building blows to bits. A group of people
dressed in black burst through the large hole and
start taking out the remaining Nabal and Vaer. The
trained soldiers with anti-dragon weapons who
moments ago had us about to surrender are now
dropping like flies. There are only ten newcomers,
but they are working together like a well-oiled
machine.

Levi and Jace crawl behind the table, and Tucker
is being helped toward us by Ashgrave. Drew stands
in front of us with his feet shoulder width apart with
his fists clenched. My fire dragon is willing to take
on this new threat.

But there's no need to fight. The new group isn't
here to kill us—their mission is obvious. When the
remaining Nabal and Vaer fall and the dust settles, I
suck in a deep breath.

Drew shakes his head like the pieces of a puzzle

are falling into place for him. He recognizes these people.

The leader of the group steps forward and pulls off the thick hood that covers his head, revealing his identity.

"Milo?" Drew asks with a confused expression. "What the hell are you doing here?"

"Is that how you thank someone who helps you, little brother?"

"Did father send you to get Rory?" Drew quirks a questioning brow.

"No. Even though Jett would never approve of me helping you. I said fuck it and did it anyway."

Drew has a sexy smirk on his lips, and his black eyes are gleaming. I know that look. He's surprised. And pleased.

Hell, I'm surprised too. Especially considering the last time I saw Milo, I was wondering which way he would go, after the incident at the arena. Either he would become someone better, with an actual moral compass, or he would become more like his father, willing to do anything to anyone to get what he wants. I'm glad he chose to be better. If Milo chose to be like Jett, I'd be forced to kill him, and that would hurt Drew.

More Vaer and Nabal burst in through the back

of the restaurant, and we're all in a fight for our lives against a fresh wave of soldiers. Shit, this needs to end. Milo and his team stop them before they can reach us by shooting the first of the advancing guards, and I'm grateful.

"Get out of here!" Milo orders.

Drew, Levi, and Jace step up beside Milo and start shooting at the new threat. Ashgrave dives toward a few Nabal men, burning them to ash using his magic. Tucker, who's now recovered from his beat down, high kicks the face of anyone who comes close to him. I throat punch those who step up to fight me. A feeling of satisfaction rolls over me as we knock these men on their asses. Tucker, Ashgrave, and I fight off anyone who manages to get around the death trap waiting for them in the form of Milo and my men.

One of the young Vaer guards darts toward the kitchen with a backpack on, and I chase him down. Is the bio-weapon in that pack? I need to know. I dart around stacks of boxes and piles of takeout boxes as I run after the guard with the backpack.

As I race around the corner of the huge walk-in freezer, something hits me from behind. My body falls to the floor, on fire. Pain shoots through every nerve of my body.

I'm surrounded by boots and kicked over, so I can see my attacker. A familiar face stares down at me. Diesel.

Diesel lifts his foot and kicks me in the head. And everything goes black

CHAPTER EIGHTEEN

I pry my eyes open and spots dance across my field of vision. My head feels like it weighs a thousand pounds, and it throbs in time to my pulse.

Trying to get a feel for my surroundings, I blink the black dots from my vision. A few dingy bare light bulbs hang overhead, and I'm lying on a smelly stained blanket on the floor. There are some boarded windows high up on the right wall, too high up to get to them without standing on something.

To my left a single folding table is set up with a few hand tools laid on top of it.

The bulb that hangs above my head is smudged with dirt and gives off hardly any light. Even with my enhanced vision, I can't see a thing. I roll over and push myself up so I'm sitting with my legs straight out in front of me. And every muscle in my body aches with the movement. The cold cuffs around my wrists are tight, and I can't wiggle out of them.

I figure Diesel has me locked in one of his warehouses, away from prying eyes.

My dragon coils in anger. She wants blood.

We will have it, today, I assure her.

"Look who's awake." Diesel steps out of the shadows as if he's been there the whole time, watching—waiting for me. Pompous asshole. "I've been dreaming of this day, Rory. This exact moment... when I would have you trapped and in the perfect position—"

"So that you can kiss my ass?" I'm seething.

I try to summon my magic, straightening out my hands and pointing my palms to the ceiling as best I can. The magic starts to pool in my hands, but it stops. My magic is being restrained by the cuffs. Damn it. I move, trying to get an edge.

"Tut, tut, Rory. That's not the way you speak to your superior."

I spit at him. "You're not my superior. I'm not a Spectre anymore."

"I know. You're a magical shifting dragon now. The irony!" He tosses his head back, laughing. "You can struggle all you want, but I'm not stupid enough to have you here without suppressing your magic. You won't be going anywhere, thanks to my new toy locked around your wrists." His tone is mocking. I hate it. I want to blast him and wipe the gloating smile off his face. "I got them just for you and Irena. By the way, where is your sister? I thought she'd be with you at the restaurant."

"Die, Diesel."

"No. Don't think I will. But I know there's a whole globe of humans who will be affected by the new and improved bio-weapon that Kinsley made. This will finally wake them all to the danger your kind poses."

I'm boiling with rage. When I get out of these magic-dampening cuffs, he's going to wish he was never born. At least Irena isn't here, shackled beside me. I hope my sister is safe, wherever she is. But she's a smart woman who can take care of herself.

My eyes have finally adjusted to the dimly lit room, and I find Diesel's surrounded by Spectres. I recognize the layout of this place though. I've seen it more than once on the maps I've gone over with Drew and Jace. This warehouse belongs to the Vaer —I'm sure of it.

"You will have a front row seat to the war I'm

going to start between humans and dragons. Once the beastly dragons start showing their true colors, I know humans will finally end them all. How do you like that, Rory?"

I ignore him. "You and Kinsley are working together? You two help each other out, that sort of thing? I wonder how she would feel about your little idea of manipulating humans to destroy all of the dragons. You do know she's the Vaer Boss, right?"

I speak in a tone that questions his capability, knowing that Spectres look down on alliances. The Spectres work alone, always have and always will. Working with an ally is considered a weakness.

The jab has him responding. "You know me better than that. I have something more powerful than the Vaer in my corner." He pats a lump under his jacket and turns slightly, revealing the outline of a small package. "I got what I want from them. The dragon race has no clue what's coming for them."

"It's clear you're not smart enough to play the Vaer. There's no way in hell you could ever manipulate Kinsley into doing anything to help you."

"It's time you learn your place, little girl." He slaps his hand across my face so hard that I fall over.

My face stings with the makings of a bruise.

I start to deliver another retort, as I push myself

back to a sitting position, and a man starts yelling outside. The thunder of gunshots cuts through the warehouse as something large slams against the wall to my right.

A loud clatter erupts from the wooden double doors as they fall inward, kicking up dust. Drew marches in with his guns trained on Diesel. He looks from Drew to me and back again as he clutches the package under his jacket.

It's the bio-weapon. It has to be.

He won't trust anyone but himself to handle it. As Drew steps toward him, I can tell the asshole is thinking about fighting the both of us. His eyes hold a look of cold, calculated hate.

Drew's eyes scan over me. He steadies the aim of his gun at Diesel.

"He has the bio-weapon. Don't shoot!" I warn him.

Diesel's gun is aimed at me, then at Drew. He's trying to decide who to shoot. He pulls the trigger, and a bullet flies through my left calf.

"Bring your sister next time, Rory." He turns and flees.

I hate that sadistic asshole.

"I'll tear him apart!" Drew's body tenses like he's ready to take off and chase Diesel through the back of the warehouse.

I motion toward the Spectres that surround us. We've got other issues to deal with.

"How's your leg?" Drew asks.

I look down to see blood running down my shin. I'm going to kill that asshole.

Drew turns his weapon on everyone left in the warehouse. I watch with satisfaction as he begins taking out every single one of Diesel's henchmen. I crawl over to the table and pull myself off of the cold hard floor. I need to get these damn cuffs off.

Drew shoots off round after round, and quickly reloads. He knocks down a couple of Spectres, but they don't go down without a fight. One comes after him from behind with a sword in his hand, bringing it down toward Drew's back. My fire dragon turns around, fast as a whip, doing a spin-kick to the handle of the blade and knocking it from the man's hand.

The four-foot long blade goes flying, and Drew pulls his fist back and lands a solid punch to the middle of the unarmed man's face. The man crumbles to the floor with a thump. He throat punches the second attacking Spectre, leaving him in a pile at his feet. Drew turns around and spins his large leg in a circle, knocking three more Spectres to the ground unconscious. The Spectres are no match for my fire dragon's skill and speed.

When a Spectre comes toward me, I know I have to do something. I'm not a damsel in distress waiting for someone to save her. Never have been. Never will be. I wait until the last possible minute and throw myself out of the way. I land a blow to the man's shin with my good leg and he goes down, grunting in pain.

The man starts to get up as he grabs for me, but Drew fires a single shot from his gun, and the man hits the floor, dead.

Finally finished taking down the Spectres, he approaches me. His hands gently lift me to my feet.

"Can you take these cuffs off?" I extend my cuffed wrists toward him.

"No time. We need to get out of here." He shakes his head. "Reinforcements are on the way."

The pain I felt when I first woke up is being replaced by the steady throb from the bullet hole in my leg. Even the slow and steady throb begins to fade as adrenaline floods my body while we escape from the warehouse and into a waiting armored SUV.

Thank the gods for Drew's contacts.

The large dark vehicle speeds through the city,

weaving in and out of traffic. As we leave the city, the bright lights start to fade, and the armored vehicle starts to slow. The SUV bumps down a gravel road, through a small neighborhood with some parks and more greenery than I thought possible in this city. I want to ask a million questions. We pull in front of a small abandoned building and the car turns off.

"We're safe here, for now."

It doesn't look like much. The small building sits in the middle of a huge field with a real estate sign posted out front. There's only one main road nearby. This place doesn't seem safe.

"This is just a holding place. We can see for miles if anyone comes this way. There's a bed and some basic necessities inside," he says, watching me.

Drew pulls out his phone to send a text. "Just letting Jace know that we're safe."

"I figured." I sit quietly and study the building and its surroundings.

His phone beeps, and he reads it out loud:

At a Fairfax safehouse with Harper. Love Levi, Jace, and Tucker. Ashgrave too. Meet us ASAP

He stops reading when another beep comes from

his phone. I figure the last text contains the address of where we are to meet up with the rest of our team. Our family.

"Now, can you uncuff me?" I raise my cuffed wrists to him again.

Drew hops out of the SUV and comes around to open the door on my side. He lifts me into his arms and carries me to the front door of the small building.

"Are you sure? You look so damn sexy with those on." The desire in his voice has warmth pooling between my thighs. Drew reaches into his pocket as he looks at the cuffs.

He gives the driver a nod, and the other man stays put in the vehicle, keeping watch. Drew sets me on my feet gently, but keeps the chain of the cuffs in his grasp. I know he has no intention of taking them off. My heart hammers in my chest as my dragon rolls onto her back in contentment and submission. She's ready to play, and so am I.

I stare into his eyes.

"You need to rest." Desire burns in his eyes.

"Maybe later," I say with determination.

"Rory, you've just been through hell. You were shot, damn it. Just rest for a little while."

"Can't we just go and meet up with the others? My leg is already healing," I argue.

"You're stubborn as hell, woman. Everyone else is fine. It's you who needs to heal. And in order to heal, you need rest."

My whole body tenses in anger.

"Are you trying to piss me off?"

I jerk my cuffed hands out of his grasp, standing outside of the building as he enters.

I'm not budging from this spot until he gives me what I want. I want to go to the others.

Diesel is planning on releasing the bio-weapon on a human population. But the asshole never told me where he was planning on releasing it. He could launch it against us. The sadistic asshole could release it on me and my men. I can't let that happen. I need to make sure all of my men are safe.

CHAPTER NINETEEN

"Rory… " He drops his gaze and rubs the back of his neck. Underneath his shirt, his muscles tense as he takes a deep breath and lets it out. I don't know what he's thinking and I don't really care. I want to get back into the armored vehicle and drive to my men.

"Drew, I'm fine. I promise."

His eyes drift to my leg, and I know he's wondering about my gunshot wound. I bend over and pull up my pant leg with my wrists still cuffed to show him the wound is already healed. There's barely a pink mark.

"I'm already healed. Now will you take these off?"

"Diesel kidnapped you. He could have killed you, Rory. You should've stayed at Ashgrave." He shakes his head like he's trying to get a horrible thought out of his brain.

"We're a *team*. We all go, or no one goes." I glare at him.

Drew pulls me by the cuffs' chain and leads me inside the small building. He closes the door behind us.

The abandoned building has desks that line two of the walls in the shape of an L. In the center of the room is a large cherry table that's surrounded by thick leather overstuffed chairs. On one of the four walls, there's a small kitchenette with a refrigerator, stove, sink, and microwave. The final wall is home to a set of double doors. I want to ask where we are, but Drew's look of concentration has my frustration growing.

"We are a team, but the problem is…. it is our job to protect our queen. You are my queen, Rory. I will do everything I need to in order to protect you and assist you in reaching your destiny."

I suck in a deep breath and take a step back. I'm irritated and humbled by his statement—I am his queen. It's no secret that all of my men refer to me as queen. Personally, I blame Ashgrave. But Drew says it with absolute certainty. Like it's a fact. I am his queen. I am my men's queen.

I can't lead a kingdom. I have half the world against me, and I'm constantly being hunted.

"Drew," I say, searching his eyes. He doesn't get it. Maybe he never will. "You don't know what you're saying." I have to make him see that I'm not what he thinks I am. I'm not a queen.

He walks toward me and my heartbeat quickens. The scowl on his face tells me he's angry, but I don't know what he's going to do.

"You are a queen. *The* queen. You need to come to grips with that fact and soon. The longer you deny it, the more we all suffer. I'm done talking about this now. You need to rest."

He walks over to a small bar that sits in the corner next to a desk. I pull out one of the over-stuffed chairs and sit down. I close my eyes and calm my breathing. The peace and quiet settles my nerves as the last of the adrenaline leaves my body.

"Here."

I take the glass of chardonnay from him. Without saying a word, I fumble slightly with the stem of the glass because the magic dampening cuffs are still locked on my wrists. I take a long sip of my wine then set it in front of me on the table. Drew leans against the back of my chair and places his hands on my shoulders. He massages the tight muscles of my shoulders and neck. His hands send sparks of fire and want through me. I start to tremble with need under his muscular fingers, and little beads of perspiration gather at the base of my neck.

Drew spins me around to face him and pulls his shirt over his head, revealing his chiseled abs as he downs the rest of my wine and places the glass near the other end of the table.

I reach out to touch him. I use a fingertip to trace the curves of his upper chest, making sure to draw my finger slowly around both of his nipples, which draws a needy growl from Drew. Then I take the time to trace his eight pack abs, which has my fire dragon panting. And I start to trace the valley that drops below the waist of his jeans, but the damn cuffs get caught on a belt loop.

My dragon is begging to be touched by our handsome fire dragon. We need to make love to him.

Drew wraps his hands around my waist and lifts me so I'm straddling him. He pushes his hard body into mine, and I feel his erection push against me.

I want to run my nails down the muscles of his back. He senses my hunger and moves his hands from my waist to my ass, and he gives it a squeeze.

He kisses my neck and whispers into my ear. "I thought I lost you today."

I grab his handsome face with my cuffed hands and press my lips against his, like his mouth is giving me the breath I need to live. Because it is. Our tongues dance blissfully together. I pull back, and we're both panting.

"But you saved me," I say. I don't like admitting it. I hate being saved. I'm the protector, not the other way around.

Drew places my ass on the cool cherry wood table.

"Does that bother you?" he asks with a voice husky with desire as he pulls my boots off one at a time. Drew pushes my shoulders back until I'm lying on the table, then he unbuttons my pants and gives my stomach a kiss. It sends shivers of need through my body. He pulls my pants off one leg at a time, and his lips leave trails of hot kisses up to my inner thighs. My back arches with need, and my dragon wants to play *now*. But I can't give in yet.

"Maybe," I tease.

The truth is, it bothers me, a lot. The thought of him putting himself at risk for me lingers as he unbuttons my blouse, leaving trails of need where his fingers brush my bare skin. I arch my back off the table and Drew lifts my blouse, wrapping it around the handcuffs and leaving every inch of me exposed.

Vulnerable.

It's surreal to me that I needed to be saved. A fact that Drew will never use against me. Hell, knowing him, he will probably never mention it. I'm his, and I'm safe. I am with a man that I love.

His eyes take in every curve of my body as he slowly takes off his boots, socks, and jeans. My fire dragon has a glorious body, and it's all mine. His strong hands draw enticing circles on my ankles. Then my knees. He draws ovals on my thighs, dipping his fingers close to my sensitive folds, teasing me. His fingers trace an oval over my stomach, and I let out a needy sigh. Drew makes large circles around the base of my breast then makes them smaller until he's teasing my nipples with his rough fingertips.

"I want you, Rory," he whispers gruffly before grabbing my hands and lifting them above my head. Drew urges my arms to relax while he holds the chain of the cuffs over my head. Part of me, the Spectre part, wants to fight against him. But I'm so turned on, my fire dragon can do whatever he wants to me.

He wraps his free arm around me tightly as his

knee gently pushes my legs apart, lowering the tip of his erection into my entrance. I immediately arch my hips to meet him. My body welcomes him as I curve my back. I take it all, spreading my legs farther apart so I can take in every amazing inch of him.

Once he's fully inside me, he pauses his slow, rhythmic pumping, so that I can savor it, grinding his hips ever so slightly to stimulate my clit.

I angle my hips upward and spread my legs as far apart as they'll go. I want Drew to have it all, every inch of me. He thrusts into me like his life depends on my pleasure, and he picks up the speed and intensity of his rhythm, the motion shooting ribbons of bliss down to my toes.

"Come for me…" he whispers into my ear.

I pull my handcuffed hands from his grip and put them around his neck. He increases his speed, thrusting harder and faster.

Drew's cock pushes me to the edge. Deep within my body, a surge of pleasure burns through me, and I cum hard on his dick.

It's bliss.

I love this. His fire. His passion. The way his entire body commands mine.

Drew rides me through my orgasm as he pumps into me even harder. I'm about to orgasm again when a hot rush fills me, like a damn breaking. I ride the waves of ecstasy, eyes closed, back arched, fire blazing through me. My dragon licks her lips, curling up into a happy little ball, as both of our bodies start to still.

Drew and I are both flush, sweaty, and satisfied.

I haven't cum that hard in a long time, and I can't do anything but breathe and stare into Drew's black eyes. He pulls my arms from behind his neck and places them on my stomach before he collapses next to me on the cool wooden table top.

My lips, breasts, and clit are swollen, and my heart still races.

"I hope no one eats on this table." I chuckle, and he pulls me into his chiseled chest, smiling that sexy ass smile of his.

"I'll have it taken care of." He kisses the top of my head and we stay curled together in the afterglow of passion.

"Now, can we get these cuffs off?" I ask.

"But they look so damn hot on you."

"Drew!" I laugh.

He releases me, and exits the room for a minute. I watch his glorious, glistening naked body as he walks back toward me. He has a small tool in his hand, and he uses it to release me from the magic dampening cuffs.

"Better?"

"Thank you," I say, shaking out my hands.

I love my fire dragon.

CHAPTER TWENTY

A buzz has me looking for the ringing phone. It's Drew's, but the phone is on the floor near my feet. I pick it up and read the text from Harper.

We have to evacuate Levi, Tucker, Jace, and Ashgrave from the safehouse. The local authorities and press are starting to circle us here. Meet us at the Fairfax safehouse in Southern California. You know where it is. Keep her safe, Drew.

I hand him his phone. "Looks like we need to get to the safehouse."

"Or, we can stay here?"

My body is still thrumming with pleasure, but we

need to meet up with our team. I hand Drew his phone and it buzzes again.

My fire dragon's fingers fly over the screen of the smart phone, then he puts it on the table while he pulls on his shirt.

I walk around the table and grab my jeans from the floor. As I shake out my pants to put them on, I notice a big, gaping bloody hole in the leg.

"You can't wear those." He points to my pants.

"I was thinking the same thing. They're a little too bloody to go unnoticed."

Drew reaches into a desk drawer and pulls out a pair of scrubs. He tosses them to me. "These will be a bit big, but they're better than traveling the country nude. I wouldn't complain, though." He smirks. "I love your naked body."

I pull on the scrub pants, tying the waist strings tightly, and roll up the legs. I strip off my dressy blouse and put on the scrub top. At least I'm not covered in blood, and now I match.

"We should hurry. Harper said she needs to talk to us."

I run my fingers through my hair to tame the tangles, and I remember the way Drew lit every inch of me on fire with his touch. I love my fire dragon, and he knows it.

I walk behind Drew, following him out the door and watching him lock up the small abandoned building with his code. He grabs my hand as we walk to the awaiting armored car.

We speed through the city, in the morning light, with smog so thick it feels like I should cut it with my magic dagger. When we are finally free of LA's traffic, we don't slow down, we fly down the freeway until we reach a beautiful mountain range that has me missing my beautiful castle. Drew slows down as we drive up a mountain pass then turn onto a single lane gravel road that leads to a small farmhouse.

Harper is sitting on the porch swing, looking agitated.

When the car stops, I unbuckle myself and jump from the vehicle, running toward her.

"Glad you're here," she says, returning my hug. "Our position has been compromised. We have to leave. Drew... I'd get your people out of here too."

He nods at her and takes out his phone. "I want to get Rory home and safe. One of my men will take us to the chopper." He walks away to make a few calls.

Ashgrave's little metal body flies toward me out of the open door of the farmhouse. "THE GREAT QUEEN OF ASHGRAVE HAS ARRIVED."

"Thank you, Ashgrave. I missed you too." I smile. "But remember, you need to keep your voice down when we leave the castle, or you could put me in danger."

"ABSOLUTELY, MY QUEEN," The cat-sized, steam punk dragon says in a hushed tone.

One by one, my men file out behind his hovering body.

Tucker picks me up in his arms and swings me around in a circle while planting a kiss on my cheek. "You had me worried for a minute."

"I shouldn't have followed that kid, but I thought he may have had the bio-weapon and I needed to know for sure." He sets me down and looks me over, checking for injuries.

"Shit happens to everyone. Don't blame yourself." He kisses the top of my head. "It's good to have you back, babe."

I shake my head at my weapons expert as he, Drew, and Ashgrave head for the armored car. I start to follow them, but Levi grabs my hand, encouraging me to hang back with him for a moment.

Jace kisses my cheek as he walks by, carrying armloads of weapons. "I knew you were safe. Otherwise none of us would be alive. I'd have gone feral—and gods help anyone around me then." He winks at me, and my horny little dragon purrs in excitement. She wants to play with her mate. My mate. Hussy.

I watch Jace load the weapons into the armored vehicle with Tucker then turn around to face Levi. His ice blue eyes are swimming with unshed tears.

I open the connection with Levi. *What's going on? Are you okay?*

He lifts both of my hands up so that our hands are palm to palm, like we're giving each other double high fives. Then he puts his fingers between mine and curls his fingers together with mine. I step closer to him, and I can feel the heat through our clothes.

I thought... Pain and loss flows from him.

I'm okay, I reassure him and send love through our bond.

This can never happen again, Rory. I can't... my dragon and I, we need you. We can't—won't live without you. I can tell his heart almost shattered when I was captured. I push my love and regret through our bond.

Levi, I'm not going anywhere. You're stuck with me forever.

You're the only thing that keeps me human, Rory. If I lose you, I'll go feral. And I'll never come back. Memories of the years of loneliness, anger, and unworthiness flood my mind.

Levi, I'm not going anywhere. I promise. I kiss his cool lips. I send him my dedication and commitment through our bond. He strengthens his grip on my hands, then relaxes. My ice dragon drops my hands and kisses me on the top of the head as he heads toward the car.

I watch as my men and murderous castle stack and restack weapons in the storage compartment of the large armored SUV.

Footsteps crunch in the snow behind me, and I turn to smile at Harper.

"They're quite a handful. I'm glad it's you and not me who has to put up with them." She chuckles.

"Can I talk to you for a minute, Harper?"

The Fairfax Boss nods her head as she watches me with a smirk.

"I want to thank you for everything."

"It's what friends are for, Rory."

"We tried to intercept the delivery of the bio-weapon and chaos broke out. Now, Diesel's out there with the bio-weapon. He's planning releasing it on innocent humans to start a war between humans and dragons," I tell her. "If he releases that bio-weapon, he will kill thousands if not hundreds of thousands of people, all to manipulate them to turn on dragonkind. It'll be a blood bath for both sides." I pace the driveway of the farmhouse, my fury building. What really bothers me is the fact that Diesel talked about his "powerful ally." Who the hell could the ally be, and could they be related to others Jett talked about?

"Rory, you can't beat yourself up because Diesel is a sadistic asshole. And my friend, don't think you're weak because Drew saved you. Allowing Drew to save you means you're brave enough to trust in your family. Family will never fail."

"Thank you, Harper." I give my friend a heartfelt hug.

"Here. Take these burner phones." She hands me a small tote bag with some phones in it. "Use these to contact me. I don't want to take any chances. I don't know who tapped my phone."

I carry the tote bag to the car and slide in next to Drew. He wraps his arm around me, and I turn around to give Tucker and Levi a wink as Ashgrave looks out the tinted back window of our armored vehicle. When I turn back to face the front of the car, Jace turns around to smile at me from the front passenger seat as the car lurches forward.

We wind through the mountain pass, and in no

time, we're speeding through the traffic of LA. I don't like this smoggy, crowded city. I can't wait to be back home at Ashgrave.

My men and Ashgrave are unnaturally quiet during our ride to the private landing strip. I know they were worried about me. I know they all love me. And I love them.

We reach the private airport where Tucker's second favorite toy waits to take us home. *Home.*

CHAPTER TWENTY-ONE

Tucker lands the chopper on the small helipad next to the landing strip, which Ashgrave created for my weapons expert's favorite toys. The tension in the air has our shoulders hunching forward and our heads hanging.

We're all disappointed. We failed at our mission.

My family is allowing their regret to weigh them down.

None of us are happy with the fact that we came back without the bio-weapon. A bio-weapon that Diesel is planning to release on the human population.

"I know…" I say softly, meeting each of their eyes. "You did everything you could. Don't blame yourselves."

Drew looks at me with fire in his eyes, and not the hungry fire that I love. "Rory, we had one reason for going to LA.—get the bio-weapon. We didn't succeed. If Diesel releases that bio-weapon on humans, there will be hell to pay."

"That's putting it lightly," Jace chimes in, his voice low and pensive.

Tucker and Levi say nothing, and I know that even though Tucker usually laughs things off, he's blaming himself. As an expert with all things weapons related, he's probably wondering how he didn't see it coming. My weapons expert didn't anticipate Diesel's kidnapping me. I don't blame him though, and I know no one else does either.

I watch Tucker's eyes from where I'm sitting on the side seat of the chopper. His shoulders are tense as he flips the switches that stop the blades from turning and turns off the chopper's engine. His eyes focus on every switch he needs to flip, and there's a downward turn of his mouth. He's thinking about something. Something that is making him upset.

I reach out my hand and touch his arm, squeezing it slightly. It pisses me off that we lost the bio-weapon. But I'm relieved that we're still alive.

I'm sure that Diesel was planning on killing me in that Vaer warehouse. But he didn't succeed. Now he's going to be looking over his shoulder, knowing that me and my men are coming for him. This might be the edge we need. The edge to get our hands on the bio-weapon before he releases it.

Tucker turns around in his pilot's seat and gives Drew a nod. Ashgrave starts to hover in front of my face as Jace and Levi start gathering the weapons from the storage cabinets under the seat across from me. They're so focused. All of them.

"Thank you," I say, standing up and hoping to divert their attention.

"For what?" Jace asks. His eyes are watching me, like he's afraid I could disappear any minute.

"You kept me alive. I had to get back to you. And now, I have a chance to stop Diesel."

"*We* have a chance to stop Diesel. Not just you, Rory. You said we're a team. If one goes, we all go," Drew reminds me.

"Okay, Drew. We have a chance to stop the sadistic asshole. Better?" I ask him, winking. My fire dragon's eyebrows dip low on his face as he gives me a deep scowl. Drew's not amused by my little tease. That's okay. I'll make it up to him later.

A shiver of pleasure shoots through me as I remember the time we spent on the cherry table of the little abandoned building. The way his hips moved against me, the way I felt so safe, even though my hands were locked in magic dampening cuffs. So free. With a smile, I tell myself that I need to remind him to loosen up like that more often.

Drew opens the door of the chopper and Jace rushes out with his arms loaded down with weapons. I'm sure he's wondering why he didn't know where I was being kept. How did Drew get to me first? Jace is my mate, and I can feel the storm brewing inside of him.

I jump out and race after him. As I grab his arm, my mate stops in his tracks.

"Don't blame yourself." My dragon watches our mate, and her eyes are filled with unshed tears. We don't like that Jace is upset. It makes us both sad.

"We almost lost you last night, Rory. When I think about what Diesel could've done to you... how you almost—"

I cut him off with a growl.

"Diesel wasn't going to kill me. Not without a fight. You should know me better than that."

It's not a lie. But I don't know what would've happened if Drew hadn't shown up when he did. I don't want to know.

"You are my life, Rory. I know that you were okay, and my dragon wasn't worried. But..."

"You're my mate, Jace. You know me better than anyone. Our plan is shit right now. We don't have the bio-weapon. Let's all go inside and figure out a plan to take the bastard out."

He gives me a nod and we start walking toward the castle. Ashgrave hovers close behind.

Diesel's going to get what's coming to him. The asshole is going down.

With four dragons and a weapons expert gunning to see him dead, Diesel doesn't have a chance in hell to get out of this alive.

"This was all a setup and we know it," Levi says as he passes us with a bazooka strapped to his back and AR-57's in both arms.

As we make our way to the huge ornate entry doors of Castle Ashgrave, my muscles start to relax. We're safe, and we're home. *Home.*

I wonder if I'll ever get used to having a home. All the years of running, hiding in the shadows, never staying in one place. To have a safe place to just be, after everything we've been through—it's almost magical.

The large heavy doors open, and we step into the huge foyer of my massive castle. The heavy wooden doors close behind us and automatically lock into place.

"A DRAGON IS AWAITING PERMISSION TO ENTER THE THRONE ROOM, MY QUEEN."

The booming voice echoes from the small bronze body of my murderous castle, making me jump. His voice is something that I don't think I'll ever get used to. Or his constant habit of calling me queen.

We just landed. Who the hell could be waiting for me?

The muscles in my back and neck tighten instantly. I know Ashgrave wouldn't let just anyone inside his walls.

Did my evil butler allow someone inside, in the hopes that I would give him permission to annihilate them? I need to know who it is before I can allow Ashgrave to kill them.

"Who is here, Ashgrave?"

"I DO NOT KNOW, MISTRESS. BUT, BRETT ASSURES ME THIS DRAGON IS AN ALLY, MY QUEEN."

What the hell? Since when does Brett get a say in who is safe and who isn't? I'm going to wring Brett's neck.

My rage builds as I march toward the throne room. I'm sure whoever is waiting will be no match for my fury—or my dragon.

"WOULD YOU LIKE ME TO EXPEL THE VISITOR? PERHAPS VIOLENTLY, MY QUEEN?"

I'm not wrong. My castle has an edge of hopefulness in his overly loud voice. Ashgrave is hoping to smite someone. Anyone.

"No, Ashgrave. I need to see who it is before you kill my visitor."

"AS YOU WISH, MISTRESS."

The wall across from me opens, and I step into one of his magical tunnels. A smile tugs my lips up as I head to the throne room.

Ashgrave's magic is amazing, and he only has two orbs. I wonder what the magic castle will be able to do with three, or even four orbs. We need the other Astor Diaries, if we're going to get Ashgrave to full power and my magic under control.

We need to get our hands on the other diaries. Without them, we're just chasing our tails. The Astor Diaries have information—answers I need. Facts that would help me understand not only my magic, but the magic of Ashgrave.

The wall opens in front of me and I walk into the throne room.

"Where's our visitor, Ashgrave?"

The wall closes, and I walk up to the center throne. A feeling of responsibility washes over me as

I sit in the large over-stuffed ornate chair. I know this feeling will never stop, not until I'm worthy to sit on this massive throne of the queen. Still, my men expect it and Ashgrave demands it. *Queen…* could I be the one they need?

I know I'll never feel worthy enough, though. I will always fight to be better, to be stronger. To be the leader—queen—they need.

"Rory," a familiar voice greets me as the large double doors open.

"Payton," I say cordially. I watch as he strides toward me with his back straight and his eyes staring into mine.

I wonder what the young Palarne general could want. The timing of his arrival is suspicious. He came when I wasn't home. Is the Palarne heir trying to learn something from my castle, or the people who call it home?

"I'm here to offer the aid I promised in the form of an alliance. And, I have a special delivery." He raises his eyebrows. His perfectly chiseled jawbone tightens with the hint of a smile pulling at his lips.

I hope his delivery will be something that will turn the tide in our favor, whatever it is.

I give Payton a small nod. "It's about damn time."

CHAPTER TWENTY-TWO

The Palarne heir quirks a questioning brow at me.

"I assure you, I am a man of my word. I didn't become the youngest general of the Palarne forces by being someone who doesn't say what I mean." There's a sternness in his voice, almost like he's warning me.

"I understand that, Payton—I know you're an honorable man," I answer honestly.

Breathe, man. I'm not trying to dishonor you or your family.

"Trust me, the Palarne army is standing by and ready to aid you in whatever capacity you need."

"INDEED, THERE IS AN ARMY OF SOLDIERS

AT THE EDGES OF MY NORTH BORDER, MY QUEEN."

"That means a lot to me. Does your army need lodging? The castle has more than enough room for them." I wonder where my men are. They heard Ashgrave say we had a visitor. I figured they would have joined me here by now. They're going to be upset that I offered to host more people. But I don't care. Anyone who's willing to fight alongside us deserves a place to rest.

"No, thank you, Rory. We can take care of ourselves," he assures me. "We have portable lodging and plenty of rations to get us through. But, I do have this for you."

Payton shifts nervously on his feet as he reaches a hand into his jacket. He starts to pull something out, but Ashgrave's metallic hand lifts up through the elegantly carpeted floor and grabs the Palarne general around the waist, lifting him up in the air and making it impossible for the man to grab anything from inside his jacket.

"Ashgrave! Put him down, now." I conceal the smirk playing at my lips. It's good to know my castle is so protective of me.

"THE INFIDEL MEANT TO PULL A WEAPON

FROM HIS COVERING AND USE IT AGAINST YOU, MY QUEEN."

"I don't think that's what he was doing, Ashgrave." I can't help but hide a chuckle with my hand. Part of me wishes he would stop this over-protective behavior, but the other part of me is delighted that he cares for my safety.

"I'm not dumb enough to walk in here armed. I have something you can use. Something I promise that is going to help you." Payton's legs and arms are flailing like he's trying to swim in the air as he struggles against Ashgrave's death grip.

"SHALL I RELEASE HIM, MY QUEEN?"

"Yes. Let him go," I order, instantly regretting my words. The metal fingers open and Payton falls to the carpeting, rolling, before he jumps to his feet and glares at me.

I should have told my castle to put him down carefully, I forget that he is very... literal.

"Are you okay, Payton? My castle doesn't have great people skills. He was just looking out for me," I say, fighting against the smile that's threatening to sprout on my face.

Payton clears his throat as he brushes himself off. "Now, if the silliness is finished, I have something for you." He reaches into his jacket again and pulls out a leather bound book. From where I sit on my throne, I can see that its pages are aged.

An Astor Diary.

I have to be sure it's an original. I don't want to become a victim of another poison, curse, or booby trap in case this book is a fake, like the one Elizabeth Andusk poisoned me with.

"Ashgrave, gently take the diary from Payton, and tell me if there are any kind of dark spells on it? I need to know if it's real."

"AS YOU WISH, MISTRESS."

The metal hand emerges from the carpeted floor again, and this time, it moves with gentle certainty as it plucks the book from Payton's grasp and brings it toward me. I feel the humming coming from the large metal hand as it stops a foot away from me.

It seems like my castle is thinking or testing the ancient looking book.

"THERE IS NO DARK MAGIC CONTAINED WITHIN THIS BOOK, MISTRESS. IT IS SAFE."

"Please, hand it to me gently, Ashgrave."

"YES, MY QUEEN." The metallic hand lifts it and smoothly places the book in my open hands.

I flip through the pages. It is a real Astor Diary. Esmeralda's diary. I lock down the emotions of excitement and happiness that are coursing through me. Part of me wants to know how the Palarnes got the diary. The other part, the part that needs it, doesn't care.

Having this diary will help us find the other orbs. And hopefully, it will tell us how to put together the pieces of the destroyed one.

"Thank you, Payton. Please tell your men that they are welcome here. Staying camped at the outer edges of my land can be very dangerous. I've got a lot of people who want me dead, and they won't stop at anything, including an ally's army. Ashgrave will behave himself."

"Thank you, Rory. I'll let my men know, and I'll warn them to not come to the castle unannounced. But I'm sure their arrangements are fine. Isaac wants me to stress that he needs to speak with you face-to-face about the diary. Even though we know it rightfully belongs to you—he still has questions."

Isaac has questions. Sure, and how long have they been sitting on this? And what would the Palarne have done with the Astor Diary if they chose not to side with me? I have a few questions of my own for the Palarne Boss.

I nod and flash him a quick smile, not letting Payton know what I'm thinking. "I understand. And thanks again for the extra soldiers."

"We're going to need more than the Fairfax army to win this war, Rory."

I've known that for a while now. "Don't forget, we have five hundred dragon rebels on our side. I'm also in the middle of upgrading Ashgrave. You'll see that I can be extremely useful as an ally."

"Make sure you teach your castle not to jump to conclusions about everyone." Payton winks at me, his demeanor softening slightly.

"He was protecting me. Ashgrave will be more dangerous when I find him more power." I roll my eyes, smiling. Ashgrave with a full metallic dragon army. That's going to be a sight to see.

"I hope you know something I don't," Payton says. There are too many factors at play here. Factors that have nothing to do with the coming war."

"Like what factors?" I have an idea, but I need to know what he's heard.

"There are alliances being formed, of people who are against any humans surviving."

"Yeah, I've seen that first hand," I admit, thinking back to Diesel and his plan to harm his own race just to spark a war. "What else?" I question.

"You do know that there is still a huge bounty on your head? I mean, there are people out there willing to pay obscene amounts of money to have you delivered to them." He shifts his weight from foot to foot, watching me. I know he's concerned —worried.

"Trust me, I know." I shrug my shoulders.

"I WILL NOT ALLOW HARM TO BEFALL YOU, MY QUEEN."

"Thank you, Ashgrave." I'm grateful for this centuries old building and the magic it possesses.

"That's odd," Payton says.

"What's odd?" I ask as my men enter the throne room.

They quickly acknowledge Payton with nods of their heads as they take their places and sit down on the thrones at my sides. They all remain silent, knowing that I'm in queen mode.

"The castle, it seems to be a sentient being. A being that's loyal to you."

"My castle has a name, Payton."

"I've heard about the loyalty that you spark in people. That spark means something. Something, *huge*." Payton shakes his head. "I think that gives you —us, an edge."

"It might. I think the Darringtons could be swayed to our side. Probably not Jett, but Milo. He helped us recently—saved our lives, actually."

Payton shifts his weight from one foot to the other, like there's more he wants to say.

"Does Isaac want anything else, besides our face-to-face discussion?"

"No," he answers, hanging his head, kicking invisible lint from the carpeting, as he refuses to look at me. His actions are setting off alarms. Alarms that tell me he's hiding something.

My intuition is telling me that it has something to do with the gods.

Maybe the Palarnes know more about the orbs and the remaining Astor Diary. And how did they get their hands on this one?

I'll have to ask Payton on a different day. Or maybe I should just ask Isaac. Either way, the Palarnes know more about the gods than they're willing to share, for now.

The buzz of a vibrating phone has me watching my men from the corner of my eyes.

"I gotta take this. I'll talk with you later, Payton." Drew stands and stalks out of the throne room and through the double doors.

Drew's getting things ready for our flight to France. Irena and I must have been added to more 'No Fly' lists, by the way my fire dragon worked his jaw as he walked out of the throne room. Fan-freak-ing-tastic.

"Rory, I'm going to head back to prepare for my meeting with the Fairfax general. We need to coordinate our efforts in the coming war."

"Thank you, Payton. Please, let your men know that they're welcome at the castle. But, make sure to tell us if anyone is planning on crossing the castle's boundaries. Ashgrave has a deadly security system for those who show up uninvited."

The Palarne general nods, turns on his heels, and leaves the throne room.

When it comes time for war, we sure as hell aren't going down without a fight.

I have to smile, holding the Astor Diary in my hands. This ancient book has information that I need. It holds the tools I need to further develop and control my powers.

Levi, Jace, and Tucker walk up to the arm of my throne with smiles on their faces.

"Is it real?" Tucker asks.

"Whose diary is it? Esmeralda's or Brigid's?" Jace questions.

Levi stares at me with a smile that makes his face light up. He needed this small victory today, too. My ice dragon thought he lost me—that he was going to lose himself again.

"It's Esmeralda's diary. I'll be able to learn more about Ashgrave's magic—my magic." I stand and make my way to my room. I don't ask Ashgrave for help. I want to take my time and appreciate my beautiful castle.

When I walk into my sitting room, I take a seat on the white settee and open the magical book in my hands.

The first chapter is on the gods and their rage. They burned people alive for not giving them what they asked for. The gods asked the people they supposedly led for things like jewels, food, and artwork. And when the villagers couldn't provide those things, they would burn them to ash in front of their families.

Why would rulers of a kingdom do those things? These are all-powerful gods, for crying out loud, they could make these things themselves by using their magic. I figure they killed people because they could. No one could stop them until... the Oracles did.

CHAPTER TWENTY-THREE

As I sit in the silence of my room, reading Esmeralda's diary, I learn that the dragon gods are rage-filled and vengeful. They used their followers as a means to an end—more riches and immense power, and in return they gave chaos and death.

The dragon gods spread darkness. They didn't even attempt to make the world a better place. I refuse to use this magic to spread insanity, death, and chaos. Magic doesn't choose what it does. The person holding it does. I choose to make this world better—more loving.

A knock on the door has me jumping from my soft settee and rushing to open it.

Drew stands with his arms across his chest and a

sexy smile on his lips. "Jace said you'd be here reading the new diary. Can I come in?"

I step aside and let him in. He grabs my hand as he walks in, closing the door behind him. My fire dragon pulls me into his arms and our mouths collide.

"Rory, do you know what you do to me?"

"Kiss you?"

"Besides that." He shakes his head with a chuckle. "You never cease to amaze me. You entice me, always. You're intoxicating."

"So are you," I say softly, amazed by the freedom of the moment. "I never felt freer than I did with you last night."

He kisses the tip of my nose and trails small kisses down my jawline.

I gasp as heat gathers in my core. My heart races as I grab his face, pulling his lips to mine.

"Maybe I should tie you up more often," he says with desire. I'm awakening the fire in him again, and as much as I'd love for him to take me, I have other things I'd like to talk to him about.

"Not right now, later," I promise.

"I've never been good at waiting." Drew tilts his head to nip at my neck, his tantalizing bites sending shivers down my spine.

"You know I can't focus when you do that."

He pulls me tighter in his arms. "That's what I'm hoping for."

"We need to talk about Milo." I walk over the settee and take a seat next to the open diary. I quickly close the diary and hold it on my lap.

He takes a seat in the overstuffed chair next to the settee. "If we need to talk, this chair might be the safest place to sit."

"Do you know why Milo helped us last night?" I ask, trying to figure out if we can count on Milo in the future.

"I honestly have no idea, Rory. He said he heard chatter that the Vaer were planning on kidnapping you and killing us." Drew shakes his head.

I wonder how Milo heard that chatter and we didn't. I figure the Vaer knew we planted some type of intel gathering device and led us into the trap. Thank the gods Milo had stepped in and helped us out. It could have been really bad if he hadn't shown up when he did.

"You know I have issues with my brother. I probably always will, but I can't deny that I saw something in him last night. There's been a change. I don't know if I can pinpoint it, but there's something different."

I reach out and touch his forearm. "I noticed it, too."

He pauses for a moment, his eyes go in and out of focus before he continues. "I suppose if I was beaten down and scared for my life, thinking that I was going to die and then be spared—that would cause me to change too. Make me question what I did to be put in that situation, and if what others were saying about me is true. I hope it sticks."

Drew reaches a strong hand up to grip the back of his neck. He's suddenly tense. I'm worried that Drew's trying to figure out what to do with Milo again.

"Honestly, I don't think we have to worry about him." The shift in Milo, I saw it too. It was hard not to.

"I don't think so either, but I would rather be safe than sorry. If you want, I can talk to my father. Even if the alliance we have with Milo and his men is temporary, I know Jett doesn't want you to fall into Kinsley's hands—even if it's for self-serving reasons."

"Yeah, even if it's just to benefit him," I say sharply, reminded by the ever-present fact that nearly every dragon family wants me for themselves for one reason or another.

Drew reaches over and picks up the diary off the

settee next to me. The book doesn't have a lock like Clara's did, so he opens it and reads the first line.

A handwritten account of the magicks and lore of Esmeralda Astor.

"I can read it!" Drew shouts. "How can I read this diary and not the other one?"

"I think it has to do with the gods' magic. Their magic keeps Clara's diary protected. I can read it because their magic flows through me. But, Esmeralda, according to her own words, was the first to betray them. So her diary isn't protected by their magic, and anyone can read it."

"Listen to this… " Drew reads Esmeralda's diary to me.

In the beginning the dragon gods gave much to their followers—land, safety, and a purpose. However, the gods were quick to have bouts of rage with their followers. Especially if the follower questioned them.

Caelan, a quiet and brooding skilled warrior, would often have tournaments where the victor would be gifted one hundred gold bars. In the beginning there were few victors, as the victor's last challenge was to face Caelan. As time moved on, Caelan would win the

tournament by simply laying a finger to the last
challenger's forehead, causing the man to die instantly.

"Stop—please, Drew." I shake my head and grab the ancient book from his hands.

Esmeralda was the first of the Astor sisters to turn away from the gods, and it's clear according her diary, that the separation wasn't an easy one. She writes about nightmares and dark enchantments that chased her.

Her decision to defy the gods came at a great price. It's evident that though the gods are powerful, their magic is dangerous.

Magic that causes death.

Illusions that drive people mad.

So much discord, darkness, and fear.

And chaos…

I feel the weight of Drew's eyes on me.

"I've warned you about your power," he says quietly, almost like he doesn't want to bring it up. "It can become chaotic if you don't get it under control."

"Must you bring that up?" I place one hand on the closed book. I don't know if I'm covering the stories about the gods and their darkness that is being told in the pages, or I'm trying to protect my heart. "I'm growing stronger by the day, and I can feel my dragon mature. I know I've had power surges and need to rein them in so I don't hurt myself or anyone else. But this diary—it will help. I can and will learn from the mistakes they made. That's why Jace is training me. That's why I'm constantly practicing. I will not become them. I will not let the chaos rule me."

Drew places a firm hand on my back, his dark eyes searching mine.

"I'll help you any way that I can," he promises.

"I know you will." I look at the closed diary next to me. "I think it's time to go to Reims and find the missing orb. Will everything be ready so we can leave tomorrow?"

"My contact in France called earlier. There were a few issues that came up, but I'm sure they can be ready for our visit in a couple of days."

"Thanks, Drew. I need the missing orbs. Ashgrave needs his full power."

"I'm going to inform my French contacts that we're heading their way tomorrow." He stands and wraps his arms around me like he's holding on for dear life. "Rory, we will figure out a way to control your magic. We have to."

"At least now we have the tools to understanding it." I kiss his cheek and wiggle out of his grip. "And soon, we will have a metallic dragon army."

Drew walks to the door, opens it, gives me a wink, and leaves to make his calls.

"Ashgrave, take me to the treasury." I hold the Astor Diary next to my chest as if by holding it close I can block the darkness of the stories inside from getting out and destroying everything. I want to protect not only myself, but those I love, and everyone in the world with the magic that flows through me.

"RIGHT AWAY, MY QUEEN."

The wall to the right of me slides open, and I walk into the magical tunnels of my castle. I follow the stone staircase down and the wall in front of me opens. I step into the hallway as the double doors of the treasury open automatically.

As I walk into the treasury, the jewels, gold, and silver glitter in the sunlight. I approach the three pedestals and place Esmeralda's diary on the pedestal next to Clara's. One empty pedestal. One diary left to find. Brigid's.

I pass the dragon armor and feel an unnatural pull to touch it. I shake my head and keep walking. Not today. This magic is mine, and I'm not in the mood to deal with selfish gods.

CHAPTER TWENTY-FOUR

I stand near the doorway of my treasury and think over all of the horrible things the dragon gods have done. The ache of exhaustion weighs heavy on my bones. I'm tired, and I know I need to rest. It would be stupid not to, and I'm not stupid.

Everything in me wants to stay here in the treasury with Esmeralda's diary, to go over every word and drawing until I have it all memorized from front to back. I shake my head and leave the ancient book on its pedestal.

"DO YOU WISH TO RETURN TO YOUR ROOM, OR PERHAPS THERE IS SOMEWHERE ELSE WITHIN MY WALLS THAT YOU WISH TO GO, MY QUEEN?" Ashgrave asks, sensing my movement.

Oh, Ashgrave. He has more understanding within his magic walls than most people have in the bones of their body.

"My room will be fine." My eyelids feel like they weigh one hundred pounds each, and I'm having a hard time keeping focused. I can picture my bed. The soft blankets, the feel of the cloud-like comforter wrapped around me as I drift off to sleep. It sounds like heaven. My murderous castle is turning out to be kind and thoughtful after all.

The wall slides open and I step into the familiar tunnel and take the steps. I can't help but think about how much I love this ancient place. The rustic stone, the plush carpeting, the maroon and gold curtains worthy of royalty.

"Thank you, Ashgrave." I follow the staircase up. I know when I exit, I'll be in the hallway just outside my room. The hallway's plush carpet and my comfy bed will be a welcome sight after my kidnapping and losing the bio-weapon.

"IS THERE ANYTHING ELSE I CAN GET FOR YOU, MY QUEEN?" His booming voice, which usually rattles through my chest like an exploding cannon, has a softer edge. Almost like he's trying to be kind. Unless I'm imagining things. I shake my head at my thoughts. I'm more tired than I realize—

Ashgrave being nurturing. Seriously. If I had more energy, I'd chuckle at myself.

A cup of tea would be nice, but the last time I asked for a hot drink, it wasn't Ashgrave who actually would have gotten it for me.

I can't hold my chuckle back, remembering Tucker's appearance as Ashgrave forced him to cater to me. I think I'll keep my request to myself for tonight.

"No, Ashgrave. I'm okay for now."

"YOU SEEM UNSETTLED, MY QUEEN. ARE YOU WELL?"

When did Ashgrave get so perceptive?

"I just need to rest."

"REST WELL, MISTRESS." He opens the door to my room, and my shoulders relax at the sight of my huge canopy bed. The large arched windows that give me a view to the surrounding land display the breathtaking sunset.

My home is beautiful. This ancient, crescent-shaped castle is amazing. The vision of the surrounding landscape is like a salve to my mind, and entering this room, I immediately grab a silk nightgown from the dresser and change into it before I walk to one of the windows and stare out.

The gentle sloping hills and the high rising

mountains to the east and west spark a sense of happiness in me. As the sun sets, it washes everything it touches with hues of light in pinks, oranges, yellows, purples, and blues. The sun and its changing colors reminds me of the second orb we placed in the Mind's Eye domain, so full of magic and light.

So full of possibility.

Even though I've been dragged, beaten, and shot at in the last twenty-four hours, I still find peace here.

Going to Reims and recovering the third orb ensures that this feeling of peace will remain. I have to find it tomorrow. I start to pace my large room, thinking about what it will mean to find it, and how it will secure Ashgrave and my dragon army. My mind fills with images of the metallic dragon army that will rise from the ground the moment the orb is placed in the Army domain.

It gives me confidence. If I'm going to be a queen, like my men are insisting, having soldiers at my command will mean the kingdom can always protect itself. I roll my eyes, wondering why I'm even thinking about the possibility.

I am no queen. I don't know why everyone keeps insisting that I am. I glance at my bed from over my shoulder, and my eyes grow heavy.

As inviting as my bed looks, and as much as I want to curl up in its cloud like softness, I know that I won't sleep tonight. I'm drawn to the enormous windows and their beautiful views. There are too many things to think about and too many scenarios to plan for.

How will we get our hands on the bio-weapon?

Will things go smoothly in France?

What will happen if we don't find the orb?

And the one question that constantly nags at the back of my mind, like a gnat that won't stop flying around my head—will Ashgrave remain loyal to me if Morgana returns?

I don't know why this question bothers me so much, but I know I'll never truly rest until I have the answer.

Thoughts of Ashgrave, Morgana, war, Kinsley, Diesel, and the what-ifs that revolve around every choice I have to make, rushes like the wind through my mind. As I stand in front of the huge arched windows of my room looking out at the beautiful scenery but not able to focus on it.

The cawing of birds brings my eyes back to the scene outside the windows. It feels like the sun was just setting, and now the sun's rays are starting to peek over the horizon. I haven't slept at all, and as the rays of light paint Ashgrave and the surrounding area in a glorious orange glow, the tender trail of fingers circling around my waist from behind has my body reacting to the only man who can sneak up on me. The gentle pressure of Levi's chest against my back soothes my nerves.

His lips trail soft kisses up the back of my neck, stopping at my ear.

"I'll go with you to get the orb—just the two of us. It'll be easier that way," he says in a low voice.

"Why do you think it should just be you and me?" I ask with a smile. I would love to have time alone with him, but I wonder what his reasoning is.

Keeping his voice low as we stare out across the landscape, his arms still encircle me from behind. "I just don't like the idea of all of us leaving our base again. Especially to go orb hunting. Even though I know we need to do it to bring Ashgrave's army online. I want to get in and out as quickly as possible, and let's face it, you and I can get in and out without being seen."

My fingers trace over the top of his, and I lean my head back against his shoulder. Levi's presence here calms me. It makes sense, but I just stressed the importance of us being a team. But my master of stealth has a point about it being easier for two to get in and out than if we take the whole team. Plus, we'd have to make arrangements for the army at our borders.

"I understand that," I say.

"Also, if our team gets spotted in Reims, our enemies will know—which will leave us open for an attack. And I know the governments will have an issue with us traveling around the world. Hell, they don't want you or Irena in over half of the European countries, and the list grows longer every day."

"I'm not willing to lose an orb, especially when we need an army more than ever."

He doesn't argue. Levi kisses the back of my head, and I wiggle around to face him. My ice dragon has bruise-like circles under his eyes.

"Levi—" I say softly, "when was the last time you slept?"

"I don't really know," he says honestly.

"Is it the dreams? The ones where you're feral?" I have to figure out what's going on with him.

"I think the thing that bothers me the most, Rory, is that I can't tell if they're dreams or memories."

I stroke his cheek, my fingertips tracing the rigid edges of his strong face in the hopes that I can bring comfort to him. Levi taught me to feel, for the first time in my life. I push my love and gratitude into the special bond we share. My ice dragon avoids looking into my eyes as his gaze roams the scene outside the windows.

"I've done things and seen things as a feral that I just want to block out and bury forever," he continues.

I know what that's like. Doing things, seeing things you wished you didn't. Wanting to scrub your brain and heart clean of all of it. But that was another life—another time.

I wrap him in a tight hug, nuzzling my nose against his cheek. "Levi, I'm here for you. I promise. We will get through this together."

"MISTRESS, IRENA HAS ARRIVED AND IS AWAITING YOUR PRESENCE IN THE THRONE ROOM."

Irena? What is she doing here? I wasn't expecting her, and considering she didn't show up in Los Angeles, I can only imagine the worst.

"I need to talk to her." I kiss his cheek.

He nods as I step back from our hug.

"Ashgrave, to the throne room, please."

"RIGHT AWAY, MY QUEEN."

My magic castle is already sliding open the wall of my room, and I step through, running down its familiar staircase. The wall opens in front of me, and

I step into the hallway as the double doors of the throne room open for me.

As I approach, my sister doesn't move. Her head tilts downward as she stares at the intricate designs in the carpeting.

"Where were you two nights ago?" I demand. I'm not mad at her, I'm just trying to figure out what happened with her that prevented her from being at my side when I faced the Vaer. It's unlike my sister to say she's going to do something and then not do it.

Irena's body stiffens, but I can't see her face. She's wearing a large hood over her head, which reminds me of our Spectre days. Like she's trying to hide her identity.

"Rory, I..." the words catch in her throat for a moment before she finally throws back her hood. Her emerald eyes are glowing with power, and I instantly realize why she didn't show. The muscles in her neck are tense as she drops her gaze to the floor again, as if she's afraid she'll blast away anything she looks at.

I've never seen her like this. My sister, who has nerves of steel, is trembling.

CHAPTER TWENTY-FIVE

"I'm sorry, little sis. I wanted to be there. I did. But when this happened—" she motions toward her eyes before holding out her hands with her palms facing upward. A shimmer of energy dances along her fingertips. "I wasn't sure if I would be an asset or a liability in the fight." As the energy moves across her hands, Irena's eyes glow brighter. Her palms suddenly start sparking with arches of brilliant green power, and she doubles over like she was punched in the stomach.

Irena's face twists up in pain, and I can tell that she's fighting her power, trying to keep her magic locked down. But I know better than anyone that trying to suppress it only makes it worse.

I rush to her side and wrap my arms around her.

"Irena, this might seem like a bad thing, but it's not. Your body is trying to learn what to do with this new power. This sudden burst of power is a fluctuation. The more you try to push your power down, the harder your body will push back to use it. Magic has to be expressed—it's like art. The more you tuck it away and try to hide it, the more it will want to escape. Magic needs an escape."

"Has this ever happened to you?" Her gaze searches mine, hoping for an answer that will put her at ease.

I nod. "It still does. I'm learning to control it, but it takes time and practice."

My big sister shakes her head. "I don't want this… magic. I need to figure out how to get rid of it, or mute it, or something. I almost killed some of my Spectres. They were standing too close when this *magic* erupted from my hands. Hell, Rory, a couple of the men that got hit with this are still in the infirmary. And I almost blasted a hole in a school, while kids were sitting in the classrooms. Imagine what people would've said if that actually happened? How many children would I have hurt… or worse, killed?"

I release my hold on her but keep one hand on her shoulder while my eyes command her attention. There's the start of dark circles under her eyes, and she blinks like she's trying to force a piece of lint from her eye.

She's exhausted.

"But you didn't, and the children are okay. You're going to be okay," I remind her.

"Rory, I can't lead the Spectre rebels like this. I need to be able to control my body." She's watching my face, wide-eyed. "I'm a hazard to myself and everyone around me."

She shrugs my hand off her shoulder and wraps her arms around herself like she's freezing. There's something in her expression, with her top lip lifted on one side and her eyes slightly squinted.

My sister is treating this new power as if it's a virus. An illness that she's caught and wants to get rid of. She hugs her body tighter and looks at me with pleading eyes.

Irena needs me. I need to help her find a way to control this, but the rest is up to her.

"We can train together. I can help you practice, so that you can learn to start controlling your power."

She lowers her head, and her eyes search the floor for a way out of this. I can tell by the way she's avoiding my eyes that it's the last thing she wants to do.

"There's no way to escape this, sis. This power is

yours. Let me help you learn to control it."

After a few tense moments of silence, she finally nods her head.

"Ashgrave, is there a room large enough to train within your walls?"

"I WILL PREPARE SOMETHING FOR YOU MISTRESS. ONE MOMENT PLEASE."

"Thank you, Ashgrave."

"YOUR TRAINING ROOM AWAITS, MY QUEEN," he says after a few minutes. The wall across from us opens, and I grab my sister's hand and pull her into the magical tunnel. As we step inside, I watch her over my shoulder. Her head is swiveling around and her eyes are the size of saucers. I don't think Irena likes moving walls.

"The tunnels are perfectly safe. I promise."

She sticks her head out of the opening in the wall and walks further inside to observe the staircase leading upward.

"What the hell? How is this possible?"

I shrug my shoulders and smile. "It's all Ashgrave." My castle never ceases to amaze me. I don't really understand his magic myself, but I love it. And I hope my sister will learn to love her own magic too.

We walk up the stairway and the wall in front of

us opens to a hallway I've never seen before. The same elegant maroon and gold draperies that hang in the common areas surround the tall arching windows. The art here seems to be more French, paintings of women being saved by white knights.

"FOLLOW THIS HALLWAY TO THE END, AND YOU WILL FIND THE ROOM YOU SEEK, MY QUEEN."

Interesting. He usually takes me to the door of the place I ask for. Irena and I walk in silence along the hallway, taking in the architecture. The lovely way the stone curves at the top of the high ceilings. Gorgeous paintings show several women in distress being saved by men in helmets and armor. But damsels in distress aren't my thing. Probably because I just can't relate.

As we pass several doors down this corridor, I notice etchings in the ornate wooden doors that I've never seen before in other parts of Ashgrave. I'll have to ask him about that later.

As we come to the end of the hallway, the double doors in front of us open.

"MY QUEEN, THIS IS THE HALL OF HEROES. THE TRAINING ARENA OF THE GODS AND THEIR HEROES. I WISH TO CONTINUE TO HONOR IT."

The Hall of Heroes? Maybe that's why there were so many paintings of knights? I want to know more, but Irena needs to train. As I turn to face her, I see that Levi has stealthily joined us. Only he can do that. His face is sober, without even a trace of a smirk, but I'm thankful for his presence.

As we step into the massive room that has twenty-feet tall walls lined with different kinds of armor, I give Irena an encouraging smile. "Okay, this is a safe place. Don't worry about damaging the walls. Ashgrave can heal himself. I need for you to give in to your magic."

"Give in?" She asks, eyes wide.

"Yeah, just let it loose. Don't hold it back."

She shifts her weight from one foot to the other, so I move to the far side of the room that could easily fit three football stadiums inside it, and I summon my magical dagger. I grip the hilt and aim it in her direction, letting it fly through the air with a flick of my wrist.

She side steps my magical weapon. "What the hell are you doing?"

"Irena, controlling your magic is going to require you to have a mind-body connection that's on a whole new level. At least, that's what I've learned so far. Instead of pushing the energy down, try guiding it. Either you will master your power, or it'll master you. Your choice."

She has a scowl on her face, but she puts her hands out in front of her with her palms facing the ceiling. The green light that flashed uncontrollably in the throne room returns and burns like a flame. For a moment, there's an expression of awe on her face as she gazes at her hands. Then, her eyes narrow and go in and out of focus as the doubt returns. Irena's top lip curls up and her eyes squint, and she cringes. I figure my sister is thinking of whose blood and magic is in her veins as she closes her fist and takes a fighting stance.

"I don't need magic to defend myself," she says with a determined look in her eyes. "Come on, little sister."

I form another magical blade and hurl it toward her. She uses her arm guards to deflect it and rushes toward me for hand-to-hand. I dodge her quick jabs and block the right hook she aims for my head. I grunt in irritation, because she knows we can spar this way any time. The whole point of this training is to help her learn to start controlling her powers, becoming in tune with them when she's under attack.

My right hand lights up with blue magic, and I

throw a quick blast into her side. Nothing that could seriously hurt her, but enough to knock her on her ass.

Irena hisses as she lands hard on her rump. She places her palms on the floor and pushes herself back up to her feet. My sister steps forward, taking a defensive stance, but as soon as her eyes light up with power, she falters and takes two steps back. This is going to take more than a day to learn. Especially when Irena isn't willing to tap into her power because she thinks it's Kinsley's.

After a few hours of back-and-forth, Irena seems to be more comfortable with the ebb and flow of her magic. I finally get her to the point where she doesn't accidently blast a hole in Ashgrave, and she even starts using her magic defensively to deflect some of my attacks, though it might have been accidental. "Good," I tell her, sweat dripping down my forehead. "But you can do better."

"Great, just what I always wanted to hear," she says sarcastically. "I'm tired, can we take a break?"

I nod. "Yeah, of course."

She leans against one of the walls and slides to the floor in a sitting position with her head hanging forward. Levi, who has been silently watching us the entire time, catches Irena's eyes before he speaks.

"I remember what it was like," he starts in a low voice, "being feral. Not having control over my own body. Feeling like I was trapped. I imagine you feel the same way, Irena, with this new power that you never asked for—never wanted. I agree, you're doing well, but don't feel like you have to rush this. Take your time and learn how to master it."

Irena gives Levi a slight nod, and my heart hungers for my ice dragon. It's this, this honesty that he has that makes him stand out in my life like none of the others. My master of stealth makes my heart feel what I would've never thought possible. And I love him for it.

"Thank you," she says to him.

"Are you ready to try again?" I ask.

Irena nods, and this time, she blasts me first. And I wasn't prepared. I fly backward through the air.

"INFIDEL!" Ashgrave's voice thunders, shaking the room, and my intuition tells me that my murderous castle is about to do something.

"No, Ashgrave! It's fine!" I yell.

"SHE ATTACKED YOU, MY QUEEN."

"Yes, but we're practicing. You know, like when Jace and I train? That's why I asked you for this room. I'm okay."

"DO YOU WISH TO CONTINUE TRAINING

IN THIS WAY?" he asks, and I think I detect a sense of confusion in his voice.

"Yes, remember, she's my sister. I trust her and you should too."

"YES, MY QUEEN. MY APOLOGIES, IRENA."

"It's no trouble, Ashgrave," she answers back, but she's trembling like a leaf.

"Do you want to keep going?" I ask.

Irena shakes her head, flexing her hands out in front of her. "I think I've had enough for one night, but thanks for helping me." She stares at her hands again, and her eyes go out of focus like she's deep in thought.

I hate seeing her like this. I give my sister a small smile. "Well, now that you're starting to get the hang of your magic, all that's left for you to do is shift." I wink at her.

"That's *not* going to happen, Rory," she retorts, and I step back because of the sudden change in her attitude. I knew she would be against shifting, but the deadly look on her face tells me she'd rather die first.

"I was just teasing. Why don't we rest? You can stay the night and head out tomorrow after you feel better?"

She shakes her head. "Thanks, maybe another

time. I need to hunt down Diesel and get my hands on that bio-weapon."

My sister knows that if my men and I had intercepted it, I would've told her. I catch Levi still watching us, and a scowl crosses his face at the mention of Diesel.

I'm almost ashamed to confess to her that we didn't get the bio-weapon, and especially how Milo Darrington of all people had come to our aid. "Just be careful, Irena. He's working with someone powerful. He got the drop on us. Whoever he's working with is stronger than the Vaer. Or, he could have just been boasting. Anyway, please be safe." I let the urgency drip into my voice.

"I will. You take care of yourself too. I'll continue practicing what you've taught me so far, and next time you call, I'll answer. I promise." She gives me a quick hug before leaving for the exit.

I walk her to the door. "Ashgrave, please escort my sister to the foyer."

"YES, MY QUEEN."

I watch as Irena walks down the hall, trusting that Ashgrave will take her to the magical door that will lead her out.

A soft brush of fingertips on my waist has me turning into Levi's hug. "Are you okay, Rory?"

I nod. "It's just…"

"She's your sister, and you're worried about her?"

I nod my head again, thankful that I don't have to explain myself with him. "Ashgrave, has Irena left the castle?"

"YES, MISTRESS. YOUR SISTER IS HEADING TOWARD THE SOUTH BORDER NOW."

"I'd like to go to my room, please," I say, suddenly feeling exhausted. The total lack of sleep last night and then training with my sister took more out of me than I realized. Tomorrow we head to Reims, France to get that orb. I know I need rest.

Levi's hand rests on the small of my back as he walks with me toward the open doors and down the hallway toward the open piece of wall that leads to my castle's magic tunnel. We move through the tunnels silently until we come to an opening in the wall. When we exit into the hallway across from the doors to my room, he kisses me softly on the cheek.

"Try to get some rest, love."

"I should say the same to you." I raise my hand to trace his strong jaw before kissing him and heading into my room to sleep.

CHAPTER TWENTY-SIX

"MY QUEEN, A LARGE GROUP OF DRAGONS HAS CROSSED MY SOUTHERN BORDER. MAY I SMITE THEM?"

I jump from my bed, pulling the thick comforter around me as I gather my senses.

What the hell is going on?

Where am I?

I'm home. I'm in bed.

Ashgrave is being Ashgrave. As the early morning sunlight shines through the windows of my room, my bloodthirsty butler's words flash though my mind.

Dragons are here. What dragons? And what the hell do they want this early in the morning? My heart is pounding against the walls of my chest as adrenaline courses through me. It's possible that Kinsley's coming to take my head. I hurry to get dressed and grab a handgun as well, sliding it into the holster at my hip.

"Ashgrave, door!" I command, and the wall slides open the moment I'm ready, and I exit my room. "Take me to Jace." The tunnel opens outside of Jace's door moments later. I pound on his door, and he answers with a sexy, sleepy smile.

"What's up, beautiful? Come to play?" He winks and his chiseled body calls out to me, waking my dragon. She's pacing. *We're up early, we can sneak in a quickie,* she tells me.

"No! No time, Jace. There are dragons at our borders. Get dressed and hurry up."

My statement sparks him to move, and he's quickly hopping around the room, pulling on jeans and a long-sleeved shirt. His boots are next, and like me, he grabs his gun and puts it in its holster.

"Let's go," he says sternly. We don't know what to expect, but the fact that there are unexpected dragons in our territory, and they've come without an invite, tells us their intentions aren't good.

We hurry to the main floor. My first instinct is to alert Drew, who is probably in the surveillance room.

Drew likes to be there when the sun comes up, watching and listening for any sort of chatter. I fling open the door and spot the back of his head. "Drew, I need the surveillance cameras for the castle grounds to get a view of our new visitors."

He turns around to look at me, and his eyes widen in surprise, but he turns back to the monitors in front of him and strikes a few keys on his keyboard. The dual monitors in front of him go black momentarily before switching over to the familiar view of the castle grounds.

"MAY I SMITE THE INTRUDERS, MY QUEEN?" Ashgrave asks, startling me.

"Wait until we know who it is, Ashgrave." I shake my head at his willingness to maim and kill.

So far, the approaching dragons are tiny dots from the view on the screen. As they move in closer to the cameras, we get a better look.

I wait impatiently, a million possibilities flying through my mind.

Has Jade's family come to take her by force and bring her back to her abusive father? Is it Kinsley coming for a final battle?

Jace and Drew are silent, though Drew gets up from his chair and starts pacing the surveillance room. Jace stands stoically beside me as he studies the group of dragons. Out of the corner of my eye, recognition dawns on his face.

"What the hell are *they* doing here?" Jace's jaw drops.

His dojo dragons beat their wings and fly in perfect formation as they make their way toward the castle. I'm just as stunned as he is, because my mate left the dojo and its responsibilities behind when he chose to start a life with me.

Jace shakes his head in disbelief. It's clear he hasn't called them. He would have told me if he had.

"Let's go," he motions, and I nod, dropping my clothes and gun in the hallway before we jump from the windows, shifting on our way down. Ashgrave isn't far behind us in his little metallic body, keeping as close to us as he can. I know he's coming along to protect me, but I don't need protecting.

I land in front of the group of over one hundred dragons, letting out a fierce roar that shakes the ground beneath us. I know they aren't hostile, but this is my home.

They need to recognize that I'm the leader here.

"DO YOU RECOGNIZE THESE TRES-PASSERS, MY QUEEN?" Ashgrave immediately asks, and I shake my head. I place my forehead against the chest of his metallic body.

Not hostile dragons, just letting them know who is boss.

"VERY WELL, MY QUEEN. WELCOME TO ASHGRAVE. YOU ARE WITHIN MY BORDERS, AND HERE WE HONOR AND SERVE THE QUEEN OF ASHGRAVE."

I watch as the dojo dragons nod to each other and then look at me. The leader steps forward, bowing. I take that as a sign of submission and press my forehead to his.

Are you the queen? He immediately questions.

That's what they tell me, I respond. He offers a toothy grin and nods to me as if to acknowledge his agreement.

The leader tilts his head over his shoulder, nodding at the other dragons that stand at attention behind him. At his motion, everyone shifts into their human forms.

Jace and I do the same, and suddenly the tension Jace was carrying lifts. His dojo dragons do not pose a threat to us, and from where I stand, Jace's face relaxes.

"Jace, it is an honor to be here in the presence of your mate, Queen Rory, and you as well."

My mate gives him a regal nod, puffing his bare chest out slightly. He's proud to be with me, and probably over the moon that this soldier called me queen.

Men.

"We're here because the Fairfax Dojo is no longer our home. We want to serve you, General. The Fairfax Boss has given us her blessing. We sincerely hope that you will allow us the honor to serve alongside you again. To go to war with you, if it comes to that.

The dojo soldiers pump their fists into the air and start shouting. "Doo-rah, doo-rah."

"It's an honor to have you here," I say. "To have you stand alongside us. With war looming, we need all the skilled warriors we can get. We will make room for you inside the castle."

The soldiers are high fiving each other with smiles on their faces, and there is an obvious energy among them.

With the dojo soldiers, and the other orb in place, we will crush any enemy that crosses us. But first, we need to get to Reims and retrieve it.

"Ashgrave, prepare rooms for these men." The metal dragon lifts his head, tilting it slightly to look at me, as if to say, "Seriously?"

I continue. "We have more than enough room, and your walls will provide the safety we need to train and prepare for whatever attack may be heading our way."

"YES, MY QUEEN."

Ashgrave takes off, flying toward the castle, and I look over my shoulder. "Men, feel free to shift and follow me."

It'll be faster than traveling on foot, and I'm not willing to walk the whole way. I can't feel the cold, but walking naked through the Russian mountains with over one hundred men is not my idea of fun. We all take to the sky, and I lead them over the small hills and valleys surrounding Ashgrave until the large ornate doors of my castle are visible.

I land in the main courtyard, shifting back, and they all follow suit.

Once we are inside, Ashgrave uses his magic to take the soldiers to their rooms quickly. Jace takes the opportunity to grab my hand.

He leads me to the hallway where we removed our clothes and guns, and we quickly dress and arm ourselves.

I grab my phone out of my pocket and dial Harper's number as Jace watches me. "Calling Harper," I mouth.

"Rory, I gave them permission to go to you and my cousin." Harper doesn't give me time to ask my question. "Does it really matter which army they fight in? We're on the same side."

I shake my head at the Fairfax Boss. "I know, Harper. But one hundred soldiers?"

"That's fine, we have hundreds more, and the soldiers that wanted to go to you, have trained with Jace since their first shifts. Jace is their first general. If fighting with you gives them an edge, then so be it." A rustle of fabric comes over the phone. "Liam wants to say thank you. Is that okay with you?"

"Who is Liam?"

"A certain little blonde boy with blue-green eyes. You rescued him from the Vaer testing facility."

"Harper, I don't know."

A heavy thud comes over the line. "Hello, Ms. Rory?" the voice of a young boy says. "I just wanted to say thank you for saving us. I have a new life now. I have a lady who cares for me. Her name is Aubrey, she's a nurse, and I have friends and go to school."

For a moment, I'm speechless. I've been so used to rescue-and-run missions that it didn't occur to me what happens afterward. But that skinny little boy who braved the dungeons of that facility with me is happy, thriving, and living a better life.

Because of me and my men.

Hell, that feels good.

"That's great Liam," I tell the little dragon boy. "I'm glad that you're doing wonderful and you're going to school with kids your own age. Thank you for your help, I wouldn't have been able to save the others without you."

"I have to go, ma'am. Aubrey is calling me."

A rustle of fabric comes over the line again, and I know he just gave the phone back to Harper.

"You should see the smile on that kid's face. I don't know what you told him, but it sure made him happy."

"Just the truth."

"Stay safe, Rory. I have a war to prepare for, and so do you." The phone goes silent and I shake my head. Harper's in Boss Mode.

I look up and see Jace's stormy grey eyes looking at my lips. "Not now, Jace. We need to get to the surveillance room and talk to Drew."

We make our way to the surveillance room so that we can talk to my fire dragon in peace. Drew gives us a side glance as we walk in, but I can tell he's busy looking at something on his tablet.

"We know Kinsley is going to strike, and soon," Jace says, pacing in front of me and running his hand through his hair.

"Good thing your soldiers are here to lend a

hand. It looks like the army you wanted is coming together nicely." I'm smiling, thankful that the tides seem to be shifting in our favor, even if most of the Bosses aren't with us. "I want a force strong enough to work alongside Ashgrave, to help defend the area and the castle. We need that. We also need enough soldiers, and if it's required for them to leave to fight, that's an option too."

"Agreed," Jace says, studying my face.

"I just got intel that indicates Kinsley is preparing to strike," Drew interrupts.

"Thanks, Drew." It's the confirmation I need. I leave the room and Jace follows.

"We need to go to Reims and get the orb," I state.

"Soon, Rory."

Not soon enough, I think, irritated that I'm not there now. Switching topics as we walk, I notice how Jace's demeanor has changed since the arrival of the dojo soldiers. He's more commanding, and he stands taller with his chest puffed out. I'm amazed at the fact that his men are still willing to follow him. He carries their respect.

"You're a natural born leader, Jace."

He stops walking and turns to face me, cupping my face in his hand and kissing me, taking my breath away.

"You too, my mate."

My blood burns with desire when he calls me that. Mate. Our dragons are soulmates. One can't survive without the other.

"You make me better, Rory," he says, and the glow of sincerity in his eyes ignites the fire of desire that rushes through me. I love this man.

"You know how to inspire others all on your own. You inspire me all the time," I tell him, trying to brush away the compliment, but he holds my face tighter.

"Woman, you drive me to be the best, because you deserve nothing less. And as long as I'm alive, I will fight to be the man, the dragon, the mate you deserve."

I kiss him fiercely. "You are, and you always will be, and now... we need to head to Reims."

And with that, I pull away from him, leaving my mate to watch as I hurry to my room to get ready for our flight to France.

CHAPTER TWENTY-SEVEN

I have a few things I need to do before we head to France. Taking a shower is one of them.

"Ashgrave, can you please let my men know that we are heading to Reims in three hours. Inform them to prepare for our trip. We can't wait any longer. I need that orb today."

"AS YOU WISH, MY QUEEN."

I'm learning there is a definite benefit to being the queen of a wickedly devoted castle.

Queen—the title still feels foreign to me, but I can't deny people are looking up to me. Depending on me, even. And every time Ashgrave announces my title as a matter of sheer fact, it reinforces the idea that I could actually pull this off. I can be queen.

For now, my conscience tells me. What about

when Morgana returns? I know the dragon goddess is still alive. I heard her and the other two gods during the vision I had about a week ago in the treasury.

I haven't mentioned the vision to any of my men. Was it a vision? A dream? I don't know what to call it, but I know for a fact that I was in the presence of the ancient dragon gods. I don't want to worry my men. We've all had enough on our minds. If it happens again though… they need to know.

In my mind, an image of the glowing and pulsating orb calls to me, like Ashgrave did. The image takes up all of my thoughts. There's no room for anything else. It pushes out the questions of Ashgrave's loyalty and the vision of the dragon gods. None of that matters. I'm running out of time. I *need* the orb.

I take a quick shower and dress, braiding my still wet hair into a thick braid that hangs to the right side of my head. I have to talk with Brett before I leave, to see if there is any chatter about my visit to L.A. I shake my head. Of course, everyone knows I was in L.A., and I'm probably being blamed for the damage to the restaurant as well as the body count that was left in Chinatown.

The Vaer has to have some great public relations

people who will spin the story to their benefit. They'll make me look like a dragon sympathizer who doesn't care about human lives at all. They'll tell the tall tale that the bodies in the restaurant are all human, but they're not. The Vaer and Nabal dragons that died were sent to Chinatown to capture me and kill my men.

But I'm here, and my men are still alive.

I sigh, heavily. This cycle is never going to end unless I do something about it once and for all.

I hurry down the stairs, choosing to take the long way to the main hallway of the castle instead of traveling through Ashgrave's magical tunnels. What if we don't find the orb? Or worse, what if we do find it and it's been destroyed or is heavily guarded?

And, I worry about the safety of my men.

I honestly just want to protect them. The ambush we suffered in L.A. cannot happen again. I have to make sure of that.

Heading toward the kitchen, I decide that grabbing a cup of coffee will give me the five minutes I need to clear my head, before I have to dive headfirst into damage control with Brett. I pour a steaming cup of caffeinated goodness and figure there are a lot of new people within Ashgrave's walls, and when I have time, I should check in with them to see how they're settling in.

I haven't spoken to Jade in a few days. I'll add her to the growing list of people to check in on, when I have time. I've only seen some of Flynn's men in passing. Now, about one hundred of the dojo soldiers are here too. I chuckle, knowing that I don't have to think about the castle becoming too full, since it seems Ashgrave is bottomless when it comes to room. It makes me wonder if my murderous castle is growing and changing from the inside to make room for all of the people we're caring for.

"Ashgrave, where's Brett?" I ask, standing in the hallway outside the kitchen.

"BRETT IS APPROACHING THE SURVEILLANCE ROOM, MY QUEEN."

"Thank you." I take a sip of my caffeinated goodness and stroll down the hall to intercept him.

"Brett," I say, catching him walking in my direction with his head down.

"Rory, I thought you were on your way to France." His eyes widen in surprise with a small smile on his lips.

He is freshly shaven without bags under his eyes, and his clothes look to be freshly pressed. I wonder if his appearance has anything to do with his blooming relationship with Jade. The way they both look at each other, hang around each other, and laugh together... I can tell there's something between them.

"You're looking good," I comment.

"Was that a compliment?" he teases, looking down at the tablet in his hand as he swipes at it. My PR expert types something and then looks back up at me. "I guess I can blame my appearance on the beds here, or the fact that I'm getting an incredible workout handling your public image." He smirks.

"So... is that good or bad?" I ask.

"Neither, just a fact. It doesn't matter if I do this for you or someone else. You could be a saint and no one would care. The media only wants to put a negative spin on everything you do. But the people, well most of them anyway, they love you, Rory. We just have to keep working their love for you in our favor. That little incident in Chinatown didn't help. All of the news outlets are holding you responsible for the destruction of the restaurant and the deaths of those people."

His words confirm my thought on the Vaer's PR team. I wonder how far the Vaer's reach extends when it comes to the news agencies. And before I complete my thought, I realize someone is telling them what to say, trying to make me look bad. The Vaer are using their political influence and the PR angle to tear my image down.

Jade walks up to us, smiling in greeting. Her face is lit from within, and she's happier than I've ever seen her. I can't help but grin at the change in her demeanor. It's like a weight has been lifted from her shoulders—from her entire body.

"Jade, I was just thinking about you. How are you doing?"

Her smile widens, making the scar over her left eye crinkle as she looks at Brett, and then to me. The hint of a blush creeps into her cheeks.

"I'm doing great, Rory," she says, and I know she means it. Brett shows her his tablet, and her smile grows even warmer as she gazes into his eyes. Jade takes the tablet from Brett and looks at me.

"Brett's been teaching me a lot about public relations and surveillance. He's really quite amazing."

I admire the sweet friendship, and maybe more, that's growing between them.

"Fabulous," I say, with an approving nod. "Well, it looks like you two have this handled. I'm heading out soon, but Jace will take care of things while we're gone."

They both nod, excusing themselves as they

hurry back to work on countering the constant onslaught of negative news. I can't help but grin as I make my way to the west wing of the castle. There's a training area there, and though it's not as grand as the Hall of Heroes, it works well for Flynn's men and the dojo soldiers.

There are days when I feel like I could walk this castle and admire its beauty for an entire day, and I would never reach the end of its magnificence. Today, is not one of them.

"Ashgrave, where are Flynn's men?"

"SOME ARE IN THE TRAINING AREA, AND THE REST ARE WITH YOUR MATE IN THE LOWER MEETING ROOM OF THE WEST WING, MY QUEEN."

Jace is preparing them for our trip to France. I stand a little taller as a weight lifts from my shoulders. Ashgrave will not be here alone, and the men here are willing to fight to protect him.

I head to the training area at this end of the castle, knowing that Jace would use the outside area for training and the small rooms at the end of the hall for meetings and teaching. As I pass one of the west wing meeting rooms, I notice a mixture of Flynn's men and dojo soldiers gathering around a large round table.

Jace rushes past me with a tablet in his hands. "I'll be right back."

He goes into the meeting room, and he starts giving orders, discussing what-ifs, and laying down ground rules. When he's done, my mate grabs my hand as he leaves the room, and we head toward the outside training area.

"Are you sure you're going to be okay heading to France with the others?" he asks.

"Of course. Will you be okay staying here?"

He nods. "You know I'd rather be joining you in Reims, but I need to get these soldiers ready in case we're attacked." Jace kisses my forehead and rushes out the double doors to correct a soldier's fighting form.

Jace is my mate, but right now he's the general of a growing army. And he's doing what good generals do.

Preparing our armies for battle.

I walk quickly toward the main entrance and head out to the tarmac where the chopper is waiting. Levi, Tucker, and Drew are already inside.

"Everything ready to go?" I ask Tucker as I climb inside and watch him flip a few switches from his pilot's chair.

His grin makes my knees weak.

"Really, babe? After all we've been through, you're still doubting me?"

"No. I just want to make sure we're ready to leave."

"Not unless you want to sneak in a quickie, with me, your favorite." He winks at me, and Drew and Levi give him dirty glances before they all erupt into laughter.

They all know I don't play favorites. I love them all, equally. Individually. Uniquely.

"Tucker, don't make me take away one of your toys for being a bad boy," I say flirtatiously.

"You never take my toys away," Drew chimes in, and I give him a wink. "No, but you've done it to me."

The fire in his eyes tells me he's thinking about the passion we shared while I was handcuffed in the little abandoned building. He winks at me. Levi leans into me and places a possessive arm around my waist before planting a passionate kiss on my lips.

Gods, these men are going to be the death of me.

"Ashgrave!" I yell out the open chopper door, and instantly his little metallic dragon body is hovering in the air in front of me.

"I AM HERE. I WOULD NOT ALLOW YOU TO

LEAVE THE REALM WITHOUT MY PROTEC-
TION, MY QUEEN."

Damn his voice is loud. It echoes throughout the
helicopter like an erupting volcano.

"Rory! Wait!" Flynn dashes toward us as we start
buckling ourselves in.

"I want to go with you!" He doesn't wait for my
answer and starts climbing inside the chopper as the
blades start to turn.

I eye him as he squeezes in next to Drew, who
looks at him from the corner of his eyes, and he puts
on the headset that was in his seat. "Ever been on a
mission like this?" I ask.

"I'm an excellent fighter. Make use of me. I need
to do something, Rory."

I nod in response, understanding how he must
feel. It's tough going from a life of training and
fighting to sitting around a castle all day, every day.
He offered his services, as well as those of his rebels.
And I did mention to him that I could use his help
with the Reims mission. While his people are
training with Jace and the dojo soldiers, he can come
with us to France.

"Fine," I say. "This should be interesting."

Levi and Drew watch him. They're squinting

their eyes, and their faces are reddening. Is that jealousy I see? I have to admit, it's kinda hot.

Flynn is a good looking guy, but he's not my type. I think of him as more of a brother, not a lover. I smirk at the fact my men still get jealous of newcomers. It's a real turn on.

"All right, get buckled in and hold tight. Tucker could kill us all if he doesn't pay attention," I joke.

Tucker looks over his shoulder at me with a sexy smirk on his lips. "You cut me, babe. You cut me real deep." My weapons expert turns back around as the chopper lifts into the air and I laugh.

"Tucker is an excellent pilot," I tell Flynn. "So sit back and enjoy the ride."

Flynn nods and finishes buckling himself in, before he rests his head on the back of the seat. The flight is peaceful enough, and we make it to Reims by nightfall.

Drew had already arranged for us to touch down at a small landing strip just north of the famous Notre-Dame Cathedral. As Tucker powers down the aircraft, I spot a sedan waiting nearby.

There are no armored cars waiting for us like in L.A.

As I stand to exit the chopper, I notice Tucker bending to get something out of the storage

OLIVIA ASH

compartment underneath my seat. "What do you have there, Tucker?"

"Only my babies that are tucked neatly away in my vest."

I look at the beige vest that I know contains many hidden pockets. "I thought it was destroyed with the dojo?"

"So did I, until Russell gave it to me when we dropped the prisoners we rescued off at the capital. But don't worry, I updated some of my babies with the guns from the castle armory. Nothing but the best for you, babe," he says with a wink.

Ashgrave starts to hover next to us as Drew opens the door of the helicopter. I walk down the stairs as Tucker puts on his vest and my little metal dragon follows closely behind. Drew is already standing on the tarmac talking to the driver of the car. Flynn exits the chopper last with a look of awe on his face.

I'm instantly engrossed in the architecture of Reims. My mind celebrates the richly constructed buildings. According to Esmeralda's diary, the orb was hidden in the cathedral, so that's where we have to go.

As I look out at the beautiful landscape of the French city, I spy a group of anti-dragon protestors, marching and yelling. It was hard enough watching these protests on the television and computer screens. But, there's something disheartening about seeing the groups in person.

We pile into the dark sedan—Levi, Tucker, and me in the back seat with Ashgrave on the floor, and Flynn next to the driver with Drew sitting in the passenger seat. We start to travel very slowly, and even though I'm in a new disguise and the windows of the car are darkly tinted, their judgement of me weighs heavy on my shoulders as we make our way through the crowd.

Something spatters against the passenger side window and slides down the side of the car slowly.

Fan-freaking-tastic! They're throwing food now?

"Jakobe, take us down a side street where we can get away from the murderous rioters, please?" Drew's tone is not happy with our current situation, and the head of the driver nods as he turns the car left down a smaller side street.

"This is exactly the kind of shit that Diesel and Kinsley want. Chaos and anger, without reason."

"I'm glad you're nothing like them," Drew says in a low whisper. "You're kind at heart, and smarter than you give yourself credit for. Even though you don't take shit from anyone, you protect those who need protecting. You have a natural sense of justice that can't be taught. You always want to do right, no matter the cost. That's truly honorable."

"That's one of the reasons I like you," Flynn interjects. "You always choose to do the right thing."

"Yeah, and I like how you know which guns are my favorite." Tucker cracks one of his familiar loveable grins. "Hope I get a new one for Christmas! It's going to be hard for anything to top my jet and chopper though."

Loveable dork. I can't help but smile, even as I shift uncomfortably from their compliments.

"Guns?" Flynn asks. "I'm a bit of a gun geek," he says, which of course sparks Tucker, and he starts pulling weapons from the pockets of his vest.

The inside of the car is instantly transformed into a gun nerd paradise as Flynn handles each of the weapons with a sort of child-like wonder. He asks Tucker what each weapon is capable of and questions my weapons expert on how long has Tucker been into weapons.

"I officially hate you less," Tucker says in the middle of their conversation.

"Wait, you hated me?" Flynn lifts a questioning eyebrow as he watches Tucker.

Tucker shrugs his shoulders. "New guy coming in, trying to make yourself at home."

Flynn nods. "I get that. But I'm not trying to take over or come between anyone."

Tucker smiles. "Don't worry about it. You can't come between us. We're family."

"How many kills do you have?" Flynn asks Tucker, and just like that, they are deep into their gun geek conversation. I tune them out and listen to the sounds of the protestors. We can't seem to escape them for long—they're everywhere.

Out of the corner of my eye, I watch as Levi's eyes search out the window at our surroundings with a scowl on his gorgeous face. The car makes a sudden swerve, and a burst of fire ignites nearby. We barely avoid being hit by a Molotov cocktail. I slide hard into Tucker who sits on my left side.

My cat-sized steam punk dragon starts to flutter his metal wings. "HOW DARE THESE INFIDELS ATTACK MY QUEEN AS SHE TRAVELS! I WILL SMITE THEM ALL!"

I can't help but smile. My bloodthirsty castle is always willing to smite anyone. "We're fine, Ashgrave. Let's get the orb and go home."

The tall graceful tower of the Cathedral stares down on us as Jakobe, our driver, pulls up behind the church. Drew jumps out and opens Tucker's door, and we all pile out of the car and head through the beautiful garden and toward the church's underground catacombs.

I follow the map in my head. According to the diary, the orb is inside an old sarcophagus deep inside one of the many tombs.

As we enter the catacombs, the smell of dust, smoke, and mildew assaults our noses. We start exploring the tombs that resemble the description from the diary, knowing this church has been built over ancient tombs and has suffered a fire recently. Despite the physical changes and damage to some of the older, deeper tombs, we make our way to the sarcophagus etched with the image of a glowing orb.

The only light we have is from ancient-looking torches embedded into the walls every ten feet or so. We have no idea how long we've been down here as we search for the proverbial needle in a haystack.

Out of the corner of my eye, I spy the circle symbol with lines surrounding it, carved into a sarcophagus that is off to my right. That's the image that was drawn in the diary.

This is the one.

We found it.

My heart is pounding and my hands are starting

to sweat. If we can get this orb, it's going to be life changing for us. I imagine Ashgrave's metallic dragon army marching into battle and finally defeating the Vaer and ending this war before any more humans die.

The orb has to be here—this is where the diary said it would be—it has to be here.

My men surround me. "I think this is it."

Drew and Levi grab the stone top and push it aside. Pieces of it crumble and fall to the ground. I don't know what I'm expecting to see inside of it—a body? Bones and old rags?

My heart falls at what we find—it's empty. Someone beat us to the orb.

"Damn it!" I shout. "I didn't come all this way to hit a dead end."

My mind races through options as I scan the surrounding area for clues. I catch a glimpse of a camera lens in one of the corners. It appears to be shattered, but there has to be other cameras in the area, to keep an eye on the ancient catacombs.

As if reading my mind, Flynn walks up to the camera. He shakes his head. "This one is broken."

Tucker scratches his chin. "I wonder if whoever took the orb also broke the camera."

"Drew," I say, pointing to the broken security

camera. "Do you think you can hack into the security system here? I'm sure this place has more than one camera."

"Yeah, give me a couple minutes." He takes his tablet out and his fingers fly over it, trying to pull up the cameras' feeds. "Here," he says.

He zooms the camera in on a blonde woman in her twenties carrying a large tote bag. She passes through the garden and slips into the catacombs. When she comes out, her bag is bulging. Drew zooms in on her face. "I'm going to send this to Brett."

I pull out my phone and call Brett. He answers on the first ring.

"What's up, Boss?"

"Drew just sent you a picture. I need her identification and contact information, please."

"Sure, just give me one second." Keyboard clacking fills the silence, and I wait.

"Facial recognition software gave us a match. Her name is Sophie Marchand. Looks like she's human, no known affiliation with any of the dragon families. That's weird. There is no known history for her until last week. No birth certificate, driver's license, or social security number. It looks like she might be a possible spy. The Vaer have been known to use their power and influence to wipe the identities of their top spies and use them for important jobs, making them unable to be traced. I'll text you her address."

"Thank you, Brett."

"Be safe." He hangs up. Seconds later, a text comes through with her address.

"I guess it's good none of us recognize her," Tucker says as he studies her picture and information.

"Should be pretty easy to take the orb from her if she's human," Flynn chimes in.

"We still need to be careful," Tucker tells him. "Humans are great at proving you wrong when you underestimate them."

He's right, and I'm not looking forward to confronting this stranger. The fact that there was no history on her until last week has me wondering who the hell this woman is.

"Who is she working for?" Levi asks. "She just came into being, last week. That's very suspicious."

Sophie Marchand is suspicious. And that pisses me off.

CHAPTER TWENTY-EIGHT

The address Brett gave us leads us into a small neighborhood on the outskirts of Reims. The houses all have brightly colored doors and big yards with picket fences in the front. Some of the perfectly mowed lawns have flower boxes that edge the driveways. Dwarf chestnut trees border the street, and swifts fly in and out of the leafy branches.

Coincidence? I don't think so. This place is almost too convenient and too quiet. I keep trying to figure out how this woman with no past knew about the orb, and what she's planning to do with it. Drew's driver expertly navigates us through the picturesque neighborhood, away from the rioting crowds in the city. At least Ashgrave isn't threatening to smite them in his loud voice any more.

I don't know what to expect, but I do know that there's no damn way some woman just popped into the catacombs, disturbing a centuries-old sarcophagus that had been dormant for years, and steals an artifact of immense power. She's either working for someone or with someone.

I rotate my shoulders in a circular motion to relieve the tension in my muscles and notice Tucker is tapping away on Drew's tablet.

"What are you doing, Tucker?"

"Just running a quick background check on our little orb thief."

"Kind of pointless, don't you think?" I ask. "We already know she's not a shifter, and she has no known connections. Hell, Brett said he couldn't find a history on her until a week ago."

"It'd be more awkward to ring her doorbell and ask her in person if she's dealing with dragons or an anti-dragon organization." He winks at me. My weapons expert has a point. "She's not an assassin or criminal. Always a plus. I don't see any ties to the now defunct Knights or the Spectres. For all intents and purposes, she appears to be just an ordinary girl."

"I highly doubt that," I say, arms folded. My

thoughts wander to Kinsley, and if this girl is related to her in some way or working for her.

"I can train one of my guns on her and you can grab the orb, babe. It'll be romantic, like in Ho Chi Minh city," Tucker says, distracting me as only he can.

"The orb belongs to me—to Ashgrave." I stare down at the little dragon by my feet. "Let's try talking to her first. And if that doesn't work, Drew, you offer her an obscene amount of money to take the orb off her hands. It's possible that she's a thief looking to sell an ancient artifact."

My intuition tells me this looks and smells like a trap. And if it's not, I know that everyone can be bought for the right amount of money. "Who knows, maybe that was her motivation for taking it in the first place," I say, rolling my eyes.

My dragon is up and pacing nervously. She doesn't like anything about this situation. She's begging me to shift so she can take control and get the orb, even if she has to tear through the thief to do it.

No, I tell her. *We can't shift. It's not the right time or place. Shifting here would cause too many problems for all of us.*

Levi shifts in his seat. "She may have just seen a

chance to grab something that might be of value, and that's why she did it. Or, she may have already sold it."

"That's possible, but I think I'd already know if someone bought the orb. Plus, Ashgrave would've sensed it. Or someone would have told me. News like a new magical orb hitting the market doesn't stay buried for long."

Tension hangs like a thick fog in the air of the car.

We pull up to the front of a small cottage with a white picket fence. There's no car in the driveway. The birds singing in the trees that line the streets are the only sounds we hear as we get out of the car.

"Time to find out." I check my holsters for my guns, and my men do the same. We're not going in unarmed. No matter how harmless she appears in her background check.

Drew knocks on the red door, and I step up next to him.

A blue-eyed blonde answers, and the first thing I notice is that her appearance is a little different from the video footage. Her eyes are wider apart and the blonde of her hair seems lighter. But she is the same height and build, and this is the right address.

"Rory? Oh my gods!"

She's so—I try to find the right word, but I can't find it in my startled brain. Perky. That's the word that describes her. Like some college chick from Kappa Delta Fluff Fluff. Gods, this girl's mood irritates me.

I give Drew a subtle nod to let him know I've got this covered.

Sophie's still beaming a blinding smile as she opens her door wider and steps aside so we can enter. "I can't believe you're here. Please, come in. It's such an honor to have you in my humble home." She bounces on her toes and flaps her arms like a bird. Her constant need to move is getting on my nerves. I've got to play nice, though. Trap or otherwise. I just don't know what to expect.

Drew walks in and I follow behind him, studying the posh foyer of her home. It has a French country cottage feel, with tasteful decorations. Pictures of flowering gardens and women riding bicycles through flowering parks line the walls, and a book shelf stands on the far wall near the staircase. We make a right turn into the living room.

A fireplace stands in the middle of the wall to the far right with a roaring fire. The adjoining walls display several posters of me in dragon form. Each image has been plastered to the wall with care and exquisite detail. Damn, it's a shrine.

I take a seat on the white canvas couch and Tucker sits next to me. Levi stands near the fireplace, subtly motioning to the posters. Drew and Flynn stand near the archway we entered the room through, as if they're standing guard over the exit. Ashgrave's metallic form waddles near my feet, watching for anything.

I can't take my eyes off Levi's face as his gaze goes between me and the girl's Rory shrine, his expression silently asking me if I saw the pictures. I give him a discreet nod, trying to ignore the way the shrine has me wanting to rip every poster on the wall into pieces. This shrine bothers me. A lot.

"Can I get you some tea?" Sophie asks, continuing to bounce. She stopped flapping her arms, so that's a bonus.

"That's kind of you, Sophie, but I'm actually here on business." I'm hoping her obvious dedication to me means she won't want to let me down.

"Absolutely, Rory. I'd love to help you. What do you need me to do?" She asks, literally bouncing on her toes with a smile so big I can barely see her baby blues.

I clear my throat. "I think that you may have

taken something from the cathedral last week. Something that is very, very important to me."

She stops bouncing and takes a seat on the couch across from us. Her body tenses, and her smile falls into a frown as she furrows her eyebrows. Sophie looks—worried.

"You're not in trouble, I promise. I just need to know if it was a round crystal object? An orb? I'm willing to pay you for it." I smile at her.

She looks at the flower-patterned carpet, not wanting to meet my eyes. "I did take it about a week ago. I knew it had something to do with dragon magic, but I didn't know what. I haven't told anyone about it because I didn't want to lose my chance."

"Your chance. Your chance for what?" I ask, my dragon and I alert for anything.

"To become a diamond dragon, like you." Her face lights up with a huge smile as she looks at me.

Tucker immediately pipes in. "Should I tell her, or do you want to, babe?"

"Shhh, Tucker. Sophie, I'm sorry—but the magic doesn't work that way."

Her smile falls. "No, that isn't true. I can be a diamond dragon, I just know it. I think you're amazing, and I want to be just like you. Please... you have to show me how."

I feel for her, but I don't have time for this right now. "Look, just bring me the orb. I promise I'll compensate you."

She looks at the posters of me on her wall, like she's contemplating what she wants to ask me for. The blonde girl turns her attention back to me. "Will you take me with you?"

"I'm sorry, Sophie. It's not that I don't want to take you with me, it's just not physically possible right now." I may have just given her some information I didn't want to. She could read between the lines and figure out that a dragon war is coming. "Tell me where the orb is, please?"

A familiar voice calls to us from outside, making every muscle in my body tense. "Oh, Rory, want to come out and play?"

Diesel.

Damn it.

I shake my head in disbelief. How did he even know we were here?

I turn my gaze back toward Sophie, and I'm disturbed by the knowing smile that's on her face. "Diesel is working with me," she tells us.

Her voice sounds older, more knowledgeable than it did moments ago.

What the hell is going on?

Drew and Flynn step over to peek out the top corners of the large window.

"Yeah, it's the sadistic asshole all right," Drew confirms.

I keep my eyes trained on Sophie, because all of my suspicions that this was a trap are confirmed. No way in hell I'm taking my eyes off her now.

And I'm glad I don't. I allow the heat to build in my hands as I prepare to use my magic against her.

Sophie jumps to her feet, and I can see the glow of magic pooling in her right hand. The nature of her magic is oddly familiar, and I can tell that it's old. Ancient.

Her lips turn upward in a sultry smile. The knowing look on her face is more than I can stand.

"Are you an Oracle?" I ask.

She responds in a voice that grates on my soul. "Dragon vessel, that is no way to speak to the high priestess of the gods."

Is this woman seriously telling me that she is Anastasia Harris? It can't be. We've been looking for her since we accessed the mural room of Ashgrave.

"What do you want?"

The woman's face starts melting, like wax as it drips down the sides of a taper candle. The high priestess of the gods starts to grow taller as she's enveloped in a blue ball of magic.

"Child, you brazenly defy them, stealing what doesn't belong to you. I will bring you to the gods myself—it's time for them to finally awaken."

CHAPTER TWENTY-NINE

When the blinding blue light clears from my line of sight, a tall blonde that looks to be around thirty years old with royal blue magic shining from her eyes glares at me. She's dressed in black robes and stands in the middle of the quaint living room.

My men and Flynn take defensive fighting stances, while Ashgrave's head swivels, looking at me and then Anastasia. My castle is confused by the magic the high priestess wields. It's similar to mine. To his former mistress's. My evil butler is trying to figure out who to attack.

I place my hands in front of me and form magical daggers in each of them, throwing the knives at the tall woman in front of me as fast as I form them. One hits her in the stomach and then another, causing her to double over. Good.

Anastasia throws herself behind the couch as a loud bang comes from the front door of the small home. Diesel and his Spectres are trying to break down the bright red wooden door.

"Go. Take care of him and his men. I'll handle her!" I shout over the crashing sound of the battering ram.

Drew, Levi, and Flynn grab their guns from their holsters and nod. They know what to do. Tucker crouches low and puts together an AR-57 from the pieces of the weapon he produces from the many pockets of his vest. He blows me a kiss, and they all race to the foyer.

I know they can handle Diesel. They're all warriors in their own way.

As I watch the brown hair of Tucker's head disappear around the corner, I secretly hope they bring me back Diesel's head—or at least the bio-weapon. A woman can always hope.

Ashgrave makes a loud whirring sound as he flies closer to me. He hovers around the room, watching both of us for a sign of who he should attack.

As I watch my evil little metallic butler flutter through the room, Anastasia sends a blue blast of magic at me. It hits me in the ribs and knocks the wind out of me. I roll behind the other couch and search for the high priestess.

I spot the top of her blonde head moving across the floor as she moves deeper into the house. As she makes it into the hallway, moving away from the front of the house, I throw two more magical knives at her, and both of them sink into her left shoulder blade before disappearing. The high priestess rolls onto her side, searching for me. She forms a blue ball of magic and throws it at my face. I fling myself sideways and notice that Ashgrave is still in the living room, flying in a circle and muttering to himself. Who knew the ancient castle could talk quietly?

Another blast of magic hits the wall near my head, and I tuck myself into a ball and roll into the closest room. It's a dining room that's connected to a small kitchen with sage green cabinets and white appliances. I stop near the island in the middle of the kitchen and look around its corner. I spy Anastasia opening a door. I throw a blast of magic at her and it hits her in the right shoulder.

A familiar feeling suddenly comes over me. I

sense it. The orb is singing to me. It feels like when I was looking for Ashgrave and he talked to me. His voice lit my soul up with happiness. This is the same, but the only thing that's different is there isn't a voice. A humming vibration resonates through me that sounds like a song written for my heart. It has my dragon cooing with happiness.

The orb is here. It's somewhere in this house.

I roll into the kitchen and watch as Anastasia tries to open a door and crawl into a small bedroom to recuperate. I stand and stalk toward her. I grab her feet, flip her onto her back, and sit on her chest, straddling her. My knuckles bounce off her face as the snap of breaking bones fills the air.

I'm suddenly thrown through the air by a burst of magic. My body hits the white granite counter top of the peninsula and it crumbles from the impact.

The high priestess is going to pay for that.

I hurry toward her again. This time, my hands fill with magic. I'm pulling every ounce of energy I have into my hands, arms, and shoulders. My power flares and then wavers, but I pull it back. I don't have time for a power surge. Not now.

Out of the corner of my eye, I watch Ashgrave hover toward me. His flight falters as I blast Anastasia.

Spots blot my vision, and I reach out to catch myself before I fall.

Ashgrave's little metallic body is under my arm supporting me.

A singing vibration hums through my mind—my soul.

The orb.

Levi comes around the corner of the hallway and rushes toward me, and he places his hand on my face.

Are you okay? He asks through our bond. *There was a blinding flash of light and Diesel and his men retreated out of the house.*

I'll be fine. I reassure him. His ice blue eyes are searching my body for injuries. *I think I might have used most of my power though. The orb is here, Levi. I can feel it.*

"Drew, Tucker, Flynn this way!" Levi shouts.

"ARE YOU WELL, MISTRESS?" Ashgrave asks. "THAT WOMAN HOLDS THE SAME MAGIC AS YOU, AS THE GODS. IT CONFUSED ME FOR A MOMENT. I AM SORRY. IT WILL NOT HAPPEN AGAIN, MY QUEEN."

The whisper of light footsteps comes from the front of the house.

Diesel.

I know where the orb is. It's calling to me like Ashgrave did.

I stand up and brush myself off.

"Come on. This way."

CHAPTER THIRTY

The harmonic song pulls me through the little house. I walk to the back of the small cottage, driven by the song inside my soul. As I open a wooden door to a set of rickety stairs, my heart bounces with happiness.

The orb is so close I can almost taste its magic. I can feel it.

The happy song guides me down the stairs. My men, Flynn, and Ashgrave are close behind. When I get to the bottom of the stairs, there's a locked wooden door. I put my hands in front of me and let the magic pool in them.

Drew rushes past me, using his massive shoulder as a battering ram, and runs into the door, breaking the lock. "A little muscle works just as good as magic," Drew says, winking. "And, you just about knocked yourself out the last time you used your magic. Muscle seems like the safer choice."

"Thanks, Drew. I can always count on you for muscle." I can't hide my excitement.

A rotting stench assaults our noses as we open the door.

In the corner of the large unfinished basement, behind the door, lies a crumpled body with long blonde hair.

Sophie Marchand.

Anastasia killed her. But why? Couldn't she have just locked her up? The high priestess is as dark as her masters. They're all willing to kill to get what they want.

I bow my head and hope Sophie didn't suffer in her last moments. My disdain for the high priestess grows ten-fold in that moment.

The orb's harmonic song is even louder as I walk across the dirt floor of the cinder block room.

I reach the center and close my eyes and allow the happy song to lead me to the orb. The harmonic vibration is so loud that it feels like it's shaking my brain, and I open my eyes. In front of me stands a door to a tiny root cellar. I open the small square door, and pink light floods the basement.

The orb.

I lift the crystal object and admire the way the pink lights dance inside the ball. The happy vibration has my soul singing with joy.

The thundering of boots on the floors overhead tells me that Diesel and his men have regrouped after their skirmish with my men. The Ghost and his Spectres are coming.

I put the orb in the inside pocket of my jacket, near my heart, and search for a way out. The door we entered the basement through is the only direct way in or out. There are no windows, and only a light that hangs in the center of the large room.

Levi, Flynn, and Tucker push old furniture from the far left corner of the basement to barricade the closed door. Drew pushes the washer in front of it too.

"I WILL DESTROY ANYONE WHO DARES TO COME NEAR YOU, MY QUEEN."

Nice to see Ashgrave back to his normal, murderous self.

"How the hell are we going to get out of here?" Tucker asks.

"We could try and bring down the floor on the far side of the house. I'm sure you have a gun that'll work, Tucker," Flynn answers.

"We want to get out, not be crushed by a falling house," I say. "You don't know the types of guns Tucker has in that vest. I bet you have Betty in there, don't you, babe?"

"Ah, shucks. You know me so well."

"Who the hell is Betty?" Flynn and Drew ask at the same time.

"I'll show you later," Tucker says with a wink. "She can't help us now. We're fighting humans, and Rory's right, she would bring the whole house down on our heads."

Out of the corner of my eye, I spy Levi kicking at the outer walls of the basement, shaking his head.

"Levi, do you have an idea to get us out of here?" I ask while Drew adds the dryer to the barricade.

"I was thinking if Drew and I combine our powers, we could possibly wash away enough of one of the support walls. But we'd have to shift for that to happen, and that could kill Tucker. I won't do anything to hurt my brother."

Tucker runs over and throws an arm around my ice dragon. "I love you too, man." Levi just shakes his head at Tucker's antics with a smile on his face.

My men—they are brothers. They're chosen brothers.

"Maybe I can try to burst it open with my

magic?" Flynn asks, shrugging. "But I'd have to shift too, and that could bring us too much trouble in a human zone."

Creaking footsteps come down the stairs, and we all spread out and take fighting stances and pull out our weapons. Ashgrave hovers in front of us, ready to destroy anyone who comes through the door.

A blast of royal blue magic turns our barricade to ash and knocks my hovering little metal dragon into the wall behind us.

Anastasia walks through the hole in the wall and stops. Her eyes are full of hatred and spite as she stares me down.

Diesel tries to push past the high priestess, but she stands her ground.

"Rory Quinn will die today. I'll be crossing your name off my list tonight, little girl." Diesel aims an anti-dragon gun at my chest.

Anastasia elbows Diesel in the head, and he drops his gun.

"Shut the hell up, you imbecile. Go back to the doorway, and stay there until I request your assistance." She turns around and points her index finger at me. "And you, you need to fulfill your role as the dragon vessel. You are but a vessel of the dragon gods' magic. The power you possess is not yours to keep—the power is not yours to wield as you see fit. It belongs to the gods. Give it back. Now!" She bellows so loudly that the support beams in the ceiling above us shake, raining dust and plaster down on us all.

"This power is mine now. I'll never give it back to the gods. They only used it to bring darkness, death, and chaos. I plan on using it to change the world for the better. I'm going to show the world true light," I tell Anastasia. "There is no way in hell anyone but me will ever wield this power again. I'll die before I hand it over willingly."

Diesel picks his anti-dragon gun up from the floor and knocks the high priestess to the side with the butt of it. He aims it at my head. "Say bye-bye, Rory."

Anastasia sends a trickle of blue magic into Diesel's back and causes him to spasm and fall to his knees on the dirt floor.

The Ghost pulls himself up using his gun and stares into her eyes.

"Control your thirst for vengeance. You can't kill her. I need her in one piece if I'm going to save my masters' magic."

"I don't give two shits about magic or vessels. That girl needs to die."

"I would think the Ghost of the Spectres would be a patient man, not someone who's short sighted and zealous. Do you fear her existence that much?"

"Oh, lady. I don't know who you're talking to but you need to shut the fuck up. Now!" Diesel yells in Anastasia's face, sending spittle onto her cheeks and eyelashes.

Diesel's only desire is to be the Ghost, but as long as Irena and I are alive, his position will always be challenged. Many Spectres have already abandoned him for Irena's rebel group because they see her as their true leader—not him. He's also a sadistic asshole, but right now, he's the unwitting ally I never wanted. He's going to get me and my men out of here alive.

The sound of metal scraping against metal has me hoping my murderous castle is okay. Ashgrave's wings flutter as he flies in front of me and meets my gaze. I put a finger to my lips, and my little metal dragon gives me a small nod as he hovers to my side.

I grab Levi's hand. *We have to use this to our advantage. When I give the signal, tell Flynn to duck. I'm going to blast a hole in the outer wall, using my magic. I'll have Drew protect Tucker from the shrapnel.*

He gives me a wink and silently moves over toward Flynn.

I look at Drew. His eyes are trained on mine. I glance at Tucker then meet Drew's eyes again. My fire dragon gives me a small nod. He understands that I want him to protect Tucker. I love Drew. He's a man who knows strategy. I'll have to show him how much I appreciate that fact when we get out of here.

Diesel brings up his huge gun and hits Anastasia in the forehead with the butt of it. She stumbles, but she doesn't fall down. Instead, she forms a ball of magic and tosses it at the Ghost. It hits him in the chest and causes him to fly to the far side of the room, crashing into the wall. A small package wrapped in brown paper falls from his pocket from the impact, and it rolls on the ground near my feet.

The bio-weapon.

It has to be. I know Diesel trusts no one but himself with it.

I take a chance that it's the bio-weapon and send a small blast of magic into it.

A grey mist rises slowly from the hole in the brown paper wrapping.

Diesel looks at me. "You'll die for that, Rory. I'll make sure of it." Diesel pushes past Anastasia as he and the Spectres run up the stairs, retreating. They flee the area in order to put as much distance as possible between the bio-weapon and themselves.

The Oracle aims her magic at the package leaking deadly mist into the air. Her power flares as it envelopes the growing grey mist. She screws up her face in concentration as she holds the poison at bay.

While Anastasia is occupied with the bio-weapon, I face her and form my magical daggers in my hands. My men and Flynn surround the high priestess, taking fighting stances and aiming their guns at her. My bloodthirsty castle hovers near my head. I throw my daggers, my metallic castle fires his magic, and the men rain bullets down on her at the same time. She forms a blue shield around her, and I allow the daggers to disappear and blast her with a steady stream of my magic.

Her shield holds as we continue to bombard her. Ashgrave and I, along with my men, continue to shoot at her. Tucker hits the release switch for the ammunition clip on his rifle and quickly replaces it with a new one. We can't keep firing at her like this for much longer. I need an idea.

Searching the area for something, anything, I look at her feet. We're all standing on dirt. I think back to the ways Jace taught me how to keep my concentration on the battle at hand, and the things he did to throw me off. My mate loved to knock me over to break my concentration so he could win. I change the direction of my magical stream. I aim for the ground beneath her feet, and her shield starts to waver. The blue shield collapses entirely as the high priestess loses her footing on the crumbling ground.

Ashgrave and I blast Anastasia in the chest and she collapses on the floor. She's struggling to breathe and barely able to move. She must've used a great deal of strength to dissolve the bio-weapon mist.

My men are panting and catching their breath. I bend over placing my hands on my knees to catch mine too, thankful for my mate and his training.

Levi approaches the south wall of the house and draws an imaginary X with his finger near the ceiling. He walks up to put his hand on my shoulder. Drew slides over to stand behind Tucker as Ashgrave circles my head, and I give a nod to Flynn.

Flynn throws himself to the floor, covering his head with his hands as Drew pushes Tucker to the floor. Levi kneels on the floor behind me as I blast the imaginary X with my power, and the wall explodes outward.

Drew covers Tucker with his huge body while

Ashgrave instantly burns the pieces of cinder block, plaster, or wood that comes near me to ash.

I cough as dust and smoke fly up my nose, and I brush myself off with my hands. My head swivels on my shoulders as I search the area to make sure my men, Flynn, and Ashgrave are okay.

My little steampunk castle is hovering around my head, waiting to see what he can smite next. The feel of fingers grabbing my waist lets me know Levi is behind me. Flynn pulls himself to his feet, coughing.

"Get off of me, Drew. Damn dude, you're going to smother me." Tucker pushes my fire dragon off him. "I'm too pretty to be squished," he says as he wipes the dust off his face and my fire dragon shakes his head, trying to hide the smile on his face.

Levi approaches the hole and starts moving the loose blocks away. Drew shimmies his way out of the damaged wall and steps aside so the rest of us can get out. Flynn crawls out next and puts his hand back through the hole to help Tucker. Ashgrave hovers through after my weapons expert. Levi gives me a boost, and I climb out. While I move to the side and observe the neighborhood, Levi exits the basement. We're all on alert—our muscles are tense and our ears are perked, listening for sirens.

The neighborhood is still silent. The only sounds are coming from us. I wonder if Anastasia murdered the neighbors. Probably, since she has no morals. Just like her masters. An entire neighborhood gone, because of selfishness.

As we rush over to the dark sedan we came here in, Ashgrave hovers close behind me, and Drew runs ahead. He runs straight for the body of Jakobe, our driver, whose corpse lies on the ground. The body is sprawled on the asphalt near the driver's side of the car. Jakobe's lifeless eyes stare at the sky. My castle flies over to Drew and we rush to follow him.

"He was a good guy," Drew says, placing a hand on Jakobe's forehead and bowing his head slightly. "We trained together from the time we were eleven. We will take care of his family, then. It's the least we can do."

"Should we take him with us?" Tucker asks.

"No. He wouldn't want us to put ourselves at risk. It just wasn't his way." Drew moves the body of his fallen friend out of the way and gets into the car, holding up the key fob. "Let's go home."

CHAPTER THIRTY-ONE

The orange glow of the sunrise washes over the chopper as we land on the helipad at Castle Ashgrave. My cheeks hurt from smiling. There are smiles on all of our faces—maybe even on my small metal dragon's. It's hard to tell, but he flutters his metal wings a little faster as he hovers near the door of the helicopter.

Tucker flips the switches that turn off the blades and turns around with a smirk on his face. "That went well. We have the orb, and we also got the bioweapon away from Diesel. Thanks to Anastasia, the grey mist was dissipated so it couldn't hurt anyone."

"But, I'm sure Diesel is planning to get more. The lab is still standing." I shake my head to get rid of the thought. I don't want anything to bring me down from this feeling of joy.

We have the third orb.

Drew opens the chopper's door as we all unbuckle and stand from our seats. Flynn gives Tucker a hi-five as he helps him gather weapons from the storage bins of the helicopter.

A soft brush of fingertips across my bare neck has the special connection between me and Levi opening. *You were amazing back there,* he says in my mind and places a gentle kiss on the back of my neck.

I grab his hand. *You were pretty amazing yourself. I couldn't have put a hole in that wall without your X.*

Aw, shucks.

You've been hanging around with Tucker too long. You're starting to sound like him, I joke as I help Flynn with a bag that he's juggling.

"Thanks, Rory," he says. "I got it now."

Jace runs up to us and places a kiss on my forehead. "Drew said you have the orb. When can we put it in its domain?"

Drew's gaze meets mine. "Now? I think we should do it now."

"Let's go get our metallic dragon army." I shake

my head and stifle the chuckle sneaking out with the back of my hand.

Tucker places the two bags he's carrying on the wooden bench just inside the front door, and Flynn adds the bag he's carrying to the pile.

"Do you want me to join you, or put these away?" Flynn asks.

"You can join us. You're the colonel of the army."

"Thank you, Jace. I'll work hard to make you all proud." Flynn smiles as a slight blush tints his cheeks.

"Ashgrave, can you show us to the Army domain, please?"

"THIS WAY, MY QUEEN." My castle thunders as the wall under the stone staircase opens.

Drew and Jace walk into the tunnel first, talking about how exciting it'll be to have an army of metal dragons to protect our home. Levi and I follow, and we can't seem to wipe the huge smiles from our faces. Tucker and Flynn take up the end of our exciting procession, mumbling about the differences between a metal dragon and a tank.

A stairway solidifies in front of my men and we all follow it downward as stone and earth rumble around us. It sounds like my castle is magically reforming itself around us. The soft glow of magic lights our way as we trek through the magic tunnel toward the Army domain in the east end of the castle.

I can't believe that the Oracle was planning on simply handing me over to the dragon gods. The very same gods who threatened me in my vision not long ago. Morgana, Caelen, and Razorus are really coming for me. They want me to give them my power.

My dragon paces and stretches her wings in my mind as I think about the dragon gods and their threats. She's growing—we're getting stronger—both of us. We're almost as strong as the gods themselves. But I'm barely becoming comfortable with wearing the mantle of queen, and goddess is on a whole other level.

The dark words of Esmeralda's diary flood my mind. The chaos magic that enables Morgana to spread negative emotions like a tidal wave. The death magic of Caelen that kills with a single touch. And the trickster magic of Razorus, who has the ability to create illusions that drive people crazy. They're coming for my power, all of it.

My men and I need to be prepared for when the

gods' servant, Anastasia, makes another move. I figure she will strike again soon, because with the coming dragon war, time is running out.

The wall in front of us opens into a large roofed stone courtyard whose surfaces are lined with huge steel weapons that bang against their supports as a wind kicks up from nowhere. My men and I shield our face from the onslaught of air, and I continue to search the yard for the Army domain. In the center of the patio is a dry fountain in the shape of a bowl with an indent in its center. That has to be it.

As I pull the orb out of my jacket pocket, the wind stops blowing. I leave my men, who are admiring the weapons on the walls, and approach the bowl. I gently place the orb in the indent in the center of the fountain.

The pink orb turns blood red as it floats in the center of the fountain, and I take a few steps backward. I can't help the nervousness that floods through me at the thought that I'm taking a risk handing even more power and abilities to Ashgrave. If the gods do manage to come back, my murderous magical castle may obey them and not me.

Gears turn, and the castle shudders as the ground beneath our feet shakes. A pit opens in the floor across from us. The fountain that holds the glowing red orb sinks into the floor, and the ground quakes. A massive steampunk dragon sticks its head out of the pit and breathes a huge plume of fire into the air.

Tucker puts together Betty, as Drew, Levi, and Jace spread out, getting ready to shift.

I hope I made the right decision. By giving Ashgrave an army, I might've brought on our deaths and the deaths of everyone in the castle.

"Ashgrave, Jace is the general of our army and they are his soldiers to command."

"AS YOU WISH, MY QUEEN."

The stone ceiling folds back on itself and we're instantly surrounded by a cloud of bees. Not live bees, but little metallic bees that keep bouncing into us like they're all trying to be close to us at the same time.

"WOULD YOU AND THE GENERAL LIKE TO INSPECT THE ARSENAL, MY QUEEN?"

"Arsenal? Now you're speaking my language, steampunk. Hell yes, we want to check it out. All of it." Tucker says.

"YOU ARE NOT THE GENERAL, PUNY HUMAN. THE GENERAL IS JACE GOODWIN."

I can't hold my chuckle in. Tucker and my castle

are still rubbing each other the wrong way. "Lead the way, Ashgrave."

The wall to the left opens up into a large room filled with all kinds of medieval weapons lining the walls and resting on wood tables. Jace and Flynn snap their gazes to each other.

"There's thunderbird magic in these weapons. It's lying just below their surfaces, but I can feel it. How about you, Flynn?" My mate takes a battle axe from the wall closest to him.

Flynn nods, picking up an ancient dagger from the table. "I can feel it too. It's shaky, but it's there."

As the thunderbirds' hands connect with the weapons, they glow with blue and silver light.

Levi observes Jace and Flynn with a smile on his face, while Drew gazes at the magic flowing through the weapons. Tucker's mouth takes on the shape of an O.

"This looks like it will turn the tide in our favor. We need to equip the soldiers we have with these."

The men all nod in agreement, still shocked by the presence of magically charged weapons.

"Ashgrave, please give word to the dragons who live inside your walls to meet us in the armory in an hour. Tell them we have new weapons for them."

"RIGHT AWAY, MY QUEEN."

"Tucker, Levi, and Drew, can you please get some of these weapons ready and take them to the armory for our soldiers? Flynn and Jace, be sure to touch as many of them as possible so they're charged and ready to be used, please."

"You had me at weapons, babe."

"My rebels are going to love these. Thanks, Rory." Flynn runs his hand over the weapons on the surface of the table.

Levi walks behind Flynn gathering the silver glowing weapons in a duffle bag he unfolds from one of his jacket pockets and gives me a wink. Jace paces around the large room, touching the weapons that hang on the walls, making them glow blue. Drew follows him, taking the glowing swords, battle axes, and maces off the wall and stacks them according to the style of weapon along the far wall.

"Ashgrave, can you make more of these weapons for Irena and Harper, please?"

"AT ONCE, MY QUEEN."

I take out my phone and dial Irena's number to give her a heads-up, but there's no answer. I figure my sister is still off in the mountains deep in solitude, stubbornly practicing to control her newfound dragon magic on her own.

"I'm going to go check in on Brett, Rory. I need to see if anything new has popped up. To make sure Anastasia's magic deactivated the bio-weapon and no one was infected by it. We need to make sure Diesel doesn't get his hands on more. The lab is still standing, so he's still a huge threat," Drew says. "I've been gathering more intel on the Vaer and it looks like they're planning something big. I want to make sure we're ready for them." He kisses my forehead before leaving the room.

Flynn and Tucker follow with their arms full of magically charged weapons. Levi puts his arms through the straps of the duffle bag and centers it in the middle of his back before grabbing several maces from the floor.

Jace organizes more of the weapons he's charged, and I walk up behind him and put my arms around his waist. "You finally have the army you wanted. What are you going to do next?"

"Make it worthy of my queen," he says.

After making sure that all of our soldiers are armed with magical weapons, I call Harper and leave a message on her voicemail, letting her know that we have some "special weapons" for her and her army, and they can be picked up from Ashgrave at her earliest convenience.

Drew and Brett are searching through the encrypted Vaer intel, trying to figure out Kinsley's next move. Flynn is taking his appointment as colonel seriously by training our army to use the thunderbird magic in their weapons.

In the early afternoon sun, Jace, Levi, and I fly in our dragon forms through the beautiful mountains that surround my bloodthirsty castle. Tucker is tailing us in his jet, doing barrel rolls. I figure since we've been using the chopper so often for our missions that he would be excited to switch it up and fly the jet.

The sun warms my scales as I watch my weapons expert play chicken with my mate. Levi, as usual, scans the area for any possible threat.

Jace pulls his wings in close to his body and charges at the cockpit of Tucker's jet. A snuffling sound escapes my dragon lips as I laugh at the silliness of my men.

A bolt of ice crashes into the mountain across from us and we look at my ice dragon. Jace pulls up from his charge and Tucker slows the speed of his jet. Levi rushes to my side, extending his front claw.

I touch his claw with mine. *We have company,* he says through our bond. *Jets are approaching. I'll keep Tucker safe.*

Four black fighter jets fire at Tucker's plane, and Levi blasts two of them out of the air with a large ice stream. He covers Tucker and follows him back toward Ashgrave's landing strip.

Jace and I blast the remaining jets with our magic. The jet hit by Jace spirals from the sky and crashes below us, sending up a plume of smoke. The plane I hit rams into the mountain side and explodes.

My dragon is pissed that someone would disturb us so close to our borders while we spent time with our men, and she is searching the surrounding hills and valleys for more trespassers. Out of the corner of my eye, I watch Jace do the same.

My mate lets loose an earsplitting roar that draws my gaze to where he's searching the snow covered hills. Ground troops tread through the snow, and an intimidating swarm of Vaer and Nabal dragons head straight toward us. Their leader is a massive white dragon with glowing green eyes —Kinsley.

Shit! I figure this is Kinsley's idea of something

big. She's bringing the battle to us, but she doesn't know that we have an army.

Jace and I fly back toward our borders as fast as possible. We're not retreating—we're going to gather our forces.

Time to kick some ass.

CHAPTER THIRTY-TWO

When we land in Ashgrave's front courtyard, Harper, Russell, and over six hundred Fairfax dragons are standing in a battle formation. Flynn, his rebels, and the newly added dojo soldiers file into formation next to them, while Levi and Drew pace in front of them in their dragon forms.

Jade and Brett run out into the courtyard, followed closely by Tucker and his favorite anti-dragon gun, Betty.

Harper, in her beautiful purple dragon form, breaks formation and approaches me, extending her wing. *We came to pick up and train with our 'special weapons,' when Tucker told us you were attacked. I'm just glad we're here to help with the fight,* she tells me.

Payton and his troops are on the way. Brett informed them that they're needed.

I'm glad you're here, I respond.

"THE ASHGRAVE DRAGON ARMY IS FORM-ING, GENERAL. WOULD YOU LIKE ME TO SMITE ALL WHO TRESSPASS ON MY LANDS, MY QUEEN?" My little steampunk dragon's voice booms as he hovers between Harper and me.

I shake my head no. The Palarne army is on its way, and I don't want them killed by mistake.

The creaking of metal and the earth-shaking footsteps of something very large comes from the east side of the castle. Hundreds of giant metallic dragons move toward us, firing plumes of magical fire into the air.

Jace shifts to his human form and steps next to me. Harper steps back to her place in the large battle formation. She's not the Boss here. I am. And my mate is my general.

Jace addresses the army in a loud, clear voice. "We are no longer Flynn's rebels, Jace's dojo soldiers, Ashgrave's metallic dragon army, or the Fairfax army—we are Queen Rory's forces. Our queen stands for what's right, and it's of the utmost impor-tance to protect those who cannot protect them-selves. This is not just about defending Castle

Ashgrave from intruders. We must also stand against the destruction of Ash Town and any of the villages that are in the path of the advancing enemy forces. The Vaer, Nabal, and Bane will not have access to this castle or its magic. We will make them pay for attempting to usurp our queen."

"For Queen Rory!" Tucker shouts.

The entire army roars in response as Jace shifts back into his glorious thunderbird form, and I step back to admire him. He was made for this—to be the general of an incredible army.

Still in my dragon form, I approach Tucker and press my forehead against his chest. *You're going to get back into your jet, aren't you?*

"You know I am, babe. I want to join the fun. Levi and I already have a plan. Don't worry your pretty head about me," he assures me as he kisses the tip of my dragon nose. My weapons expert turns and runs to get back into his plane with Levi following behind him silently.

Jade places her hand on my leg. *I want to fight, Rory. You said yourself that I'm strong, so let me prove it. Brett can stay in the castle, keeping an eye on the fight in the surveillance room and inform Payton where his help is needed when he gets here,* she says with no hint of a smile on her face.

Brett must have told her that he suspects the Nabal have allied with Kinsley. Jade's words from our conversation days ago enter my mind. *"I don't want to be a burden or a charity case."* The young woman wants to show that she's useful to us.

I give her a quick nod of my head and Jade shifts and joins the formation. My anger at Kinsley burns through me as I roar into the sky, signaling my army to head into battle.

Jace and I pump our wings as we take off into the sky with our forces, and my little metallic castle follows behind us.

As we approach the northern border, a blast of fire nicks one of my horns and has me losing some height. Jace remains near me and pulls up. Our army spreads out, firing their magic at the oncoming enemy, forcing them further away from Ashgrave's border.

The huge metallic dragons unleash their magical fire onto hundreds of Vaer fighters, turning a few hundred of the dragons to ash instantly.

Russell, Harper, and the Fairfax soldiers break off and attack the Vaer fire and ice dragons, blasting them with their thunderbird magic. A black dragon hits Harper with a blast of ice, causing my friend to crash into the mountain side. Russell is by her side instantly, standing over her as she shakes off the blast.

Jade and Drew break away and blast the ground soldiers who are shooting at us with anti-dragon guns. They destroy six of the ten huge ground-to-air guns. Jade gets knocked out of the sky by one of the remaining guns. I send a blast of my magic into the gun's giant barrel, and it explodes into a fireball, taking out two more of the deadly guns. One left.

The high-pitched whistle of a missile screams through the air, and the last anti-dragon gun flies into the sky, flipping and tumbling, until it crashes into the valley below. I turn to check on Tucker, and I'm hit in the back with a blast of ice. The ice freezes my wings instantly, and I start to plummet to the ground like a rock.

I roll over onto my back and tuck myself into a ball to absorb the impact as much as possible. Snow, ice, grass, rocks, and trees scrape my scales as I push my claws into the soil to slow myself down. A white dragon with glowing green eyes circles above me. Kinsley.

As I push myself to my feet, the Vaer Boss lands near me. She sticks the tip of her wing out toward me, asking me to talk to her. I growl low in response, and she throws herself at me, pinning my back to a large oak tree. The bark scratches my scales, and I snap at her face, biting the top of her nose.

Kinsley opens the connection between us as her blood drips down the side of her face. *Rory, you don't deserve the power you have nor the opportunity of becoming a goddess. You're just a thief. The dragon gods are still alive and they'll never allow you to keep their power.*

Look who's calling who a thief, I laugh in her face. *Kinsley, your opinion doesn't count. Especially not to me.*

My opinion matters a lot to the news agencies I own. Be careful, little Spectre. You don't want me on your bad side. You've already seen what public opinion can do.

I slam my head into her face, and she drops the connection. Kinsley returns the favor and hits me in the side with her tail, knocking the breath out of me.

As I fight for air, green ice magic pools in her throat. I throw my large dragon body to the side to escape the blast of ice aimed for my chest. The ground I was just standing on freezes over. Not giving me a second to get to my feet, Kinsley blasts me with her magic, and spots dance in front of my eyes. Hell that hurt. I can't take another shot like that.

Two huge steampunk dragons land in snow

behind Kinsley. "GET TO SAFETY, MY QUEEN," my castle's booming voice demands.

The massive metal dragons fire at the Vaer Boss and she turns to fight them. She pools her magic and fires it at the dragons, hitting the one on her left in the claw. It falls over without a claw to balance on, but a new one starts to grow back instantly.

I pull myself up and catch my breath, and my vision clears. I'm not leaving. I refuse to run away. This is my fight, and I have to see it through.

Kinsley has no idea who she's messing with. But she's about to find out exactly who I am and meet my power first-hand.

CHAPTER THIRTY-THREE

The earth shakes as the massive metal dragon summons its magic and blasts it at Kinsley. She falls to the ground and grabs at her left leg, trying to stem the flow of blood pouring through. The Vaer Boss roars in pain and takes to the sky to escape the steampunk dragons of Ashgrave.

The flap of dragon wings has me searching the sky, and I spot a black thunderbird with silver magic flying overhead with a troop of golden dragons following him in tight formation. Flynn and a small group of rebel Andusk dragons are heading west, toward Ash Town. A few of the golden dragons roar out in pain as they're hit by blasts of fire. Flynn flips in the air and tucks his wings to charge the troop of black Nabal dragons that snuck up behind them.

The thunderbird's silver magic blasts five of the Nabal soldiers near the front of the rapidly advancing group, causing them to drop to the ground dead.

Trees slam to the ground on my left and I observe a huge silver dragon slam his shoulder into a black dragon with spikes that resemble black ice, pushing the Bane Boss back into the forest as he slams the end of his black-striped barbed tail across the fallen dragon's stomach. Victor roars in pain as the hole in his abdomen drenches the ground beneath him with blood. Payton gives me a wink as he takes to the air to continue the battle.

I shoot a blast of my magic at a group of three Vaer soldiers that fly overhead, and they all tumble to the valley below, dead. As the battle rages on, my heart pangs with dread at the thought that I haven't seen my men for a while. My eyes search my surroundings. I have to find my men. My *family.*

A jet's screaming engine has me scanning the skies for my weapons expert in his favorite toy. I spy the white fog that the plane leaves in its wake followed closely by my fire and ice dragons as they battle fifty Vaer soldiers together. Drew blasts fire at the outside of the enemy soldiers' formation while Levi sends a stream of ice into its center. The Vaer formation scatters. My mate and Jade drop from the clouds and start to blast their magic at the Vaer as they retreat.

My men are fighting the enemy together, and they've added the ex-Nabal to their ranks. My family is fine. They're together.

I spread my beautiful diamond wings and take to the air. Time to end this. I need to find Kinsley.

"YOU ARE NOT PERMITTED TO ENTER MY WALLS, KINSLEY VAER!" My evil butler's voice booms from the massive steampunk dragons waging war near the castle.

The Vaer Boss is trying to breach the castle walls, and I have to stop her. As I flap my wings harder, my speed increases, and I search the ground over the army's outdoor training area for her.

An earsplitting roar of pain comes from the front courtyard of my castle, causing me to increase the beat of my wings and head toward the center of Castle Ashgrave.

When I get to the front of the ancient castle, I find Ashgrave's cat sized metal dragon firing at the white dragon with glowing green eyes. Kinsley rolls forward, sending pieces of marble from the fountain that stands in the center of the football-field sized courtyard flying through the air. She turns onto her back and releases a stream of ice at my castle's little body. Ashgrave deflects the blow with a blasts of his magic, but the Vaer Boss doesn't let up. She blasts his right wing with ice and freezes it instantly. The small steampunk dragon falls from the sky like a rock as I rush to catch his metallic body in my claws. I place his little body on the ground gently and take off into the sky again. She could have hurt him. Who the hell does she think she is? This is my castle.

My diamond dragon pierces the air with an angry roar. She's pissed. Hell, we're both pissed.

I tuck my wings tight to my body and dive for Kinsley. I don't even try to slow down as I collide with the massive white dragon who's trying to break into my home. She drags her front claw across my cheek, causing blood to well up from my face. She's going to pay for that. The Vaer Boss damaged my scales and made me bleed.

As an angry roar escapes from my mouth, making the whole courtyard shake, I pin her to the hard stone floor. This needs to end. Now.

Kinsley's muscular tail swings toward my head and I duck. As I shift my weight to get away from the battering tail, she throws her massive weight to the left side, pitching me off her. The force of the throw has me sliding across the ground and into the base of the castle steps where my head slams against the marble. I fight the darkness trying to pull me under as I attempt to rise from the cold hard stone. My magic sparks and sizzles as it pools in my throat. But my body isn't listening. And neither is my magic. I can't move or access my magic. If she fires her magic at me, I'm dead.

An earth shaking roar signals a new dragon joining the fight.

Fan-freaking-tastic! Kinsley has another ally.

The new dragon's bronze scales glitter in the late afternoon sunlight as it stares down Kinsley. When the dragon turns its massive head to gaze at me, I notice its glowing green eyes, just like the Vaer Boss's.

I know those eyes. Irena. A swarm of thoughts, ideas, and questions about the woman I've known and loved for my entire life rush through my mind. The last time I saw her, she vowed to never shift. And now, she's charging into battle in her stunning bronze dragon form.

As Kinsley stands with her dragon mouth hanging open, she narrows her eyes at my sister, defiant as Irena's magic pools in her throat. The Vaer Boss ducks to the left, narrowly missing the blast of my sister's ice magic.

I pull myself off the hard ground and step up beside my sister as I fire a blast of magic at Kinsley, forcing her to back out of the courtyard. Irena sends another blast of ice magic toward the Vaer Boss's chest, but Kinsley ducks and the ice crashes into her already injured calf, causing blood to pour from it again.

The Vaer Boss searches the area and shakes her head as she notices that her soldiers' numbers are dwindling. Kinsley's leg leaks blood onto the ground, washing the area outside of Castle Ashgrave's front courtyard in bright red. She roars an order of retreat into the sky, and the skies surrounding my home fill with her remaining army.

An eruption of victorious roars fills the air. My mate is leading the procession of my family, followed closely by Drew on the left and Levi on the right, with Tucker in his plane in the middle and slightly behind the fire and ice dragons. Jade's white dragon glides behind my weapons expert. They fly in a formation that resembles a diamond.

As my men and Jade land, shaking the ground beneath my feet, Tucker flies off toward the landing strip.

Jace's eyes narrow as he rushes my sister. I put

my wing out to stop him and brush its tip against his chest. *It's Irena. She came to help.*

She shifted? He asks, shaking his head in confusion.

Tucker's feet slide across the stone as he comes to an abrupt stop. "Rory, did you see me explode those massive anti-dragon gu--?"

I silence his question by pressing my large forehead to his chest. *You did amazing, babe. I knew you would.*

"Hey, who is our new dragon friend?" Tucker asks.

As Levi approaches my sister, he lowers his head, so he doesn't startle or offend her. While Drew stands to my left shaking his big red head, Jade observes my ice dragon and Irena, standing tense and ready to jump into action if Levi needs backup.

"MAY THE ARMY OF ASHGRAVE RETIRE, MY QUEEN?" My murderous castle booms as he paces by my back claws.

My eyes search my mate's face for an answer. Jace is the general of my army, I figure it's his call. My thunderbird nods at me and an earsplitting roar erupts from my lips.

The over three hundred massive steampunk dragons converge like a metallic cloud on the east end of the crescent shaped castle and disappear from sight.

A silver bolt of thunderbird magic explodes the stone in front of my sister's feet, and my dragon rumbles in anger. How dare Flynn fire at my sister?

The black thunderbird and his golden rebels circle overhead as the only lavender thunderbird I know lands next to Jace and extends her wing to touch his. My mate is informing his cousin that Irena shifted. I can tell by the way her mouth drops open as she stares at my sister's bronze dragon form.

A thunderous bang echoes throughout the courtyard and has every set of eyes in the area looking at the ornate entry doors of my castle as they swing open.

"Gods, Ashgrave, the battle is over. So nice of you to finally let me out!" Brett bellows at my castle as his little metallic form paces at my feet.

"I AM RESOPONSIBLE FOR YOUR SAFETY. YOU WILL STAY INSIDE, UNTIL MY QUEEN ORDERS ME OTHERWISE, HUMAN."

Brett catches my gaze. "Will you please tell him that I'm allowed outside now?"

I notice Brett is carrying four huge duffle bags as I extend my claw to touch my little steampunk castle. *It's safe for him to come outside now.*

"FLYNN AND HIS REBELS ARE STILL FLYING IN A BATTLE FORMATION OVER- HEAD, MY QUEEN. HE ALSO JUST FIRED AT IRENA. DO YOU WANT ME TO SMITE HIM, MISTRESS?"

At my murderous castle's words, Flynn and his rebels land next to the new dojo soldiers. Flynn shifts his weight from foot to foot while his massive black head hangs so low that I'm afraid he's going to topple over.

My general roars the order to shift, and within minutes, we're all human again.

Harper's eyes are the first thing I notice as I shake my arms out. Her beautiful baby blues are still widened with shock as she stands in front of me. "What is up with you Quinn gir—"

Jace elbows his way past his cousin and envelopes me in his strong arms. "Thank you, Rory. I have a purpose again."

"Hey, you could at least say you're sorry," Harper quips with a smirk.

"Can we compare notes from the battle?" Jace asks Harper.

"Sure, as long as you stop pushing me around," she says, smiling. "I'll go get Russell and meet you and your colonel in the war room."

The Fairfax Boss looks at me. "Rory, this victory is yours. Enjoy it." She smiles. "Kinsley and her allies know she can't attack your home—your capital again."

Flynn, dressed in a set of sweat pants, approaches Irena with a pair of sweats that he retrieved from one of Brett's duffle bags. "I'm sorry I shot at you. I didn't know that you were a dragon."

"Thank you, Flynn. I didn't know I was a dragon either. I shifted for the first time last night."

A soft touch of fingertips on my left hip has me turning my head to look into Levi's ice blue eyes. *We're safe.*

Yes, we are. As I put my head on my master of stealth's shoulder, I look out at my family, friends, and allies.

Drew and Payton are slapping each other on the back with huge smiles on their faces. When my fire dragon catches my gaze, he gives me a heat filled wink. I blow him a kiss.

Irena is staring at the stone beneath her feet as Flynn talks to her. Every few moments, she raises her gaze to his face, and a blush climbs up her cheeks.

Tucker is being patted on the back and high-fived by some of our dojo soldiers and a few from the Fairfax army. The young leader that I met at the north border has his arms spread wide and circles the group like he's imitating my weapons expert's flying skills. I figured Tucker was a good pilot, but by watching the way the dragon soldiers are acting, he's better than good. He's great.

"SHALL I DISPERSE THE BEES, GENERAL?" My castle asks as he paces in front of me and Levi.

"Yes please, Ashgrave," Jace says as he walks over to me and Levi.

A loud buzz comes from the east end of the castle as millions of bees drown out the last of the daylight, filling the sky and spreading out.

The shuffling of footsteps has me looking over my mate's shoulder. Brett is holding a naked Jade in his arms as blood drips down her side. Her normally toffee colored skin is as white as the freshly fallen snow.

I tense. "Brett, get Jade to the infirmary."

As I look out over the front yard of my castle, I notice we're missing almost one hundred soldiers. Those men died defending our home. Nothing can bring them back or replace them, just like Jakobe the driver. I'll get with Drew, when he's finished celebrating with the Palarne heir, and figure out how to honor our fallen soldiers and deliver the news to their families.

I know this isn't over. Not by a long shot. But at least Kinsley knows she and her allies can't come near Castle Ashgrave ever again.

My home is safe. My family is *safe.* And it looks like my family is growing.

CHAPTER THIRTY-FOUR

The orange rays of the rising sun shines through the large arched windows of the infirmary. The twenty beds in the makeshift hospital room are filled with soldiers. *My* soldiers.

Jace's left arm is in a cast, with cuts and bruises on his face and neck. He crash landed during the battle, but he should be fully healed by lunch.

Drew's left eye is swollen shut and is a deep purple color. He walks with a slight limp, but my fire dragon is a natural born leader, so he won't complain. He never does.

Levi and Tucker both have bandages around their left biceps, while every time I move, my body screams painfully in protest.

None of us are as injured as Jade. She has a large

bandage wrapped around her chest and stomach. The wounds on her right arm are covered with gauze. She has to sit at an incline, propped up against her pillows in bed. But her toffee color is coming back and her almond shaped eyes have their glimmer back. Even her left eye is looking better with its silver scar that cuts through her eyebrow and onto the top of her eyelid.

A blonde nurse approaches us, handing Jade a steaming cup. "Jade, please drink this. It'll help you heal faster."

"What is it?" I ask.

"A chamomile and peppermint tea, my queen. It'll help Ms. Nabal's muscles relax and speed her healing," the nurse answers. "I also have your anti-pregnancy tea prepared for you, mistress." She hands me the other cup in her hand.

I take a sip from the steaming mug and shudder at the bitter taste.

A deep chuckle has me looking at the doorway to the infirmary where Tucker's standing like he's on guard, but I know my weapons expert remembers his time in the infirmary back at the dojo. He doesn't like being here.

"It's better than chasing a toddler around, babe," I jest.

Drew, Levi, and Jace all jump to attention as a bald fifty-something man in a white lab coat enters the room. "Can I do something for you, doctor?" My mate asks.

The doctor rubs the back of his neck with his hand. "General, I've already told you the last fifteen times you asked that I need space to treat your soldiers. Thank you again for your offer." He slips away to tend to a soldier who's covered from head to toe in gauze.

These men of mine are going to drive me crazy. "Hey guys, don't you have somewhere else to be?" I ask them. "I'm inside my murderous castle, surrounded by soldiers. I'll be safe here with Jade. I promise."

"Are you sure?" Drew asks, winking.

"Yeah, let's go find a way to pay Kinsley back for her little attack," Jace interjects, kissing me gently on the lips. He turns and heads toward the doorway.

"I thought you'd never ask." Tucker walks over and kisses me on the top of my head. "Take care of little Jade, babe." My weapons expert exits the infirmary.

The feel of fingertips on my shoulder has me looking into the enchanting blue eyes of my ice dragon. Levi places a heat filled kiss on my lips and follows Tucker out the door.

Drew gazes at me, ensnaring my eyes with his. "Have fun, ladies," he says, kissing me on the forehead and leaving Jade and me to talk.

"How do you deal with those four?" Jade asks, shaking her head and chuckling.

"There are days I ask myself that same question," I say, shaking my head at their antics. "But I don't think I could live without any of them. I love them all. Deeply. Uniquely. Irrevocably."

"I think I feel the same way for Brett."

"Really?" I ask, downing my bitter tea. I figured they had feelings for each other, but finding out that they're in love has me beaming a huge smile at her.

Jade left her father and found love here at Castle Ashgrave. But… we just battled against her father. Her *family.*

"How are you feeling, Jade?" I take her empty tea cup and help her sit up so I can fluff her flattened pillows.

"Better now," she says as she leans against the full pillows. "Thanks, Rory, for everything. Seriously, everything." She gestures around us and at her bandages.

"I mean about fighting against your family."

Jade sighs and winces. "I don't consider the Nabal my family anymore. My father only wanted to use me and my strengths. He never told me he cared for me—loved me."

I raise my arm to place my hand on her shoulder, but a sharp flash of pain travels down my arm.

"My father has never tended to me when I was injured or sick. But you do. You're more of a parent—role model than he ever has been."

"I'm sorry, Jade. I know what that feels like." I shake my head to rid my mind of the times I sat in an infirmary with Irena as my only visitor.

"Rory, I believe you, your men, Brett, Flynn, hell... even the castle itself is my family now. This is the family that I'm meant to be a part of, not the Nabal." She grabs my hand.

Dress-shoed footsteps clack against the stone floors, as Brett walks into the infirmary carrying a bouquet of red roses. His stern brown eyes search the room until they land on Jade, and the seriousness falls from his eyes, replaced with a shine. My PR expert and Jade both have huge smiles on their faces as they gaze at each other like they're the only two people in the world.

Whoa! They *are* in love.

I clear my throat, grabbing their attention.

"Oh. Hi, Boss. How is everyone doing this fine morning?"

"Doing better, thanks Brett. I'll visit with you again later, okay, Jade?" I painfully push myself out of the chair next to Jade's bed.

"You don't have to leave. I can come back later, Boss."

"No, Brett. You're fine. Take care of our girl." I walk out of the room, smirking.

As I stretch my sore, aching muscles, Jace and Irena's voices echo in the hallway. I follow their voices to the doorway of the war room, and I look inside.

"About damn time." My sister catches my gaze with hers. "I've been waiting all night for you."

I walk into the large meeting room and spy Jace and Drew sitting next to each other looking at the same tablet, whispering. Levi's eyes are trained on a stack of papers that are spread out in front of him. My ice dragon has a scowl on his face, like the papers are making him angry. Tucker is swiping furiously at the tablet in his hands.

My men start sharing their information with me all at once. "I have the location of the Vaer's weapons suppliers. I can wipe it from the face of the planet whenever you want, babe," Tucker pipes up.

"Drew and I have a plan laid out to attack Kins-. ley's private home," my mate says.

"Let's reciprocate what she tried to do to us. Make her homeless," Drew adds with a smirk.

"I'm trying to figure out how to rip her news agencies away from her," Levi interjects.

These men of mine are amazing. We defended our home yesterday, and first thing this morning they're all strategizing how to rip Kinsley to shreds. My men will do anything for me. But Kinsley is mine to defeat.

"Hold on a minute, guys. Let me say good morning to my sister before you bombard her," Irena says, pulling me into a life strangling hug. My men's eyes all turn back to their information, making it look like they're ignoring us. But I know they'll be listening in.

"So, you're a dragon too?" I ask my sister, pulling out of the hug and gazing at her face.

Irena's eyes drop to the floor. "I was on my way to see you when I saw all hell break loose." Her voice cracks. "The moment I saw Kinsley throw you into the stairs, and you didn't move." My sister looks at me with tears in her eyes. "I thought she was going to kill you. My magic went wild, and I instantly shifted. I don't know why I got this magic, little sister, but I knew in that moment that I needed to use it to help you."

I put my hands on her shoulders and stare into her eyes. "You're always welcome to continue training and learning about your dragon with me. I've been through the same thing. You don't have to go through this alone. I'm here for you, sis."

Irena's eyes narrow a bit, but at least they don't have the same look of disgust she used to display. She doesn't argue either as she smirks at me. "I wasn't just coming for a visit, little sister. I came here to tell you that I found out where the bio-weapon lab is located, but Diesel abandoned his original plan. He's moving his Spectres around. It looks like he's switching gears."

"What's Diesel's new plan?" I ask, removing my hands from her shoulders and studying her eyes for a hint of insight into the Ghost's plan.

"Diesel still wants to go through with his plan to harm as many innocent people as possible and use those deaths to destroy us. But, the plan has changed to exploding a chain of massive bombs that will kill thousands."

"How will that even be possible?"

"I don't know the details. Just that he has a

weapon of mass destruction, and he plans on using it."

Brett enters the room and clears his throat. "I'm sorry for interrupting, Boss. But I know that a weapon of mass destruction exits."

Irena and I narrow our eyes at him.

Brett releases a deep sigh. "When I was a Knight, I helped create it," he says, examining the stone floor. "I'm not proud of it. It's called the multitude trigger or MT-bomb. This bomb is one of the few weapons the Knights made that is truly advanced and destructive by design. It was meant to be a type of doomsday weapon for whenever the Knights needed to go kill themselves, kamikaze style. But even the General wasn't crazy enough to use it."

My sister shakes her head and kicks at the stone floor. I figure she's thinking the same thing I am. "How did Diesel get his hands on this MT-bomb?"

"The Ghost has been buying up black market items, some of them from ex-Knights and governments willing to participate in a shadow war against dragons," Tucker pipes in. I figured my men were all listening in on our conversation.

How will we stop Diesel? The last time we saw him in France, he teamed up with the Oracle. And does that mean they're allies now? No. The way they argued in Reims, they can't be. They each had their own agendas and seemed to be using each other.

"We can lure Diesel out in the open. He won't be able to resist Rory and me in the same place." Irena draws me from my thoughts.

"I agree. He has to be stopped once and for all. But if we're both out in the open, in the same place at the same time, I think Diesel won't come. He might suspect it's a trap." I shake my head. "Unless we make it look otherwise."

"How do you plan to do that, little sister?"

"We hit the bio-weapons lab and let your Spectre rebels leak our plan to Diesel's people, or Drew can leave a digital bread crumb trail for him to follow," I say. "The lab needs to be destroyed, regardless."

"You're right. We need to hit the lab and burn it to the ground. Diesel will come. He won't pass up the chance to try and salvage what he can from the lab. He would do anything to take out both of us without putting himself at risk. When he shows up, we can take him down and prevent the MT-bomb from ever going off."

"Diesel does seem to have some kind of deal with Anastasia, though. We need to be prepared for her to show up at the lab too," I add. "The Oracle seemed almost desperate to grab me back in France."

"We need a solid plan," Jace suggests.

"Where's the lab, Irena?" I ask.

"Poland."

"*The* Poland? The country that outlawed you both, and put you on their terrorist list?"

"Fan-freaking-tastic!"

This whole things smells like Kinsley.

I don't like the idea of going to a country that hates me. But there aren't a lot of options, and we're running out of time.

CHAPTER THIRTY-FIVE

The pink, purple, and orange hues of sunset flood through the windows of the van that my men, Ashgrave, and I are stationed in. We're parked across from the Vaer laboratory. Irena separated from us when we landed at a private airstrip on the outskirts of Warsaw, Poland. She's giving her Spectre rebels some last-minute instructions.

As we wait for Irena to rejoin us, I observe the inside of the huge white waste disposal van we sit in. The vehicle is tricked out with two desktop computers with dual monitors, a ham radio system, a full comm system, and multiple cameras that are linked to the computer monitors. We can see and hear anyone who comes and goes from the lab.

Jace and Drew are busy typing away furiously at

the keyboards, adjusting the camera angles and watching the computer screens. Tucker pulls parts of guns out of his vest of many pockets and replaces them in different pockets. I figure he's moving them around to make it easier to grab his favorite toys in the heat of battle. Levi's sitting next to me, swiping away on the tablet in his hands, while Ashgrave paces at my feet.

I don't know how Drew accomplished getting this all set up in less than twelve hours, but I'm grateful he did. My fire dragon has connections everywhere, even in a country my sister and I are labeled as enemies of the state in.

The back door of the van opens, silently, as my sister finally joins us.

Drew turns his computer chair around to face me. "I left some digital breadcrumbs, so Diesel will pick up on where we are and head straight for the lab."

I give him a small nod, letting him know that I understand our plan is in action.

"My network estimates that Diesel should be here in an hour or two," Irena adds.

"Good! That gives us time to destroy the lab," I say. "That way, neither he nor Kinsley can ever use the bio-weapon again.

"Locked and ready to roll when you are, babe." Tucker pats the pockets of his vest. He stands and tightens the strap of the bazooka on his back, giving me a wink.

Jace stands from his overstuffed chair. "Does anyone have any questions?"

"I think we all know what we're doing, dad. But thanks for double checking," Drew says as he stands and clasps my mate's shoulder.

"Ashgrave, remember while we're on this mission I will need you to stay silent. Say nothing," I order my small steampunk castle.

With a small squeak, he nods his head.

These men of mine are ridiculous, but Jace and Drew have come a long way. They aren't trying to kill each other anymore. They're more like brothers now. And that makes me smile.

Levi places his tablet in his seat and gives me a quick nod as he opens the back door of the van. We all quietly escape into the rays of sunlight.

Drew and Tucker approach the security door of the lab, while Levi, Jace, Irena, Ashgrave, and I stick to the shadows of the large surrounding buildings.

From behind a little stone alcove near the door, I observe Drew as he scans a forged security badge. Tucker's gaze sweeps across the surrounding area as he presses his back to the door with an AR-15 in his hands. The light on the door turns from red to green and Drew raises his right arm in the air, signaling us to rush the doors.

Sticking to the shadow of the wall next to me, I make my way to the door of the Vaer lab, and we all enter together.

A loud creak comes from the large, glass double doors as Jace pulls them open. My muscles instantly tense up, and my dragon is awake and wanting to battle. I search the inside of the building.

Just inside the doors is a bare glass foyer with a big black rubber mat on the floor, and another set of doors. As I pull open the inner set of doors, a high pitched wail pierces the air.

Damn it! Now they know we're here.

We walk into the building. There's a counter to our right, but no people. No soldiers. No noise, except for the screaming alarm. All that's here is a long hallway ahead of us that's lined by four doors, two on each side.

I nod to my murderous castle, signaling him to start heading down the corridor.

Ashgrave flutters ahead, with Drew and Tucker right behind him. As we rush down the large hallway, their gazes scan left and right for danger. Irena and I follow behind them, and I glance over my shoulder a few times at Levi and Jace who are doing the same thing.

As I search the hallway, I catch Irena's eyes and mouth to her, "Stay alert." I'm rewarded with an eye roll and a curt nod.

Something about this feels wrong. The Vaer know we're here, but they haven't attacked. Why?

Ashgrave reaches the set of double doors at the end of the hallway, and the corridor is instantly flooded with light as men in security uniforms barge out of the four doors.

I scan the hallway and count twenty guards surrounding us.

As Irena and I step back into fighting stances, Jace lashes out at the two men closest to him with a magically charged dagger. Their heads instantly roll from their shoulders.

Levi's light brown hair is ruffled as a bullet passes near his head, and he reaches for the man's gun. He grabs the barrel and makes a quick upward thrust, knocking the security guard unconscious with the butt of his own weapon.

Four guards surround Irena and me, and we both pool our power into our hands.

I concentrate to form a battle axe in one hand

and a dagger in the other. The curved wooden handle of the axe takes form, and my magic burns hot then suddenly cold as it wavers. I pull my power back and center it in my hands again. The curved wooden handle of the battle axe forms in my left hand, and the cool metal of the dagger forms in my right. I throw the dagger into the chest of the guard on my right and grab the handle of the axe with both hands, swinging it at the man on my left. His head instantly thuds to the floor, washing the concrete with his blood.

Irena unleashes her green magic at the two guards standing near her. It sparks wildly, instantly freezing the men into solid blocks of ice that my sister shatters with a single roundhouse kick.

Ashgrave turns the security guards that come near him or Tucker to ash while Tucker stands with his back to the large wooden double doors guarding my fire dragon.

Drew huffs loudly as he struggles with the computerized lock on the wall by the doors. The alarm's loud, high-pitched wail is cut off as the light on the lock turns from red to green. Drew opens the doors. I send two magical daggers at the only two guards standing inside them, and blood darkens the chest of their blue uniforms, and they fall to the floor dead.

As we enter the large lab, we separate to cover more ground. We have to destroy everything. The samples, serums, and formulas. Every single trace of the bio-weapon needs to be obliterated, so no one can ever use it again.

Levi, Tucker, and Drew approach the left side of the chemical lab that is full of stills whose coils are full of a green glowing liquid. Jace, Irena, Ashgrave, and I approach the right wall with transparent refrigerators full of vials and flasks of the glowing green poison.

I silently nod as we aim our guns and magic at the deadly bio-weapon.

Gunfire and magic erupts in the room. Out of the corner of my eye, I spy Irena's glowing green eyes full of tears.

As my sister and I make our way to the back of the room to deface the white boards with formulas written on them, I grab her hand. "Kinsley won't win. We've got this."

My sister's face becomes the emotionless face of a Spectre as she squeezes my hand. "I know little sister. We will never let this poison change anyone else."

Irena and I step away from each other as we pool our magic in our hands. I smile at my sister and release my magic, and she does the same.

The back wall of the lab blasts outward, spewing concrete and chunks of the destroyed wall over the alleyway, making a huge hole in the outer wall.

Ashgrave flutters through the opening first, scanning the area and with Levi and Tucker closely behind him, doing the same. Irena and I exit as Drew and Jace leave the building last.

We all search our surroundings with our ears perked for any noise at all. Drew, Jace, and Tucker scan the rooftops, and Levi, Irena, and I search the shadows for anything that moves or just doesn't belong.

We are all listening. Looking. Waiting. On guard.

That was too easy. The night air is too quiet.

CHAPTER THIRTY-SIX

As I observe the empty businesses around us in the cool night air, a light shuffling of footsteps lets me know we aren't alone. I catch my sister's gaze and give her a silent nod, and I do the same to my men.

The dark night is suddenly flooded with light and the chak-chak of cocking rifles. "The Quinn sisters in the same place at the same time. I'm one happy man." Diesel's voice echoes off the surrounding buildings.

The Ghost plants his feet on the roof of the building about one hundred feet in front of us. He brandishes a huge anti-dragon gun, and Anastasia stands by his side as footsteps surround my family.

Our plan worked. Diesel is here. And so is the Oracle, unfortunately.

Now I can get revenge on the asshole for locking me in a Vaer warehouse and using magic dampening hand cuffs when he kidnapped me. But I don't see him with those cuffs now.

Diesel gives my sister and me a smug smile.

The new Ghost doesn't realize this was a trap set to take him out. He's planning on taking us both out. I'm just salt in his wounds, but my sister is Zurie's true heir. Hell, the great Zurie Bronwen trained my sister to take her place. Diesel has never had Irena's capabilities. And he never will.

He needs to kill Irena to ensure the Spectres follow him, and only him.

But we have to show restraint—we can't indiscriminately kill the Spectres surrounding us. Some of them work for Irena.

Tucker and Levi put their backs together, swinging their AR-15's like bats and knocking the men next to them to the ground unconscious. Drew and Jace shoot the ground at the silent army's feet, sending pieces of asphalt into them and forcing them to take cover. Ashgrave hovers over my and Irena's heads, instantly turning the bullets the Spectres are firing at us to ash. We fire blasts of magic into the surrounding buildings, raining chunks of debris down on the Spectres in the shadows.

Diesel fires his large gun at Tucker and Levi, and they throw themselves to the ground beside us to evade the shot aimed for their heads. Diesel will pay for shooting at my men.

My evil butler flutters his metal wings above my head as he returns fire at the Ghost. His magic blasts a hole in the roof top, forcing Diesel to drop his gun. Anastasia just watches with a sneer on her face.

I grab Levi's arm and pull him toward the hole in the Vaer lab, and Irena does the same thing to Tucker. My murderous castle stands guard, blasting any bullets aimed for us with his magic.

As we enter the Vaer lab through the nonexistent back wall, I notice Drew is already inside, typing away on one of the surviving computers while Jace stands guard with his gun, aiming it at the Spectres. Levi, Tucker, and Irena rush to the side of the crumbled wall and guard it to make sure none of the surrounding soldiers enter.

My fire dragon types away on the Vaer computer as if we aren't in the middle of a deadly battle. He looks at me, and I raise a questioning brow at him. "I'm using the network and piggybacking from our surveillance room back at the castle. It's the same one that stores a lot of the Vaer intel, and I'm using it to search for the locations of the MT-bombs." He growls. "The bombs need an internet connection to remotely activate them. I'm using the system to locate and shut down the MT-bombs before Diesel gets a chance to use them."

"That's my genius hacker." I wink at Drew.

The army outside presses closer to the building's opening, shooting at my men.

I wonder when Irena will give her rebels the signal to show themselves and turn on the Ghost and his Spectres.

"Irena!" Diesel's voice thunders. He's right outside the opening. "Come out and settle this. Let's show the Spectres who the one true Ghost is."

My sister looks at me. Her face is a stoic mask as she stands tall and walks out into the alleyway.

"About time you decided to do the right thing, Irena. You've been causing me too many problems, and it's time to end this."

"Diesel, you're the real problem. Put your gun down and let's settle this like Spectres."

The Ghost throws his recovered anti-dragon gun to the side and takes a fighting stance as the men and women surrounding the area step back, watching and waiting.

Irena charges Diesel and punches him in the middle of his forehead, knocking him to his knees. He grabs her by the knees and she falls onto her back. Diesel straddles her upper chest with his knees and she draws her knees up, stretching her back so only her shoulders and upper back stay flat on the ground, and grabs his shoulders with them, flipping him onto his back, pinning his shoulder blades to the ground, and bouncing his head off the asphalt.

My mouth drops open. My sister who stands at five feet nine inches tall and weighs one hundred-thirty pounds, just pulled a professional wrestling move on a man who's taller and out-weighs her by over a hundred pounds. Whoa.

Diesel grabs Irena's neck with his calves and starts to choke her. She throws her weight to the side, loosening his grip on her neck, which allows Diesel to pull his arm out of the shoulder lock Irena has him in. He kicks her in the face, and her head bounces off the hard ground.

The glimmer of metal in Diesel's hand has me tackling him and pushing him away from my sister's still form.

Irena's a dragon now. But she's still my sister, and I'm not going to allow Diesel to stab her as she lies on the asphalt.

Irena pulls herself up, shaking her head as I stand over Diesel. "You wanted us both. Now you got us," I tell him.

Diesel rolls himself to his knees and hatred leaks from his eyes as he stares at me. The Ghost of the Spectres wants me dead.

Not tonight, Diesel.

Irena joins us and lands a hard kick to his solar plexus that has him falling over onto his back. His head bounces off the ground and starts to pour blood.

My sister stands over him. "Who was it that was going to die tonight? Me? Rory? It looks like you're the one lying on the ground bleeding, Diesel. You're not the Ghost. You never have been, and you never will be."

Something glimmers in his hand, and I lift my foot, ready to stomp his head into the ground. Irena stands next to me and leans forward with her hands on her knees, catching her breath and forcing her dragon down as green sparks race up and down her arms.

A blast of magic to my chest suddenly throws me backward. The burning magic that hit me feels familiar. Almost like mine.

Anastasia.

I lean on the brick wall that I just crashed into and pull myself up to face the Oracle.

Anastasia stalks toward me with blue magic in her hands. I form my magical mace in my right hand and swing it in a figure eight like I did while training with Jace. She sends a blast of magic at my head. Her power bounces off the swinging mace and knocks my sister to the ground unconscious.

This has to end, before someone I love dies.

While I continue to swing my mace, I form a magical dagger in my left hand, forcing as much of my magic into it as possible. I throw the magic-infused knife at Anastasia. It hits her in the stomach, and she stumbles.

The Oracle pulls her magic into her, trying to make another shield like she did in France, and I form my battle axe in my left hand, slow the swing of my mace, and gather all of my strength. I make a one-handed throw with the huge axe at Anastasia. It lands with a loud thud in the center of her chest. Anastasia falls to her knees, trying to pull the magical axe from her chest. I release the magic that I used to make the axe, and it disappears.

Anastasia falls down on all fours, panting. "That magic belongs to the dragon gods. Not you, little girl."

I approach her as I bring the mace to a complete stop, and the spiked ball dangles over her head as she kneels on the asphalt. "I've already told you that this magic is mine."

She sneers and fill her hands with magic. I lift the handle of the mace and infuse the weapon with my own. The ball burns brightly, and the blue light arches off the spikes as I swing it over my shoulder and bring it down on the Oracle's head with a deafening crunch.

She goes down in an explosion of magic and slumps to the ground. I watch her chest for any signs of life. After a few moments of watching her lie still, I let out a low breath.

Anastasia is dead.

I'm thankful for my murderous castle, my men, and my sister. And I'll do anything to protect them. I figure Ashgrave proved his loyalty today, but it still bothers me that I question it. He stood against the Oracle, who has the magic of the dragon gods. But will he remain true to me when Morgana returns?

I know the dark ancient dragon gods will return soon. My dragon and I are growing stronger, which means they will come for me. Soon.

Irena moans as she rolls over. "Did you get the

license plate number of the bus that hit me, little sister?"

I shake my head and push my chuckle down. My sister is trying to tease me, but we're not out of this yet. We still need to take out the Ghost.

"Hey. Where did Diesel go?" Irena asks.

"The asshole probably ran away," I say.

"Oh girls, you know better than that." Diesel and the Spectres surround Irena and me. "Aim for their chests," Diesel orders. "I want them to die nice and slow."

CHAPTER THIRTY-SEVEN

My sister and I meet the eyes of each Spectre that surrounds us as we stand in the middle of the alleyway behind the now burning Vaer lab. My men and Ashgrave are making sure that there is nothing to be salvaged of the bio-weapon.

I catch Irena out of the corner of my eye, raising her left fist into the air. In one smooth motion, half of the Spectres train their rifles on Diesel and his followers.

It's about time Irena signaled her rebels to step in. The Spectres have anti-dragon guns. If they had fired on us, we would've been maimed—or worse.

As the street lamp casts a halo of light onto the alley, the glimmer of dragonscale armor shines from beneath the shirt collars of the rebels closest to me.

My heart fills with gratefulness at my sister's need to protect her soldiers.

I scan the Spectres surrounding us and notice that we are evenly matched. And by the red color of Diesel's face and the way his mouth hangs open, he's shocked at the turn of events. The Ghost must have thought he had a few moles he would eventually uncover and punish, but having half his forces declare themselves as Irena's rebels—he's stunned— he's pissed.

The thundering footsteps approaching lets me know my men are finished with destroying any trace of the bio-weapon. They're coming to aid us, and they're bringing hell's fury with them. Some of Diesel's Spectres' eyes widen as my men push them aside. They clench their jaws and ball their fists, but as long as Irena's rebels have their guns pointed at them, they dare not move.

The Ghost and his followers are going down.

A brush of fingertips across my lower back tells me Levi is behind me. Out of the corner of my eye, I spy Tucker and Jace on our right with Ashgrave flying in a tight circle over our heads. Drew moves to my left and takes a fighting stance. I gaze into his eyes, and he gives me a wink.

Diesel pulls his wrist close to his face, looking at his smartwatch, and smirks at us.

The Ghost swipes the screen on his watch. I figure he's triggering the MT-bombs.

Drew laughs. "Did I forget to tell everyone that I managed to remotely shut down all of the MT-bombs?"

The vein in Diesel's neck bulges. He dives toward my sister's knees and crashes into her, making her fall hard onto the asphalt.

Gunfire explodes through the night air as some of the Spectres and rebels fire at each other. Those who are too close in range with an opponent resort to using the butt of their guns or switching to hand-to-hand fighting.

A deafening bang echoes through the night, and I look over my shoulder to find my fire dragon slamming a garbage dumpster into a group of Spectres, knocking them unconscious and trapping them behind the huge metal box. Levi creeps silently behind two Spectres aiming their rifles at my murderous castle, and he slams their heads together. They're knocked out instantly and fall to the ground in a heap. Tucker slams the butt of Betty into the Spectres who are attempting to sneak up behind him. Ashgrave blasts a steady stream of blue fire at

Diesel's followers that come too close to me or Tucker, instantly turning them to ash.

The soft patter of footsteps has me pooling my magic into my hands. As the curved wooden handle of my magical battle axe forms, I grab the handle with both of my hands and swing it at the three Spectres approaching my left. My axe knocks their weapons from their hands. I lift the large axe over my head, and Diesel's followers drop to their knees, surrendering.

The surrendering men's eyes widen as their gazes rest on the weapon I created with my magic. Two of Irena's rebels rush forward with their guns and order them to their feet and lead them away. I turn to the side so I can keep an eye on Diesel and Irena as they battle. I allow my axe to disappear, but I keep a ball of blue magic in my hand.

My sister's magic arcs through the night sky, hitting an electrical pole, and sparks light up the air. While Irena tries to control her magic, Diesel pulls back his fist and punches her in the forehead, making her stumble and fall to the ground. She shoots a bolt of her green magic at the Ghost, but it slams into the huge warehouse door across the alley.

Diesel is taking cheap shots at my sister. I have to do something.

I pool my magic into my hands and shoot it at the Ghost. My blue magic slams into his chest, knocking him to the ground.

Diesel instantly jumps to his feet and drops into a fighting stance. "Come on, little girl. I'll kick your ass too."

I'm so over Diesel and his asinine ways. He wants to start a human-dragon war and eliminate all of dragonkind. He wants to kill everyone I love. I won't let that happen.

I lift my palms to the sky, drawing on my magic and pooling it in my hands. A magical dagger forms in each of them. I flip the glowing blue daggers over in my hands so I can hold onto their hilts, and I throw them at the Ghost as he stands against the warehouse fifty feet away. Both knives hit him in the chest, making him fall to his knees. As I release my magic, the knives disappear, and Diesel falls to the ground with a thud.

I approach the fallen Ghost and kick him to roll him over. I'm repaying him for the time he did it to me when he and his Spectres kidnapped me in Chinatown.

As I stand over his head, he looks up at my face, his lips pull up at the corners, allowing the bloody teeth in his mouth to show. Diesel turns his head and spits a glob of blood on my boots.

I glance at my sister. She's shaking her head and pulling herself up. Irena's eyes meet mine, and she gives me a small nod.

My sister is giving me permission to take her kill. A kill we both want more than anything right now. A kill that will stop the monster who wants to start a human-dragon war.

A gurgling laugh has me staring at the man struggling to stand. "What's the matter little girl? Are you afraid the Spectres won't follow your sister if *you* kill the Ghost?"

Diesel doesn't understand that my sister—my *family*—is what matters the most to me. Not the Spectres. Not even the dragon gods. Nothing is more important than those I love.

As I stare down Diesel, I pool all of my energy into my hands, arms, and shoulders. The Ghost attempts to grab my arms, but he stumbles against me in the cool night air. I pin him against the corner of the warehouse with my blue magic trailing up and down my arms, and I stare into his narrowed eyes.

"You're not a big scary dragon. Just a sniveling little girl who cried when I held her mommy's head while Zurie slit her throat," Diesel growls.

I'm reminded that Zurie and Diesel took my mother from Irena and me. The mother who died trying to save us from a life of being Spectres—assassins and thieves—for hire. She was murdered for trying to save us from a life of obedience and servitude.

The only image I have of my mother—the woman who died for me—is of a woman with a kind face, loving smile, and long dark hair.

My blood boils with rage at the thought that Diesel helped Zurie take my mother from me. From Irena.

I unleash my magic on Diesel, and his body instantly jolts. As stubborn as he is, he refuses to scream, but his expression contorts into one of pain. My power burns so brightly that it lights up the night sky, and my brilliant blue magic turns him to ash at my feet.

I knew that Zurie killed my mother. But Diesel's last words make my heart pang with grief as I'm reminded of my mother's sacrifice. She was only trying to get me and my sister away from the Spectres. She wanted a better life for us. Now we finally have that chance.

The shuffling of footsteps has me rushing to my sister's side. She wraps her arms around me like she's trying to squeeze the ache out of my heart.

I have no idea how long Irena and I embrace each other. We're both lost in our hurt.

Levi's strong chest presses against me from behind, and I lean into him. A loud whirring sound comes from above our heads as my little steampunk dragon circles us. Two sets of strong arms encircles us both—Drew hugs us from the left while Jace embraces us from the right.

"Hey, I want to get in on this group hug," Tucker says.

Irena releases me from the bone-crushing hug, extends both her arms, and makes room for my weapons expert.

"That's better," Tucker mutters while my family and I encircle each other.

"I think it's time to get out of here," I say, after standing in our family embrace for a few minutes.

As the first rays of sunlight filter through the clouds, I observe the carnage in the alley. A few bodies litter the ground, but none of them are Irena's rebels. She's still making sure they're all accounted for, but they were all wearing dragonscale armor which is indestructible for the most part.

And the Ghost? Not so much. I glance at the pile

of ashes he's been reduced to. It won't bring my mother back, but at least I've finally dealt him the hand he deserves.

Diesel tried to not only destroy me—he tried to destroy my family.

I'm extremely grateful for my sister, my men, and my evil butler. They're all important to me. Each of them have carried me through this time of change and growth since I became the dragon vessel. And I know that they'll be with me until the end.

Gods help anyone foolish enough to mess with me and my family. Even the ancient dragon gods themselves.

CHAPTER THIRTY-EIGHT

After showering and changing into black jeans and a black sweater, I walk into the dining hall of my murderous castle. I'm greeted by the warm rays of the mid-morning sun shining through the tall arched windows.

Levi is sitting at the large table between Flynn and Tucker, nodding his head and wearing a smirk on his face. I figure Flynn and Tucker are talking guns and Levi is stuck in the middle, literally. My lips tug up into a smile. My men, they really are brothers.

Jace, Drew, and Irena solidify that belief by sitting together with their chairs pulled into a small circle in the far corner of the room, looking at the same tablet.

A throat clearing at the doorway draws my attention to Brett and Jade. "Should we see what's happening in the news world today, Boss?"

I drop my gaze to my feet. "Way to ruin my morning, Brett."

The Vaer control the news agencies. Kinsley admitted it when we faced off a few days ago. There won't be anything positive from any of the news outlets. I'm sure of it.

My PR expert walks over to the large flat screen television and turns it on. "I think you'll be pleased by what the news is saying."

"...the Spectres are being held responsible for the previous attack on humans. Our sources have produced a list of items purchased by Diesel Richards, the leader of the dangerous anti-dragon organization. The list includes a multitude trigger bomb. This set of bombs is said to be a doomsday weapon that if triggered would cause a death count in the hundreds of thousands," the anchor man with dark skin who appears to be forty-something says. "Law enforcement officials have traced the bomb deactivation to Rory Quinn and Drew Darrington."

Brett changes the channel. My mouth hangs open as I point to the TV. "Over eighty percent of the countries who have started anti-dragon legislation have actually put those votes on hold. Most have outright abandoned those articles of legislation." A blonde woman announces.

So many questions run through my head that they'd come out a jumbled mess if I were to ask them, so I stay quiet. I can't separate them enough in my mind to ask.

A high-pitched laugh has me looking at my sister. "You should see your face right now, little sister. It is hilarious."

Drew approaches me. "Are you okay? You look a little dumbfounded. It's cute."

"Did you?" I look into his beautiful black eyes.

My fire dragon nods his head while a smirk tugs at his lips. "Brett, Jade, and I sent the list of items to Kinsley, reminding her that she is tied to the Spectres. She removed her name from all of the correspondences then forwarded them to her news agencies. The Vaer Boss needs to separate herself from Diesel."

"But Kinsley would never acknowledge me or any of you for saving people. She wants to destroy my public image," I interject.

"That was where Drew's hacking abilities shine, Boss." Brett smiles and pats my fire dragon on the back.

"I left a digital trail for law enforcement agencies to follow, so that they'd know it was us who disabled the bombs."

I wrap my arms around my fire dragon. He is a computer genius. I'm grateful to have him on my side.

Brett changes the channel again. "...that's right you heard it first here on World News Now. Rory and Irena Quinn have been removed from all of the 'No Fly' lists. They are no longer considered terrorists in Europe or Africa," a thirty-something man with short brown hair tells the camera.

The channel changes again. Images of people with signs that say, "Leave Rory alone," "Humans for Rory," and "I love Rory," parade across the television. "Here in Warsaw, Poland they're having pro-Rory marches," the voice of a male newscaster announces.

My shoulders lift and my back straightens as the invisible weight I've been carrying lifts off me. Our public image has been restored. I take a deep breath.

I tighten my hold on Drew. "Thank you."

He kisses me on the top of my head and wiggles his eyebrows at me. "I have an idea how you can thank me."

I chuckle and step out of his embrace. "Later. I promise."

The sound of brass horns, drums, and shouts of·
victory comes from the main hallway. I rush out the
doorway and observe Payton and Edgar leading a
procession of Ash Town villagers, Flynn's rebels,
Jace's dojo soldiers, and Palarne army forces into the
foyer.

The eight tapestries that hang in the large
entryway suddenly start to change. The one closest
to the throne room changes to an inspiring image of
the sunrise as its golden rays wash across the
grounds of the castle. The tapestry next to that
changes from a dark image of Morgana to one of me
and my men, standing with arms linked, smiling in
the blue moonlight. The tapestry furthest away from
the center of the crowded foyer, where I'm now
standing, changes from an image of the three dragon
gods to an image of a glorious sun as it sets over the
castle's grounds. Each of the tapestries change from
dark images to those of natural beauty, or they
depict me and my family.

"Thank you, Ashgrave. The tapestries are truly
beautiful."

"I HAVE A FEW MORE DECORATIONS I
WOULD LIKE TO ADD, IF IT IS ALL RIGHT
WITH YOU, MY QUEEN?"

"Of course."

A decorated Christmas tree emerges from the ground. Magical metal hands wrap garlands embellished with pinecones and red bows around the huge stone staircase. Cedar wreaths are placed onto the large entry doors by metallic hands.

My eyes tear up as I feel my sister's hands pull me into a hug. "Let's celebrate Christmas for mom."

"Did you teach Ashgrave about Christmas?" I ask my sister.

She nods her head. "I suggested a few pictures from a magazine Jade has."

I turn to gaze at her tear-filled eyes and can't say anything. We haven't celebrated the winter holiday since I was young. I can barely remember myself, Irena, and a woman with dark hair and a loving smile gathering around a pine tree in the woods and exchanging small homemade gifts.

"Ashgrave, it isn't Christmas without music. Can you give the makeshift band a break and get some tunes going for us, please?" Tucker asks.

The loud squelch of metal rubbing against metal has me releasing my sister and covering my ears.

"Stop!" I demand. "Thanks anyway."

"Maybe I should just find a radio?" Tucker shakes his head.

"Let's move the party to the ballroom," I suggest.

We head for the huge room with a bar, dance floor, and couches set up inside. Crystal chandeliers hang from the ceiling—this breathtaking room is made for parties. We finally have a celebration.

After I throw open a huge set of ornate double doors to the ballroom, the music from the makeshift band starts up again, and the revelers follow me in.

They all spread out and start to make this a real celebration.

I take a break and stand back to observe the people in my life. The people I would die to protect.

Brett and Jade are snuggling in each other's arms while they watch some of the villagers dance an entrancing waltz to the music. Flynn and Irena stand behind the bar, mixing drinks and talking with my ice dragon and Payton. My sister's face beams with a smile I haven't seen in a long time. As she catches my gaze, she gives me a wink. Drew and Jace flex their muscles like they wouldn't mind going out to run some drills with the army. And Tucker, oh my sexy weapons expert, is swinging the little girl who gave me the pink pearls in a wide circle, making her squeal with happiness as her parents watch with huge smiles plastered on their faces.

My men are amazing in their own ways. But

together, they are awesome. So are my friends. I wish Harper could join us.

Feminine hands on my shoulder has me looking into my best friend's blue eyes. Like I just wished her into existence at my side.

"Don't look so shocked. Jace called me when you landed this morning and filled me in on your adventures in Poland," Harper says. "I had to come and congratulate you on a hard fought victory."

I shake my head, dismissing her need to congratulate me. "I was just wishing you would join us for the celebration."

"Can I steal you away from the party for a minute?" The Fairfax Boss asks.

I link elbows with her and lead her out into the hallway so we can hear each other. I give a small nod to Russell as he stands talking with Drew and Jace.

Harper puts her hand on mine as I hold her elbow and walk down the corridor. "Thank you for being so loyal, Rory." She pats the top of my hand. "You really are a Boss and a queen. You know how to care for your followers, and you do your best to protect them."

I pull my friend to a stop and wrap my arms around her. "I learned how to be a good Boss from watching you, Harper."

"Am I being replaced?" Irena voice carries to us as she silently approaches.

Harper pulls out of our hug. "I could never replace you, Irena. And I'd never want to. I'll leave you to some sister time, and I'll go see what Flynn is mixing up." Harper winks and heads back toward the ballroom.

"How are you doing with being a dragon, really? And don't lie to me, or I'll know," I ask my sister.

"I don't honestly know. It feels like it's growing. Is that normal?"

I nod. "My magic is still growing and changing."

"Really?"

"Listen, Irena. This is all new to both of us. We're the only two humans in history to be changed into dragons by magic and blood."

"But it's so different. I don't know if I'll ever be comfortable using my magic. Did you see what happened when I was fighting Diesel, Rory?"

"I did. But we can work on that—*together.*"

"All I have to do is accept that Kinsley's blood runs through my veins, right?" Irena asks.

"Not necessarily. Your blood is still yours. It's just that Kinsley's is added to it, giving you the magic of an ice dragon."

"So let me get this right, little sis. You're saying that I'm not Kinsley, I just have her magic."

I nod my head and quirk an eyebrow at her. "Exactly. Did you think this entire time that if you embraced your magic that you'd become her? Never. You're still my sister. You saved me."

The apprehension in her eyes melts away, and I can tell that whatever nagging worry she held onto has just been let go. "You're right. I stepped in when Kinsley was trying to kill you. Maybe this is a benefit, not a curse."

I wrap my sister in a tight hug. "Well said, Irena."

CHAPTER THIRTY-NINE

I stand on my private balcony watching the sun set and listening to the music that travels throughout the castle from the ballroom. I don't think I'll ever get enough of the natural beauty that surrounds my castle. The way the sun's rays bounce off the mountains, making it appear as though the mountains are capped with diamonds instead of snow and ice.

"A DRAGON APPROACHES, MY QUEEN."

"Do you know who it is, Ashgrave?"

"IT APPEARS TO BE THE PALARNE BOSS, MISTRESS."

"Have Isaac meet me in the throne room, please?"

"WOULD YOU LIKE ME TO TAKE YOU THERE, MY QUEEN?"

"Yes, please."

I walk into my sitting room and the wall to my left opens. I step into Ashgrave's magical tunnels and follow the stairway that leads downward. As I get to the bottom of the stairs, the wall in front of me opens and I step out into the hallway across from the double doors leading to the throne room. I approach the doors, and they automatically swing open.

The huge doors slam closed as I approach my uncomfortable throne and take a seat to await the arrival of the Palarne Boss.

Moments, later the double doors open. "ALL HAIL THE QUEEN OF ASHGRAVE. THE QUEEN OF ALL MAGIC. BOW IN HER PRESENCE, INFIDEL."

My eyebrows ride up my forehead as I watch Isaac. I am the queen here, no matter how much I still struggle with this fact. However, I need him to bow. Just this once he needs to recognize that this is *my* kingdom. He has to acknowledge that fact or our alliance is going to fail.

The tall, dark-skinned handsome Palarne Boss lowers his black eyes to the floor and gives me a deep bow.

I smile. "You may rise."

"Rory, I'm here to congratulate you on your latest

win. You not only defended your kingdom, but you also defeated a madman and destroyed the bio-weapon."

I raise a questioning brow. "You didn't travel all this way to congratulate me. Why are you really here, Isaac?"

He gives me a curt nod. "You're more clever than even I imagined. Can we talk frankly?"

"Please do."

"You promised my brother that you and I could have a discussion."

"I did."

"First, can I please see the first Astor Diary that you have? I believe it's Clara Astor's diary. Am I right?"

"You're correct, and I'll consider it if you share what you know about the dragon gods?"

Isaac's eyes go in and out of focus as his head drops to face the ornate carpet under his boots. He bites the inside of his cheek as he contemplates sharing the information he has.

He raises his gaze to mine. "I know they are no longer asleep."

As I remember the vision I had in the armory, the dragon gods told me they are coming for me. For my magic. I nearly shudder as I remember

Morgana's voice, the way it wants to burrow inside my body.

The beep of a cell phone draws me from my thoughts. "I'm sorry, Rory. I have to leave to attend to some issues at the capital. But I'd like to visit again, if that's okay?"

I adjust myself as I sit in my uncomfortable throne. "Sure. We are allies, after all."

He may be my ally but I still don't trust him. I can tell by the way he made hamburger out of the inside of his cheek. The Palarne Boss knows more than what he's saying.

Isaac Palarne gives me a bow and then rushes out the door.

I leave the throne room and walk into the ballroom. The celebration is still going strong. There are now tables scattered around the room where people are eating venison and roasted vegetables. A huge six-layer cake with white frosting stands on a table in the corner near the arched windows.

The loud guffaw of laughter has my eyes going to Payton, who is slapping Edgar on the back near the bar. Levi is serving a glass of wine to a young blonde woman from the village who is trying to get his attention. I catch my ice dragon's gaze and he blows me a kiss.

Sitting at a table to my right is Flynn and Irena, who are sharing a drink. As Flynn talks to her, she smiles up at him.

It's nice seeing Irena smile at someone besides me. My sister deserves to love and be loved.

The loud clomp of footsteps to my left has me turning my head to watch Drew's approach. He's wearing a big smile on his face.

He places his arm around my waist. "We've been kicked out of the Vaer intelligence network. But I've already begun analyzing and cataloguing the information that we managed to steal."

"Was any of it useful?" I ask.

"I think so. But we can always try another hack." He chuckles. "I love a good challenge."

Brett approaches us with his chest puffed out.

"So you have a crush on Jade?" Drew asks, wiggling his eyebrows at Brett.

"I have no idea what you're talking about, Drew." Brett's cheeks turn pink as he gives us a smile.

The piercing ring of a cell phone has Brett looking at his phone. "It's an unknown number. I wonder if it's a reporter or some crazed fan club member," he says as he pushes the answer button.

My PR expert's jaw tightens and his eyes narrow as he mouths, "It's Kinsley." He places the phone in his palm and hits the speaker icon so Drew and I can hear.

Kinsley's voice comes over the line. "Now that I know Irena has powers, this will make things even more interesting. Tell your sister to watch her back, Rory. She's a dragon now, and she has Vaer magic that flows in her veins." The phone goes silent.

I *really* hate that woman. Kinsley can never let anything be. She always has to start trouble. *Always.*

Drew wraps me in his strong arms and holds me close to his chest. "Kinsley will get what she deserves. Don't let that crazy bitch ruin your amazing night. We're celebrating a huge victory. And our next victory will be taking her down."

I can't help but smile. My fire dragon is right. I won't let Kinsley ruin this celebration.

Drew drops one of his arms and steers me toward the dance floor. "Dance with me, beautiful?"

I nod. My muscular fire dragon holds me in his arms, swaying to the music. He kisses me on the forehead then spins me out toward Tucker, and my weapons expert pulls me close and waltzes me until I'm dizzy. Jace taps Tucker's shoulder, and my weapons expert bows then kisses me on the cheek. My mate twirls me around the dance floor then dips me as my ice dragon stands nearby with an expectant look on his face. Jace pulls me up and holds me close while he plants a kiss on my lips. He places my hand in Levi's and walks away, leaving my ice dragon and I to share a dance or two.

As I dance with Levi, I can't help but think that I'm the happiest woman in the world. My men are amazing. Each one of them give me what I need. They all bring me joy.

I need to return the favor to each of them. No matter what is heading our way, my men's happiness comes first.

Dragon gods and Kinsley be damned.

Hey, babe!

This book was an exhilarating ride that I didn't want to end.

My fingers couldn't type fast enough, getting out the heart stopping action as Rory and her team go up against the Vaer, and delighting in the hot love scene between her and Drew, which revealed just how much she truly trusts him. It was more than gratifying to watch Rory step into the role she's meant to fulfill by becoming a queen and finally building her army. She's coming to grips with her new place in the world and the fact that it's never a sign of weakness to depend on her family.

And though she questions her evil butler's loyalty, she's extremely grateful for him. Ashgrave is, after all, vigilant and protective of his queen, even when she's away from the castle. The way in which he just swoops in and turns Rory's enemies to ash makes me want a cat-sized mechanical Ashgrave to take along with me at this point. Who wouldn't?

Kinsley and Diesel can scheme all they want, as they spread suffering and death in an attempt to stir up conflict. But Queen Rory refuses to let them unleash weapons that can kill thousands—not while she has the power and will to oppose them.

She knows she has to step up and not only become a queen but also a hero.

In *Reign of Dragons,* for the first time in her life, she defied her master.

In *Fate of Dragons,* she learned how to give up a bit of control. How to compromise.

In *Blood of Dragons,* she learned what it means to have a family. To trust, to let down her guard to her inner circle, and grow as a person.

In *Age of Dragons*, Rory finally accepted who she is: a dragon, a warrior, and someone worthy of being loved.

In *Fall of Dragons*, Rory realizes she's not prey—she's a hunter, one who doesn't need the shadows to survive.

In *Death of Dragons*, Rory steps up as a role

model, she learned to live not just for her close-knit family, but for others as well.

In this book, Rory takes up the mantle of queen, learning that it's those around her—her family that enables her to carry the burden of protecting others.

All while remaining her beautiful badass self, of course.

Tucker makes me smile with his adorable charm and snarky quips. The way he masters the air with his jet and chopper has been an invaluable resource to Rory, and he's a constant source of joy for her. Now, if only Ashgrave can stop pulling him away from nighttime grooming to make cups of coffee.

Drew's love for Rory grows in this installment, as she encourages him to keep his family ties and he teaches her that she can be strong and be helped by those she loves.

Once again, Jace is ready to serve as Rory's general. When devoted dojo soldiers show up and pledge loyalty, Jace is ready to train them to protect Rory's kingdom. He assists Rory in learning to control her growing and changing power. He knows she will have to control it for that battle that is to come.

And Levi, *awwww!* Even when he silently stands next to Rory, the heated looks he shares with her lets her know that he's fiercely and passionately in love with her. His one and only desire is to protect her with all that he is.

As for the universe of Dragon Dojo Brotherhood? I love how Rory is fearless and smart and kind. Especially as she faces the threat of war. But there are unseen forces still edging their way into the scene, but our badass heroine refuses to be toyed with, manipulated, or captured. She puts her enemies on alert—mess with her and those under her protection, and she *will* come for you. No matter who you are.

Her enemies are learning exactly who they're messing with.

I couldn't play in this world so much if you didn't love reading it. So, from the bottom of my heart, *thank you.* Thank you a million times over. If I ever get to meet you in person, I'm going to give you a huge hug.

You are a true gift to me.

I know you're probably chomping at the bit to find out how Jade is getting on at the castle. Will her budding relationship with Brett continue to grow? And how fiercely will she continue fighting for Team Rory, even when that means going up against her father? Milo Darrington is turning out to not only be a staunch ally, but the brother Drew wished he had. Will he stand with them in the face of the oncoming battle? And now that Irena can shift—*hello*—will she start training more with Rory and accept her amazing new gift? And finally, all signs are pointing toward a final showdown between Rory and Kinsley, and the dragon gods who are coming back with a vengeance.

Good thing Rory and her men are such brilliant fighters, and Ashgrave is well-equipped to help face any enemy that dares attack Rory's family.

The next book will be available soon!

Make sure you **join the exclusive, fans-only Facebook group to get the latest release news & updates.**

Until next time, babe!
Keep on being your beautiful, badass self.
-Olivia

PS. Amazon won't tell you when the next Dragon Dojo Brotherhood book will come out, but there are several ways you can stay informed.

1) **Soar on over to the Facebook group, Olivia's secret club for cool ladies,** so we can hang out! I

designed it *especially* for badass babes like you. Consider this as your invite! We talk about kickass heroines, gorgeous men, our favorite fantasy romances, and... did I mention pictures of *gorgeous men?*

2) **Follow me directly on Amazon**. To do this, **head to my profile** and click the Follow button beneath my picture. That will prompt Amazon to notify you when I release a new book. You'll just need to check your emails.

3) **You can join my mailing list by going to** https://wispvine.com/newsletter/olivia-ash-email-signup/. This lets me slide into your inbox and basically means we become best friends. Yep, I'm pretty sure that's how it works.

Doing one of these or **all three** (for best results) is the best way to make sure you get an update every time a new volume of the *Dragon Dojo Brotherhood* series is released. Talk to you soon!

City of Fractured Souls

City of the Enchanted Queen

Demon Queen Saga

Princes of the Underworld

Wars of the Underworld

Sentinel Saga

By Dahlia Leigh and Olivia Ash

The Shadow Shifter

ABOUT THE AUTHOR

OLIVIA ASH

Olivia Ash spends her time dreaming up the perfect men to challenge, love, and protect her strong heroines (who actually don't need protecting at all). Her stories are meant to take you on a journey into the world of the characters and make you want to stay there.

Reviews are the best way to show Olivia that you care about her stories and want other people discover them. If you enjoyed this novel, please consider leaving a review at Amazon. Every review helps the author and she appreciates the time you take to write them.